THE PURE HEART

BY: HANNAH POTTER

Book Cover by Hannah Potter

ISBN-13: 979-8862289657

First Edition: September 2023

This book is dedicated to Jordyn and Bedika, my cherished friends. Thank you for supporting me through this journey.

Prologue

Before Midsummer, 1349

The ground began to crackle as the roots of an old oak ripped upwards revealing a circular wooden door. A large man with a grisly scar across his right eye stood above. His auburn long hair filled with silver lay tangled and wet upon his back.

“Finally,” he said, scratching his beard. He looked around cautiously before placing his hand upon the door. “Bumblesnatch.” The door shook and fell, hanging by the skin of a snake.

The man dropped into the room. Rain drizzled through the hole. Chairs, clothing, and bloodied cloth scattered the ground. A cauldron simmered atop a green flame.

“How did thou find us?” A scrawny man stood, his leg bleeding through his bandages. “Show thy face!” A large orange energy flew towards the man. The man raised his hands; his blue magic encapsulating the spell and dwindled its effect. He smirked and walked towards the scrawny man. “Stand back!”

“I come to help,” he said, placing a hand upon the scrawny man’s shaking shoulder.

“Wulfric? Is it truly you?”

“Aye, Elias. Tis I.”

“They said thou were dead!” Elias cried.

“My friend, twas but a ruse.” He hugged him. “Where are the others?”

"The others? Oh!" Elias clapped his hands. Suddenly, dozens of magical beings lifted their invisible veils. "'Tis Wulfric! He hast come to help us!" The crowd rushed to Wulfric's side, howls of joy filling the air.

"My friends. Please, let us settle. Man, as thee know, hast captured our families. We must act fast. Before long, we will be found. When that time comes, we will be easy prey."

"How long do we have?" Elias asked.

"'Til morn," said Wulfric. Screams and cries rose from the crowd.

"How could they have discovered our refuge?" a man asked.

"What about the children?" cried a mother with a suckling babe.

Wulfric raised his hand and the crowd hushed. "My friends, please settle down. Someone has betrayed us. Worry not, I have a plan."

"Do thee!" a slithering voice snapped behind them. Wulfric turned to find a hooded figure with glowing yellow eyes. A blue whisp encircled his hands. "Make not me laugh. Thou art in no position to fight. I must thank thee, for thou have revealed thy secret path."

"Milady, where hast thy gone?" a young man called from above the door.

"Humans," she hissed. "They are quite dreary simpletons, yet so delicious. Quite the trick, having an invisibility potion soaked into the soil."

"Who are thou?" Wulfric barked.

“Who am I?” she cackled. She snapped her fingers and Wulfric was drug to her. The crowd shrieked. She grasped his chin. “I am the evil within.”

“Thou would betray thy own kind?”

“My own kind? Thou are mistaken. I only showed the truth behind the façade.”

“And what may that be?”

“No more games,” she hissed. A black thorny wall blocked the second exit that the crowd headed towards. “The fun is just beginning. All of thee out, now!” The crowd skittishly exited the burrow to the forest above. Wulfric broke free drawing his blade.

“A silver blade will barely do any damage to me,” she laughed. “A word of advice: dragon’s blood is always worth the price. Too bad thou will not have the time to find any.”

“Thou wicked-”

“Indeed.” She leaned down to Wulfric’s ear. “I can only wait to taste your flesh.”

Wulfric’s eyes widened. “What are thou?”

“Thou will see,” she said. With the last of the crowd through the wooden gate, she shoved Wulfric up to the forest floor. Hundreds of humans stood amongst them with ropes and weapons. They watched in amazement as dozens of magic folks appeared from the hidden door.

“Now, let the fun begin.”

Chapter 1

A Note of Friendship

Darkness fell as the last of the remaining lamp posts shattered, scattering fragmented shards of glass across the dusty unfinished road. A sudden burst, followed by the grinding of rubber against dirt, rang through the air. The tumbling began down the grassy hill until two trees blocked its metal frame. Two lights glistened betwixt the foggy night, providing little help to the half-conscious woman inside.

A flash of green cast its shadow and, in its disappearance, only silence remained.

~:~

Two Days Earlier

Eva sat at the corner table, flipping through her yearbook. Lines of her peers waiting for their copies filled the other side of the cafeteria. She enjoyed searching for her friends amongst the hundreds of pictures and articles.

"Phew, finally got through that line," Maddie said, resting her book on the table and pulling out a sandwich from her backpack. "See anything good in there?"

"Just a bunch of advertisements from school sponsors and clubs. *Two-hundred and fifty trees planted by students on Arbor Day, band gains new teacher, pretty-miss-popular wins for the third time in a row being prom queen*, the usual," said Eva. "They always seem to take pictures of all the popular kids in everything they do more than...OH here's one of you!" She turned the book around to show a picture of Maddie swinging a softball bat.

"Not my best game."

"Maybe not, but hey, you won the game after that for the team! You're a great player. I bet you could get a scholarship!"

"Oh, please," Maddie said, rolling her eyes playfully. "I don't even know if I want to go to college. I'm not book smart like you, yet alone know what I really want to do in life."

"You are too smart, and don't you deny it!"

"Oh, hi Eva" a short blonde girl said. Her hair was flawless, and she wore only the most expensive clothing. A tall thin girl stood beside her, texting.

"Hi Brooklyn, Natalie…" Eva said meekly.

"I see you got your yearbook. How about I sign it?" she said, smiling smugly.

"No, it's okay."

"Brooke said she wants to sign. We don't want to cause any issues, do we? Don't forget all it takes is a picture and help from the journalist club to prove you're nothing more than a low grade, boyfriend-stealing slut!" Natalie said.

"Hey! Who are you calling a slut, bitch!" Maddie said, rising from her chair.

"I wasn't flirting with him. He was my partner for our science project. I did most of the work anyway. It's not like-" Eva mumbled, nervously.

"Shut up! You even so much as look at my boyfriend again, I'll make sure everyone knows what type of girl you really are," said Brooklyn. She smiled then grabbed her yearbook. "Now, let's see. Oh, no signatures? What a shame. Looks like you must not have many friends."

"Give it back!" Eva said, reaching over Brooklyn's shoulder.

"Don't be such a dweeb," Natalie said. She pulled out a marker and wrote along with Brooklyn. Maddie got up and grabbed ahold of the yearbook.

"That's enough! Give it back, or else."

"Fine," said Brooklyn. "You can have it back. Here, Eva." Brooklyn closed the book and held it out for her. As Eva reached for it, Brooklyn shoved her aside and tossed the yearbook in the trash. Eva rushed over to the bin, scrambling through the multiple lunches that oozed over the sinking book. Natalie took a picture of her. "Wow, you're so pathetic. If you were *that* hungry, you could have just asked your mommy and daddy for some money. Oh wait, they don't have any." Brooklyn laughed.

"GET OUT OF HERE!" Maddie yelled, pushing them back.

"Come on, Natty, let's leave these two dorks."

Eva grabbed her yearbook and went back to the table, wiping off the slimy food remains off the edges. She opened the first page, tears rimming her eyes.

SLUT
UGLY
TEACHER'S PET
WHITE TRASH
GOODY 2 SHOES
SEE YOU NEXT YEAR, BITCH. X-X-O-O

Maddie sat by her friend. "Don't pay them any mind. Here, you can have my copy."

Eva closed her eyes and shook her head, pulling her book close. "No. It's okay. It's not like these things really matter anyway," she said with a sad laugh. "You know sometimes I just wish I could escape this place. I just feel…nevermind, it doesn't matter."

"Feel like what?"

"Like I don't belong," she said slipping her yearbook into her bag.

The bell rang, signaling lunch to be over.

"Ah, I better head to class. I'll meet you by the lockers after the last period."

"I can't. I got practice after school today, but I'll catch you this weekend! I'll pick you up for the renaissance fair at 9:00AM," Maddie said.

"Okay."

"Here bring it in." Maddie hugged Eva tightly. She grabbed Eva's bag and handed it to her. "Don't forget this."

"Thank you, Maddie. I'll see you later."

~:~

Eva made her way towards class with books and assignments in her hands. She was reviewing equations for the final calculus exam. Heading up the stairs she accidentally bumped into a girl heading in the same direction. "Pardon me," she said. The girl scoffed and came behind her, pushing her down upon the stairwell. Eva winced as her knees hit the edge of the step, her papers scattering all over. People walked by as she scrambled to pick up all her stuff. Shaking, she rushed to class just before the teacher closed the door.

"You, okay?" said the girl who she sat beside.

"Yeah, I'm okay, Rina. How are you doing?"

Rina rested her head on the table, covering her short boyish hair with her hoodie. "Just tired. I stayed up all night studying for this exam."

"Then let's ace this together."

"Thanks. Is that the yearbook?"

"Yeah." Eva handed her yearbook to Rina. "Just avoid the first page."

"Why? It's blank. Oh, there's a piece of paper folded in here."

"What?" She pulled the book back and found all the writings gone and only a small message left on a torn piece of paper from a notebook.

Hey Bestie,

Never worry about what other people think. You're absolutely amazing! You're going to make a difference one day! You're going to be so successful that one day those suckers will regret having ever messed with you. You're stunning, smart, and unique. We will always be friends forever. And don't you dare think about returning this book. It's yours now, got it?
You've got this, chicka.

- *Maddie*

Chapter 2
The Majestic Rune

It was June 2nd, and her day started just like any other. Eva brushed through her long wavy hair, that remained frizzy from the heat. She put it part-way up and topped it off with a black headband, as usual before getting dressed.

Freshened up, she opened her window to view the morning sky and listen to the robin's chirp. The fresh air filled her with ease, but it seemed too quiet. Not a single bird resided in the yard. An orange tabby cat sat in the tree next to her window, cleaning its paws. A few feathers rested in the crumpled nest beside him.

"Oh, you bad kitty! You leave the birds alone! Shoo!" Eva said.

The cat hissed at her and hopped to the ground, running away. She noticed beneath where the cat had sat was a small crater in the tree. Its edges shined with an emerald-green luster. Eva touched the crater, feeling an electrical pulse. Eva jumped back as her fingers began absorbing the green energy. She turned her hand around to find it completely normal.

"What the heck was that?" she said. She glanced towards the tree branch again, to find the crater completely gone. "I could have sworn...nevermind. I must be tired."

Heading downstairs to the kitchen, Eva poured herself a bowl of cereal and a glass of milk, then sat at the table. Her parents sat across from her; her father was reading the newspaper and drinking his morning coffee while her mother dug her nose into one of her romance novels.

"Good morning, Eva."

"Morning Mom."

"Something bothering you? You look a little pale."

"The neighborhood cat ate the robins in the tree." she said.

"I'm sorry, sweetie. That's awful."

"It's okay. Hey dad, anything new in the paper today?"

"Another kidnapping over in Michigan," he said. "I'm telling you; this makes at least thirty cases now."

"No new leads?"

"None. And the kidnappings are getting closer. I think you should stay home today."

"Your father's right. Maybe you should reschedule things with Maddie."

"Mom, Dad, you're overreacting. I seriously doubt the most wanted criminal across the world would come to the renaissance festival."

"I don't know," her father said.

Eva shrugged and placed her now empty bowl in the sink.

A knock came at the door.

"Is that Maddie?" asked her mom.

"Yep. I better get going."

"I really think you should stay home. You and Maddie can stay here," suggested her father.

"Come on! Maddie and I have been planning this for a whole month! Look, I promise I'll be careful. Trust me, there's nothing for you to worry about," Eva said before she kissed her parents' goodbye. "I should be home before dinner."

"Your father and I have a business meeting, so we'll be out late."

"Okay!"

"Have fun!"

Eva greeted Maddie at the door with a hug. Maddie's wild smile had a touch of elegance from the beauty mark upon her upper lip. They squeezed each other tight as if they hadn't seen each other in years.

"You made it. I thought you'd never come," Eva laughed.

"Sorry," Maddie said. "I overslept a bit."

"No worries."

They hopped into her car and headed off.

~:~

A man walked through the dusty paths of the renaissance festival. His taupe suede cloak covered him from head to toe. He glanced around at the various people in costume and performing circus acts. "Quite unrealistic if I do say so," he muttered. "Good performances, but this is nothing but a simple market with overpriced fake trinkets and weaponry. And they call themselves medieval folk."

"TURKEY LEGS, MEAD, AND BEER! FINEST IN ALL THE LAND," yelled a merchant.

"Well, it never hurts to take a break and get my senses back in order." The man said. He made his way through the line.

"What'll be, rogue?"

"Mead please," he said.

"Coming up." The bartender turned to grab a cup. As he filled the plastic cup, the man snapped his fingers. Suddenly one of the kegs' taps fell off, spewing beer all over. The bartender quickly rushed to save all the beer he could whilst trying to plug the keg. The man reached over, grabbing his mead, and hurried off.

"Hey, you! Wait! Ugh!"

The man sat down at one of the picnic tables watching the crowds surrounding him. He took a sip of his drink, spitting it out. "Son of a bunkaroo, that's terrible! What the hell is in this? Tastes like a dirty washbowl." The man sighed, scanning the area. "I'm never going to find that...Hello, who do we have here?"

Across the way stood The Majestic Rune, a shop full of jewelry and weapons. An armored guard cautiously placed a piece of jewelry behind a glass box. "Looks like Bertram finally showed himself." The man snuck through the crowds and into the shop. Hiding behind the shelves of weapons, he waited for the perfect time to set up a distraction.

One of the shopkeepers asked Bertram for his help with the weapons. Awkwardly, he obliged, grabbing the saber from the top shelf. The man snapped his fingers again, and the whole shelf collapsed upon Bertram. The shopkeeper came to assist him.

"GET OFF OF ME YOU WENCH!" Bertram screamed.

The man took this moment to sneak by the glass case. A lustrous glow came from the simple necklace that lay in the box. Its orange gem, swirling with sparkles. The man's emerald-green eyes widened. "I finally found it."

Reaching for it, he felt a sharp point center at his spine. A scruffy beard came close to his ear. "I suggest you leave that alone, Finn."

Finn turned around. "Bertram! What a surprise to see you here! I thought I might find the King's jobbernowl here." He drew his dagger. "I'm sad to say that the gem is coming with me."

"That's where you're wrong." Bertram raised his blade to swing and the two began clashing their blades together. The shop customers gasped, backing away from them. Finn smiled, blowing a gust of green dust upon Bertram. He stumbled back, rubbing his eyes as Finn leaped for the necklace.

Chains wrapped around Finn's legs, pulling him to the ground. Bertram grinned, dragging him out onto the road. Finn yanked on the chains and with a flick of his hand, wrapped them around Bertram's body. The crowd clapped, excited by the sudden performance.

As the two continued to wrestle, Maddie entered the shop, glancing at the various jewelry. Her eye caught on the orange gem necklace. "Miss, how much for this necklace?" she asked. The shopkeeper struggled to carry the swords, dropping a few in the process. "Here let me help you."

"Thank you, my dear. Now, let's see," the shopkeeper said, grabbing the necklace. "Hm, no price tag. Usually, the items in this case are rather expensive. It doesn't look too fancy. Since you helped me though, I can offer it for, let's say, ten dollars?"

"I'll take it!" Maddie left the store with the necklace in her pocket.

Finn wrapped his arms around Bertram's neck until he passed out. The crowd screamed in enthusiasm. Finn bowed awkwardly and pushed past the crowd to the shop. He went to the glass box only to find the necklace missing. "Ma'am? Where is the necklace that was just here?" he asked.

"Oh, I just sold it. I'm sorry."

"YOU SOLD IT? DO YOU KNOW WHAT YOU HAVE DONE?" Finn said before running out of the store. Bertram groggily stood up. "Shit! I got to find that necklace, and fast!"

~:~

Maddie climbed to the lowest branch of a maple that stood seven feet off the ground. She lowered her hand down to Eva and pulled her up. They sat on opposite branches to make it easier to talk to one another.

"Oh hey, I got something for you. Close your eyes and hold your hand out," Maddie said. Eva closed her eyes. "No, cover them all the way. I want you to be surprised."

Eva chuckled, placing one hand over her eyes. Maddie pulled out something of her pocket and placed it into Eva's open hand. Eva took her hand away and opened her eyes to see a beautiful necklace with an orange quartz gemstone dangling from the corded chain. Wires wrapped around the spherical gem and three tiny silver beads dangled below it.

"Happy birthday!" Maddie smiled.

"Oh, it's beautiful! Thank you, Maddie!" Eva said, hugging her friend before putting it on.

"My family decided to head out to the coast next weekend, and I won't be back for two weeks, so I figured I'd give it to you now. Besides, it's not every day you turn eighteen!"

"Thank you! I love it!" A moment passed and Eva sighed, leaning back. "I've missed this."

"Yeah, school's a pest, isn't it?" Maddie grinned.

"I guess, but it's fun to learn new things."

"Psh, nerd!"

"Hey, you won't be saying that when I've got a job and become filthy rich."

"True, I'll just have to become famous then and we can be *filthy rich* together."

"Fair enough."

"Seriously though, I'm fine with whatever happens as long as I'm happy. Which reminds me, I have something big to tell you. I've been thinking about this a lot, and I think I want to join the military."

"What?" Eva said, her heart sinking in her chest. "B-But what about college? We always talked about getting into the same school and studying together!"

"I don't know, Eva. School just isn't for me. I was never as smart as you. I don't really know what I want in life, and I feel like joining the military could help me find my path. I figured it would give me something to work on and do what I am told without having to really worry about finding a job I like and financing an apartment. I'd live for the country. Do something good with my life."

"Something good? Maddie, you can do so much good with your life through college! I could help you! I-I mean what about us being dorm roommates and-" her voice lost itself amongst her tears.

"Eva, please don't cry. It's not like I'll be leaving forever. I'd still visit you while in college and at the flower shop. And when you have time, you could visit me. We'll still be able to text and send letters to one another. Besides, we still have senior year together."

"But what if you get sent off to war?"

"That won't be likely, but even if I do, I'll promise to give it all my might."

"I understand. I just don't want you to go. What will I do without you?"

"Girl, you got this. You're going to be so successful, become the best botanist there is, and make loads of cash with your green thumb. One day, someone's gonna come around and scoop you up and love and marry you and you'll never have to worry about a thing." Maddie said, hugging her. "But sometimes life throws us for a whirl, and we must take the path it leads us even if we're scared and unsure of what's to come. Now dry up those tears. I don't want you getting all mellow on me."

Eva gave a pitiful laugh. "You better visit me, okay? And you know I'll always support you in anything you do."

"I know."

Finn rushed over to the tree. "Hey! You two up there! Where'd you get that necklace?"

"Over at The Majestic Rune. Why?"

"Thank goodness. How's about a trade? I could give you any necklace you want."

"No, thank you," Eva said.

"Please? I really need that necklace!"

"She said no. Go find another necklace. I'm sure the shopkeeper has plenty of others," said Maddie. Finn grumbled, walking away.

"That was weird,"

“Yeah, but did you see his eyes? They were beautiful,” Eva fawned.

“You’re such a romantic,” Maddie laughed.

Chapter 3
The Man with Green Eyes

Eva was placing the last two marigolds in the bouquet order she was making for Rina. She had placed the order well in advance but would not let her know of the occasion. Only that it was very important that there be six dozen, no more and no less.

"Eva, are you almost done with the order?"

"Yes, Mrs. Greer."

Mrs. Greer came from the stockroom carrying empty boxes. "Here are the boxes you can put the vases in. Be sure to pad them."

"I will, don't worry."

"Eva, I got to step out for a bit to take a phone call. Think you can watch the store for a bit? We've still got tons of orders to fill."

"I'll be fine, Mrs. Greer. The store is empty."

"You're the best, dear,"

The doorbell rang. "Hello, welcome to Roses and Blooms, how can- Oh hi Rina! I didn't expect you for another hour!"

"Well, I figured I'd come early and hang out for a bit. Wow, these flowers look great! Thank you so much for helping my family out!"

"Oh, it's no trouble at all, really. Want me to help you pack them into your car?"

"That'd be great thanks." As they loaded the plants into the back seat, Rina caught a glimpse of the necklace around Eva's neck. "Where did you get that?"

"Oh, do you like it? Maddie gave it to me for my birthday!"

"It's very pretty. I've only seen a necklace like this once before. You don't know, by chance, who sold it to her, do you?"

"No, but there was this random guy-"

"Here we go again, ha-ha. What's that make, three crushes now?"

"I don't have three crushes," Eva blushed.

"Mhm, sure you don't."

"There's nothing wrong with finding someone attractive. Besides, a girl's gotta dream. And I'd like to be married sometime in the future."

"Oh please! We both know you will be married before me. I don't mind though. I'm totally happy becoming an old spinster."

A spider crawled onto the tabletop towards the flowers. Eva let out a yelp. "Oh, I hate spiders! Get it away Rina."

"It's just a little spider."

"That thing is *huge*!"

Rina laughed, gently scooping the spider into her hands and took it outside. "You're so silly. Heck, you'll probably jump into a guy's arms before you have a chance to meet him. Very ladylike."

Eva pointed her nose to the ceiling, crossing her arms playfully. "Hmph! Some lady you are. Speaking so rudely to another. Why, thou shalt be disgusted!"

"I know," Rina replied with confidence.

"Besides I'm ladylike enough. One day my Prince Charming will come and sweep me off my feet and grant me a kiss of true love and we'll live *happily* ever after."

"Yep, and I'll be the one to care for all your cats."

"Rude!" Eva said, pursing her lips.

"Anyway, what happened with the guy?"

"He kept asking me to trade my necklace."

"Man, that is weird."

"It was. Part of me feels kind of bad, since he seemed kind of desperate, but Maddie gave it to me, so there's no way I'll ever trade it. He had beautiful bright green eyes though."

"Bright green eyes?" Rina said, a look of worry striking her face.

"Yeah...why?"

"Dingus!" she muttered under her breath.

"What's going on? Is something wrong?"

"No, no it's fine! I better be going. I was supposed to be home ten minutes ago to go to the market with my mom. She's going to be mad, so I better go. See you later!" Rina said quickly, leaving the shop.

"Okay, bye, I guess."

A few minutes passed, and the door rang again. Bertram walked through the door, gripping his cloak. "I can feel it. It's nearby," he mumbled.

"Hello, sir. How can I help you? We have plenty of roses, daisies, snapdragons-WOAH! Nice outfit! Are you heading to the renaissance festival? I hear its romance weekend, perhaps a flower for your maiden?"

Bertram's face reddened as he gripped the edge of his cloak. "Ahem, I am here to-um…yes! The renaissance festival. I need a-a golden orchid?"

"I don't believe we have any of those."

"N-None of them? What a shame," he said. His eyes focused on her necklace, its gem-core shining with white wisps. "Tell me, where did you get such a *lovely* necklace?"

Eva blinked, confused by the man's assertiveness. "From my friend."

"She does have good taste, doesn't she?"

"I didn't tell you-"

"No need for explanations, how about I buy it from you? I could really use something for the, uh, festival" he said. The man's gloved hands were filled with gemstones. "These are some of the finest gems you could find. I'm sure that would make do for the sentiment."

Eva backed up. "Sir, I'm not interested in selling my necklace. I don't know why people keep asking me to sell it, but I'm not. Now, if you would like flowers, I could help."

"Someone else has asked for it? Please, miss, I must have that necklace. It is quite important that I have it."

"Sir, I'm going to have to ask you to leave," she said.

The man grasped her wrist tightly. "Now, you listen here! I want that necklace, and if you can't give it to me, I will take it for myself. If he finds out I misplaced it again, he'll-"

"Get off of me!" Eva screamed, trying to pry his hand off.

"Eva, is everything alright?" Mrs. Greer said, coming around the corner.

"Mrs. Greer, call the cops! This man-" said Eva, but before she could finish the statement, the Bertram was gone. "Where did he-"

"My dear, what are you going on about? There hasn't been anyone here for a half hour. I heard you talking to yourself from the back."

"But the man! He was just here!"

"My child, you must be so exhausted you're seeing things. Why don't you go home and come back tomorrow? I can close shop once the last order comes in."

"Yes, ma'am."

~:~

Maddie's car horn sounded from outside the shop. The flower shop was a couple of miles from Eva's home and was not always the easiest to get to. The few streetlights in the suburban area made it difficult to see upon the dark windy roads.

“Thanks for picking me up, Maddie. I would have asked my parents, but they had a last-minute project that came up.”

“No worries, chicka. You want to get some ice cream?”

“No. I just want to get home. That man really freaked me out.”

“Well, if he comes back, you call me, and I’ll beat the shit out of him. No one messes with my bestie.”

“Thanks, Maddie.”

They went up the Trailwinds pathway. Although confusing, it made a quick trip. Eva had gone through it many times, so she knew her way around. With only a turn left, Eva expected to see the hill that would lead her home, and instead saw a dirt path.

“That can’t be right...I must’ve made a wrong turn somewhere," Maddie said, very confused. She slowed down her car and read the signs as she passed the coming streets.

“Okay, there's Heartfield. The next street should be Jackson and I turn there," she said, trying to keep herself calm. She came to the next street and turned left. She continued straight for a while and made another turn, then quickly came to a halt. They were on the same dirt road. In the center of the road, stood a cloaked figure.

“Maddie! That’s the guy from the renaissance festival!”

“You got to be kidding me.”

The man started walking towards the car. A green aura encapsulated him.

“Holy shit!” said Maddie.

Maddie quickly drove around the man, his eyes watching their every movement. Following the path, they soon came upon the dirt road again. Maddie halted, grasping her forehead.

"How are we still on this road! I didn't even think they intersected!" Eva said.

"They don't!"

Two hands slammed on the passenger window. It was the man. He banged on the window once more and rattled the door latch. Eva let out a yelp, clinging to Maddie's arm. The man's eyes glistened with frustration and an essence of fear. He kept muttering words neither of them could understand. The window began to crack.

"Drive Maddie!" Eva yelled.

Maddie sped off. "Call 911! Now!" she said, tossing Eva her phone.

Eva shakily dialed the number. She attempted to calm down, following the operator's orders. "They want to know where we are."

"Hold on, I'm coming up to the next street…no way…"

"What?"

"It can't be… We're back on Monroe! I know I turned on the right street!"

"No, I don't see him anywhere. Okay. Yes, ma'am," Eva said with a quivering lip. "They're sending a cop our way. They said we should stay on this street unless we see that lunatic again and to let her know where we are headed if we decide to move."

"There's no way we're on this street again! This is like some shit out of a horror film!"

"Maddie...look." A dark shadow began to form through the rearview mirror. Static filled it like a cumulonimbus about to burst open.

"Screw this!" Maddie said and pressed on the gas. The car squealed, tires digging into the dirt, as if being pulled back. A slight humming resonated followed by a sharp crack. Tiny bits of glass landed on the windshield.

"The streetlight busted! There's glass everywhere! I just want to go home!" Eva cried.

"It's okay! Try to stay calm and avoid-" The man jumped on the car, banging his hand upon the windshield. They screamed, clinging to one another.

"Maddie! I just want you to know you're my best friend and if anything happens-"

"Don't talk like that! We're going to be fine! Just breathe and everything will be okay." The man searched his bag. "That's it!" Maddie said, grabbing her softball bat from the back of her car.

"Maddie, no!" Eva pulled at her shirt, but Maddie slipped through her fingers.

"YOU WANT TO FIGHT? COME AT ME!"

The man stepped off the car, and with a second glance, threw a bright green orb at her. Maddie flew across the road, somersaulting into the grass.

"MADDIE!" Eva screamed. The man came towards the passenger side. Eva scrambled to the driver's seat and fumbled to the ground. She winced as scuffs covered her knees. Scrambling to her feet, she ran towards Maddie. She lay unconscious, a few twigs in her ebony hair. Eva lifted her head into her lap, tears streaming down her face. "Maddie, please be okay," she said. Maddie shuffled slightly. Eva struggled to lift her, attempting to drag her to the car. She gasped as a dark cloud rushed towards them. They were trapped. "Come on, Maddie, wake up! We got to get out of here!" The dark cloud surrounded them, and Maddie's body slowly faded within the cloud. Eva screamed.

Suddenly, she was thrown back into the car. She groaned as she lifted herself off the gear shift. Two hands grasped her wrists. "Let me go!" she said, wrestling under the man's grip.

Green ribbons wrapped themselves around her lips, silencing her cries. Eva kicked and squirmed, finally landing her heel into the man's stomach. As he stumbled back, Eva took the opportunity to slam his head against the car door. The man crumpled to the ground, clutching his head.

Eva tore the ribbons off, shut the door and sped off. "Okay Eva. We'll just make a U-turn, find Maddie, and hope that the cops come soon. Ha-ha! Everything will be okay!" A popping sound came from the side and the car flew across the road, making a full circle before coming to a halt.

The headlights shined bright against the misty air. The man ran towards her. Eva gasped and pulled the shift in reverse and swerved backwards trying to escape him. The streetlights started shattering one by one as she passed them until darkness surrounded her. She kept moving back, soon losing sight of the man again. All of a sudden, a gush of electric-like darkness hit her car followed by a green light. Eva screamed, losing control of the car. She went off the side of the road and tumbled down the grassy hill, leaving muddied streaks. The car slammed between two trees, holding still at an angle.

Eva's head seared with pain as a hot substance flowed down her right temple. She breathed slowly, trying to focus her vision through the dusty air that the airbags let loose. Everything seemed so fuzzy.

A shadowed figure headed towards the car. He mumbled something foreign to Eva's ears. He opened the door and stared down at Eva intently. She felt woozy and could barely see through the blurriness that her eyes created. Her heart pounded in her ears and her breath became shallow. The man leaned forward towards Eva his eyes glowing brighter.

Then everything went black.

Chapter 4
Another Realm

A soft whistling echoed through Eva's ears. She turned her head away from the sound, giving a groggy moan. The mattress crinkled releasing a tangy, musty smell that reminded her of a horse ranch. She opened her eyes to find she was in the comfort of a soft straw-tick bed wrapped in a thick toffee-colored woolen blanket. An old English-style cottage made of aged wood and cobblestone surrounded her.

A small table sat next to the bed with a ceramic pitcher and basin. Beside it laid a pewter candlestick holding a candle, still smoking from being recently blown out. Across the room sat a wooden chair cushioned with a maroon feathered pillow. To its left rested a stone fireplace with blackened wood still sizzling in the hot embers, making the whole room smell strongly of pine.

Across the room was a bookshelf filled with many leather-bound books in a variety of colors. Bright light shined in from the open window, letting in fresh air from outside that gently moved the sheer material used for curtains.

Eva quickly sat up, only to feel a searing pain shot through her head. She winced, placing her hand on her throbbing brow.

"You shouldn't sit up so quickly. You took quite the tumble back there. Been out for about twelve hours now." A man's voice came from the side of the room. A tall man filled the doorway, his curled dirty blonde hair falling over his face. He carried a pewter tray and tea set in his hands, looking at Eva intently with his green eyes.

"You!" She screamed. She scooted herself backward until her back hit the wall, trying to keep as far away from him as possible. "Don't you come near me! You-you-"

"Calm down. I'm-"

At that moment, Eva grabbed the closest item near her and threw it at the man. He dodged the basin swiftly, which shattered into pieces when it hit the wall behind him.

“Woah! Hey! What are you-”

The pitcher ended up in the same fate as the basin. Eva threw the candlestick, finally hitting the man in the arm, causing the tea set to tumble to the ground, spilling hot tea over his leather vest. “Ow! I’m not trying to hurt you, so calm down!” the man yelled, brushing the tea off.

Eva pulled off her shoes and threw them, one by one, towards him, being the last thing close to her reach.

“Okay, that’s it!” he shouted. He threw up his hands before the shoes came near him, and a transparent green energy surrounded Eva’s sneakers, causing them to hover a moment before falling to the ground. Eva gasped and started to run, but the man grabbed her by her wrists, making her face him.

“No! Stop it!” she screamed, struggling to break free from his strong grip.

“Calm down, alright! No one’s going to harm you!”

“That’s what they all say before they murder you and throw you in a ditch!”

“Look at me," he said sternly. Eva looked at him, still in a panic. “I’m not going to hurt you. Calm down, okay," he said. He sat her down on the bed, kneeling on the floor to be at face level. “You are safe here," he continued. Eva eased up a bit, staying alert. “Now, I’m going to let you go. I mean you no harm, so please, just hear me out," the man slowly loosened his grip, taking a step back.

He rubbed his arm. “Gee, you sure threw that well.”

Eva sat there looking at him, catching her breath. As the man took a couple more steps backward, Eva darted for the open window across the room. She got one leg out the window when the man grabbed her, wrapping his arms tightly around her, pulling her back into the room as she thrashed her legs back and forth.

"Oh no you don't! Get back in here."

"Help! Help!"

"Be quiet!" he scolded, placing a hand over her mouth. Eva bit down hard on the meat of his hand and stomped on his foot.

"Son of a bunkaroo that hurt!" the man yelled, gripping his hand. "Fine if that's how you want to be, we'll play this the hard way!" He snapped his fingers then waved his hand towards him, as if summoning someone. A long rope floated through the room and into his hand. With a great struggle he pulled Eva to the wooden chair, still holding tightly onto her. After a moment he tied her to the chair and walked in front of her.

"You know, you're pretty stubborn. I'm trying to be nice to you, but I guess that's not good enough. I rescued you from that car crash and took you into my home to keep you safe, and I got a measly bite on the hand. I hardly call that fair!"

"Save me? You nearly killed Maddie and I causing that crash! Oh my god! Maddie! Where is she? Is she okay?"

"She's fine. Home with her family by now, I assume."

"You assume? What did you do to her?"

"Nothing, I swear. I just knocked her out for a bit. She will be okay."

"I swear if you hurt her, I'm going to kill you!"

"You mean like this? All tied up. I find that hardly practicable," he smirked.

Eva's face reddened. She rocked the chair side-to-side trying to free her hands. "Why you! I swear, when I get my hands on you, you're going to regret kidnapping me!"

"I saved your life, no thanks to you! Besides, it's not entirely my fault. I was trying to stop you from crashing, but obviously that didn't happen. You're lucky I got to you before someone else did."

"Someone else? Who else would be coming after some stupid little nobody like me? The only one I can think of is you! And don't you go thinking you can put this all on me! If you hadn't come after me like a maniac, the crash wouldn't have happened!" she spat.

"I was trying to protect you!"

"From what?"

"The King, you stubborn chit!"

"Don't think I'd fall for that! We live in a democracy!"

"Not here we don't."

"What do you mean 'not here'? Where are we? Where did you take me?"

"That's not important right now. Would you like some tea?" the man said, trying to avoid the subject.

"What?" Eva snapped, flabbergasted.

He gently grabbed her chin to examine the right side of her face. "Hmm...Yep, I did a good job. Not even a scar. Maybe that crash was a little harder on you than I thought," he said tilting his head. "You know what? I'll just make some tea," he stood up and walked towards the door. As he snapped his fingers the green energy reformed the pitcher and basin flying them back to the bedside table. It then took the candlestick, placed it next to the basin, and with a small orange spark, circled around the broken candle, forming it to its original state. Afterwards it picked up the tray and tea set, hovering them on a green cloud that stayed close to the man. He stopped at the doorway and turned his head to face Eva. "I'll just let you stay here and think things over for a bit," he said with a small smile and walked away with the tray following behind him.

Eva just stared at the entryway, gaping. *WHO DOES HE THINK HE IS? How dare he treat me like this? I can't believe this! What am I going to do! Here I am, stuck in a chair, God only knows where! On top of that, I've been kidnapped by this crazy...wizard?* Grief overwhelmed her and before she knew it, tears streamed down her face.

A whistling sound came from the other room and stopped seconds later. The man walked back in. "I made some tea, and the raspberry tarts are fresh out of the oven. So how about we talk about-" he stopped in his tracks when he saw a tear drop from Eva's face. "Are you alright?"

"No, I'm not alright. I'm tied to this stupid chair. I don't know where I am or if I will see my family and friends ever again," she sniffed, turning her face away from him.

The man scratched the back of his head. "Well here," he walked over to Eva. "If you won't run away, I'll untie you. Deal? And if you don't run off, I will take you home once all this ends. After that, you'll never see my face again. I give you my word," he said looking straight at her.

"Why should I trust you?"

"Because I just want to protect you," he said as he started untying her ropes. Once they were off, he gently took her hand and smiled at her with sympathy. "Come on. I'll explain everything over breakfast." and he led her out of the room.

~:~

Heading into the room next door, Eva gazed at her surroundings. The place filled her with warmth. Faded red stones lined the floor, giving rise to lime covered walls. The ceiling rose about ten feet tall, with connected long wooden beams supporting its curved structure. A metal chandelier dangled from the ceiling with eight candles lighting the room. A large fireplace lined the east wall, the wood still crackling releasing smoke through the tall chimney. Around the fireplace, hung copper and pewter pots and pans. Shelves filled with spices, herbs, flour, sugar, and potatoes, stood against the adjacent wall full of cabinets. Next to the cabinets stood a five-foot-long box. Its thick silver metal seemed to be sweating.

"Oh, do you like it? It's been great having it around here! My food stays fresh about ten times longer than it used to. Merik, the blacksmith in town, made it a couple years ago. He calls it an icebox, although I'm sure it looks quite different in your world," the man said. He opened it to reveal many wrapped up pieces of linen-lined meats all covered in crushed ice. Milk bottles lined up against an enclosed compartment. "The meat lasts for about three weeks now as long as I replenish the ice once or twice a week. Merik likes to yell at me though. He says the ice is supposed to go in the box, but I find the food lasts longer when it's crushed. Although, I think a lot of it has to deal with how the meat's preserved. I lather it in salt and fresh wine and let it ferment before drying it in the sun. Then I just wrap it up in some linen and put it in here. Once it's cooked though, oh man, you can believe it's about the best thing you've ever had," he grinned, shutting the door.

"That's interesting. At home we generally use a refrigerator."

"A refrigerator?"

"Yeah, it's like an icebox but it uses chemicals and electricity to keep food cold."

"Electricity? Wow! Wait until I tell Merik! He'll be so shocked. It's hard to come by these days, but then again, most people just use magic. Makes things easier," Finn grinned.

"Magic? So, it is true. You're a wizard," she stated.

The man blushed, staring down at her as if deciding whether to be embarrassed or insulted. "Not exactly. I'm a sorcerer."

"What's the difference?"

His face stiffened peevishly. “What’s the difference? There’s a big difference! Wizards learn how to use magic over time studying spells and shadowing a wiser, more powerful wizard. Sorcerers, like myself, are born with powers. It’s an innate oddity that allows us to channel energy from ourselves or outside sources and bend it to our will.”

“I see…”

“Anyway, I’m sure you have a lot of questions. Here, sit down," he continued, pulling out a chair for her at a red oak table, centered in the room. Eva stared at the chair warily before sitting down. The man walked over to the counter above the cabinets, grabbing the pewter tea kettle, with a cotton potholder, and two matching cups. He set a cup next to Eva and the other on the opposite side of the table. He filled her cup and looked at her. “Do you want any cream or sugar?”

“Maybe just a little sugar.”

The man nodded and snapped his fingers. A quarter teaspoon filled itself with sugar and flew itself over to Eva’s cup, while the man prepared his own tea. A tray of raspberry tarts lay on the table. Eva stared at them with caution.

“They’re not poisoned, you know. You can eat, and you should. You’ll need your strength.”

Eva looked at the man, then back at the tarts, and took one. She took a small bite. The crispy crust filled her with comfort, for the soft berries were sweeter than any she ever tasted.

“See. I told you,” he smiled, taking one for himself. “I picked the berries fresh this morning.”

“They’re delicious.”

“Thank you," he said, then rested his elbow on the table with his left hand touching his chin. “So, what do you want to know?”

“Well for starters, who are you, and why were you following me?”

"The name's Finn Barrett. I've lived here for twenty years now, and care for my family's ranch. On my free days, I like to hang out in the town and talk to the local folk. And I told you, I only followed you to protect you. Your life's in danger. You see, King Valdof, ruler of this world, has an interest in you. He's been trying to find you for quite some time. If I hadn't gotten to you when I did, he surely would've taken you."

"Why would he want me?"

"That's what I'm trying to figure out myself. There's something about you that's got him interested. He's too eager. You must be special if he's willing to cross the barrier into your realm. If he finds you, your life will be in grave danger, and that's why I can't let him get to you."

"But wouldn't it be easier to hide in my world then, since it sounds like it's not a common place to go from here?"

"No. If we did, he'd find us in a second. He's able to sense any magical folk, so even if I protected you over there, he'd find us instantly."

"Woah, that's a lot to take in. What if he does find us?"

"I won't let that happen. Just stay with me and you'll be safe, but we'll need reinforcements. We need to head out soon. I arranged for us to meet a friend of mine. He should know how to help."

"And where exactly are we?"

"In a place that people can only dream of," he said with a mysterious smile. "But first you must change. You can't be wearing whatever that is in these lands. It's way too provocative and makes you stand out too much."

"It's just shorts and a t-shirt."

"Maybe to you, but that'll get you stoned in a moment's notice," Finn said with a scoff. He walked over to the corner of the room and opened a door to another room. He came back a moment later holding a long dress for her. "I picked this up in the market and boy, did I get some strange looks. Believe me, you'll fit in perfectly here," he handed the dress to Eva. "I also placed some shoes in the bedroom. I hope I picked the right size. Oh, and best to put your hair down or something. You don't want anything from your world to be seen here. The locals are pretty picky about human items. If they catch you with those, you'll find yourself before the Twelve Superiors, and trust me when I say a dungeon would be preferable than meeting them."

Eva looked at him for a moment, questioning hers and his sanity before heading back to the room she woke up in. She closed the door behind her and held out the dress for her to see. A maroon overdress surrounded the cream ankle-length chemise, its gentle design both charming and durable.

"This is so unreal," Eva said before changing.

The dress, simple but beautiful, felt more like a costume. She looked at herself in the mirror beside the bedside table. Her hair was ratty and unruly. She leaned closer. Finn must have been honest as her head showed no sign of injury. She took her hair tie and headband off and ran her fingers through her hair in hopes of detangling it. Although frizzy, it would do.

She lifted the necklace Maddie gave to her in her hand to look at it. She questioned whether to leave it, in fear of what Finn might say. She thought for a moment, figuring if she could hide it, there would be no harm. It would be her secret, and thus she stuffed it between her bosom where she knew it would be safe. She looked at the shoes beside the bed, made of fine leather of an intricate design, with a sewn pattern and laces to tighten them. They were a bit snug, but comfortable at least.

She laid her clothes on the bed, nicely folded, then opened the door. Finn packed a cloth bag with various items. He looked up and just smiled. "Perfect," he grabbed his bag and wrapped it around his shoulder, then placed a knife in his belt. He grabbed a slightly smaller bag and handed it to Eva. "Here. We'll be gone for a while, so I packed you a bag. It's not much, but it'll last us awhile. Just some flint, linen, and food, the essentials," Eva took the bag and wrapped it over her head, letting it dangle on her hip. He led her to the front of the house, giving her a smile, as he opened the door. "Welcome, to Aloncia."

A tall, dark figure approached a cell gate which held a ragged woman. Bruises wrapped her body like that of a jacket. Although unable to see, she cowered before him. The figure summoned her forth.

"She arrived in Aloncia. Tell me where she is!" he spat.

"I see a girl with hair of chestnuts and eyes of anise. Her body is thin and frail, but her heart is pure as light. She..."

"Where is she?" he barked, latching his hand around her wrist.

"I-I cannot tell!"

"You will tell me, or you will suffer the consequences! Must we repeat our little game once more?"

The woman shivered then looked around, searching for a sign. "She cannot be traced. Finn cast a protection spell around her and-"

The figure let go of her with a scoff. "How pathetic! You're absolutely worthless! I ought to dispose of you right now!"

"W-Wait! I-I'm sensing something!" the woman pleaded.

The figure raised his brow in suspicion.

"She goes by the name of Eva."

"Eva, you say?" he smiled.

"Yes, yes! Eva Dawkins!"

"Thank you, my pet. You shall be rewarded, as promised," he grinned sinisterly, digging his sharp nails into her cheeks. He let her go and held a warty citron before her. She gasped, reaching towards the fruit. The man smiled. "Now, now,

patience be you. No one likes a beggar," he said, taking a bite out of the fruit.

"Yes, master," she said, resting her hands in her lap. "Forgive me for my insolence."

He spat out the chunk of citrusy flesh and tossed the rest through the cell bars. The ragged woman rushed towards the fruit, tearing it apart as if she had not eaten in days. "All is forgiven, my pet. Just remember, there are worse things than this measly life of yours." He turned around to exit the dungeon. "Well, Eva Dawkins, if it is a chase you want, a quickening feat you shall receive. There will be a day when our paths cross, and when that day comes, you will not escape me."

Chapter 5
A Story Untold to Man

Eva stood there with her jaw ajar. Hundreds of people crowded the village. Men and women carried bales of hay over their backs, two men lugged a hog ready to roast over the village fire pit, and women at the wells summoned water into the buckets. To the side stood a bakery. A man with fiery red hair stood against one of the posts supporting the hut, baking the bread with the fire that inflamed his hand. Within minutes the bread finished baking, and the man's hair cooled off into a shade of dusty black.

"Oh, that's Terrowin. He makes the best bread in the village. Although, try not to get on his bad side or you'll feel it for a week," Finn laughed. He walked her over to the shop. "Good Morrow, Terrowin."

"Good Morrow. Who do we have here? Another girlfriend perhaps? You always did know how to handle the ladies, eh Finn."

"Haha, you could say that...This is Eva. She's a family friend. She traveled all the way from Laurik. She'll be staying with me for a while as we are on a quest. We will be gone for quite a while, so we'll be needing the freshest bread you've made today."

Terrowin smiled at Eva before handing Finn the bread he made only moments ago. Finn graciously paid the man four silver coins, and he pocketed them quickly. Terrowin grabbed another loaf and baked it right before their eyes. The crust crackled as the smell of fresh sourdough filled the air. Terrowin extinguished the flames and handed the warm loaf to Eva with both his hands clasping hers. "And one to the fair maiden. On the house. I know these are troubled times for thee. Good luck on thine quest."

"T-thank you," Eva said blushing. She placed the sourdough in her knapsack and she and Finn continued through the village.

"Laurik?" Eva questioned.

"Tis an island off our shore. A poor village of magic-ridden folk. They've struggled for the past few years, or that's what I've heard."

"Why doesn't anyone help them?"

"It's been rough on everyone here with the rule we're under. We make the best of what we have."

~:~

The butcher set up shop next to the bakery. A huntsman entered the building to gain his daily wages. Next stood the fishery and fruit and vegetable stands where men were yelling about the low prices of the day. On the other side of the town rested the Tailor and Drapery shop. Five women stood outside dying fabrics as the looms, behind them, magically wove tapestries and rugs. The colorful dyes followed the women's movements, and danced around the white fabrics, staining them evenly to produce vibrant material. Watching the women made Eva wonder if they made her dress.

A giant fountain stood in the center of the village. The water synced with the music played by a man on flute. A few coins sat in his hat that lay upon the rim of the fountain. Two kids ran around the town, throwing little balls of energy at each other. Sparks flew as they hit one another, both of them giggling.

At the end of the village was the usher house. The undertaker, dressed in white, laid out newly furnished coffins, ready to be used. The local parish stood beside it, the bells ringing for the afternoon mass. A sharp clanking sound came from the area, clashing with the bells soulful tune.

"Hey, fellas! Look who's here! Oi, Finney boy!" a scruffy man yelled, leaning out the window of the pub. Two other men rushed up, practically leaping out to get a look.

"Oh, no. Why now?" Finn groaned.

"Ooh, and it looks like he's got himself a new girl! Hey, Finn! Why don't you come in for a pint?" the one said.

"Not today guys. I'm on strict business."

"*Strict business* he says with the lady," the other mocked.

"Come on, Finn. Let's share a round! You can bring the lady with you! We'll show her a good time!"

"No, thank you. She's with me," Finn said, keeping Eva close. "Just keep going. Don't pay any attention to them."

"Can't be any worse than that one with the golden locks. You know, the one with th-"

Finn quickly pushed Eva through the door of the blacksmith's shop next to the pub, snapping his fingers before shutting the door. The green energy pushed the men back, sending them flying, slamming the pub window tight.

Darkness filled the room, with the only light coming from the window and fireplace. The heat was overwhelming. The smell of burning coal and sulfur filled the air. There were many tables filled with various metals, some molded into bits and pieces of different tools and objects. A large man hammered a piece of copper on an anvil as they entered.

"Oi, Merik! Did you get the stuff I needed?" Finn said.

Merik turned around to face Finn. He wiped his scarred hands on an already dirty rag. "Sure did, you pompous pig," the man grunted. A thick graying beard covered his face. "I've got 'em in that sac over there," he said tilting his head towards the back table where he kept pre-ordered items. He proceeded with his work, grabbing a large log and splitting it with his bare hands. The fire hugged the halved wood like a blanket when he tossed it in.

"Thanks, you old bastard," Finn replied snarkily. Finn walked over to the table and opened the bag. He pulled out a dagger and slipped it in his boot. Then he took a couple charcoal orb-like items, a small hatchet axe, and a thick rope, throwing them into his bag. The last item was a smaller drawstring bag. He opened it, smiled, and closed it again, tying it to his belt. "Thanks, Merik. This will help a lot. Just put it on my tab."

"Will do, but I expect full payment when you get back. No more jokes this time, Finn." Merik said, then nodded his head towards Eva. "That the broad you were talking about?"

"Yep."

"Doesn't look much like a fighter, nor prepared for anything as dangerous and adventurous mind you. You sure she's up to this?"

"She will be."

"Excuse me! I'm right here," Eva snapped.

"Sorry miss. Don't take this the wrong way, but have you ever been out on your own? The forest isn't some place a little peasant girl needs to be going."

"For your information, I've traveled through many forests," she said, pursing her lips. Of course, she referred to the safe forests in her own world, but she figured he need not know that.

"Uh huh, sure you have. Rule number one missy; don't go into the forest without some sort of protection," Merik said. He took a piece of steel by its wooden handle from the fire, wrapped in a resistant material. The red-hot metal glowed brightly. Merik looked at it once, hit it with the hammer, then held it up to his face and blew hard on it. His breath cooled the iron instantly, making the metal smooth and shiny. He took off the material to reveal a wooden handle to what could now be determined as a dagger. He looked at Eva and threw the dagger into the wall, the blade just inches from her face. Eva flinched, paling. Merik scoffed and walked past her, pulling the dagger out of the wall, its edge having sliced one of the steel nails that held the wall in place. He faced Eva holding the knife between his two index fingers.

“This is a chevalier dagger. You use this for defense. If someone comes at you, don’t be afraid to use it. Finn will teach you the rest," he grabbed the blade gently in his palm, showing her the handle. A small spiral looped itself through the four-pointed star in the middle. “I’ve engraved the symbol of luck in the handle. The way I see it, you’ll need a lot of it," he said. Merik placed the dagger into a leather sheath then into her hand. Eva gulped looking at the weapon she held in her hands. She shakily strapped it around her waist.

Finn placed a hand on Eva’s shoulder, giving her a soft smile. “Come on. Let’s go," he said. Eva gave a small nod, and they headed out, away from the village.

~:~

“The forest is a dangerous place to travel through. There are many creatures here that are protective of their territory. I've made arrangements to meet a friend a little way in. He'll know how to help us. Just follow my lead, and we should be fine," Finn said as they entered the wooded area.

“So, how did you know my name?” she asked.

“Oh, didn’t you tell me?” he chuckled nervously. “I could’ve sworn you did.”

“No. I never told you my name. I would’ve remembered.”

“That’s right.” Finn sighed. “I heard that other girl scream your name when I was trying to get you two to stop your car.”

“Maddie…I hope she’s okay. She must be so scared!” Eva said. “You’re sure she made it home safely?”

“Honestly, I don’t know. I didn’t see her when we left.”

“WHAT?”

"I had to get you out of there! I'm sure she's alright."

"We must get back! I have to know she is okay! What if she's hurt, or worse!"

"I can't take you back. Not now when we've come this far. If I take you back now, King Valdof will surely find you and all of this will be for nothing."

"But-"

"I know you're concerned for your friend, but if you truly care for her, you will keep your own hide safe and keep your concern for her low. If King Valdof finds out you care that much for her, he'll use her against you."

"What if-"

"No. There's nothing we can do now, Eva. You need to let it go. I'm sure she is safe at home. You can see her when you get back."

"How long should that take?"

"That depends on how long it takes to get King Valdof off your back. If I calculated correctly, it should be about four to five days."

"Four to five days! Everyone will think I've been kidnapped, or dead! My parents probably already set up a search party!"

"Well, no one will be able to find us here."

"Fine," she pouted, forfeiting. Eva gazed in awe at the forest around her. Golden dust of light sprinkled around the trees and through the air. Birds chirped and rustling sounded where woodland animals danced their paths creating whimsical music. A bucked-tooth red squirrel whipped its prickly tail, gazing down at her. She paused for a moment as it made its way down the tree. Eva glanced at Finn, who kept walking, and sneakily broke off a piece of her sourdough. She knelt, holding out the piece of bread to the tiny creature. It crooked its head then shyly sniffed her fingers.

“It’s okay,” she whispered. The squirrel quickly wrapped its paws around the bread and nibbled it. Its tail shook playfully as it stuffed the bread crumb into his cheeks. The squirrel nudged its head to her hand. “You’re quite welcome, little one,” she chuckled. The squirrel groomed its tail and pulled out three quills, placing them into Eva’s palm before running off.

“Don’t get too far behind.” Finn called out.

Eva quickly pocketed the quills and rushed to keep up.

“Why do magical folk hate humans?”

“It’s kind of a long story,” Finn said. “Magical Folk and humans used to be on good terms for thousands of years. We would help man survive, teaching him our wisdom and the new techniques that made our colonies stronger. In return, Man would tell stories of our kind, and tell their young about our mysterious ways that man, himself, could not fully understand. Most of them were based off true events, with an addition of thrill to excite the storyteller’s audience.”

“So, what happened?”

“Let’s just say humans became fearful of us and started a war to destroy our kind.”

“I’m not sure I understand. Why would they become fearful? If Man and Magical Folk were bonded for so long, it just doesn’t make sense why they would start a war.”

“Does war ever truly make sense?”

“No, I guess not. But-”

“It doesn’t matter what changed. What matters is that Man killed thousands of our kind and didn’t even blink an eye!”

“There has to be some reason.”

“There’s no excuse to enslaving, torturing, and brutally murdering anyone, Man or Magic Folk! Anything can be resolved peacefully. We lost so much those seventy years ago: our homes; families; friends; everything we knew. Even in battle, my grandfather used to say, we fought with peace in mind. All Man could do was fight for blood. Even magic wasn't enough to stop their brutality," he said, fist clenched.

"I'm sorry, Finn. I couldn't imagine losing all you own because you were different. I know Man has done horrible things to his own kind, and it's not surprising that the same would happen to magical folk, but it's a shame it couldn't work out. I've always been fascinated by the so-called 'urban legends.' It allowed my imagination to explore new realms of thrill, mysticism, and magic. Now that I can see it in real life, it almost makes me glad the King wants me."

Finn stopped to face her; his cheeks were as red as fire. "Don't you ever say that again! You don't understand what Valdof is capable of! We've had two kings rule over us now, and ever since Valdof seized the throne, he stricken the rules and caused terror amongst various village tribes!"

"What do you mean?" Eva asked, stepping back.

"He altered the ways of the kingdom. When we first chose our leader, there were set rules of how our realm should be ruled, and everyone agreed upon them. Although the king has power to change said rules with the flick of a finger, he must think of his public and follow the path of the Newmark Agreement. He's a monster, a vile being that doesn't deserve to live in this realm! He's killed hundreds of people without a care in the world, but as our ruler we must obey his orders." A look of rage filled Finn's eyes. His jaw tightened as he looked away.

Eva stood there quietly; her stomach tied itself into knots. *You idiot! How could you be so naïve?* She quietly scolded herself, biting her lip. "Look, I'm sorry. I didn't mean to upset you. It was stupid of me to think-"

"Don't apologize! Just stand still!" he said sternly. Finn carefully drew out his dagger. Eva's eyes widened. "Don't move," he said. Finn's eyes focused on something beside her. A small red flower sniffed around her head. Just as he closed upon the stem, the flower turned its bud to face him, then, in an instant, wrapped itself around Eva's waist, pulling her backwards.

"Shit!" Finn yelled, throwing himself onto Eva, dropping his dagger in the process. The flower made a squeaking noise, and suddenly eight more identical flowers showed up. They quickly wrapped themselves over Finn and Eva. Their grip tightened as they lifted them up into the air and through the dense foliage. A growling sound came from behind them, where the mother plant stood, reeling in its vined bait. Its greenish-red bloom curled like a glass pitcher capped on the top with leafy flaps full of spiny teeth. The flower opened its mouth as the vines brought Finn and Eva closer. The vines pulled them through the hole, releasing them into a giant pit that was its stomach. The flaps shut tightly, intertwining their teeth together, making it impossible for Eva and Finn to pry out of it.

"Oh my God! We're going to die!" Eva cried.

"We're not going to die!" Finn said, placing his hands on her shoulders. "We'll get out of this together." He pulled out his knife and started slashing the walls. "Start trying to find a way out."

Eva looked around at the plant. Not seeing a way out, she started pushing the plant's sides, hoping to possibly force it open. The plant reeked of rot with the sweet smell of death. Yellowish fluids bubbled through the bottom, filling the stomach up fast. It simmered over the edges of their boots, eating away at the material. Finn's knife grazed the plant causing a green substance to ooze out. The plant growled, and stretched itself upward, tightening its body around them.

"Why don't you use your magic?" Eva asked, feeling their bodies coming closer.

"The flower's bile cancels out any magic. Besides, even if I did, we'd both go up in flames," he grunted, trying to cut the flower. "Shit! The walls are too thick! Give me your chevalier."

"Okay," Eva squeezed her hand towards her sheath, trying to pull out the dagger. "I got it!" The moment she grasped it, the plant squeezed harder, allowing them little space to move. Eva lost her grip and the dagger fell into the fluid below. "Oh no…"

"What? Where is it?"

"I dropped it!"

"You what!"

"I'm sorry! I'll look for it."

"No! If you touch the bile with your bare hands, you'll burn yourself. We'll find another way out," he said, examining the plant. "Whatever happens, I promise you, we'll get out of here alive!" he continued, thrashing his knife into the plant's flesh.

"This is it! We're going to die! All those years of following the rules and studying hard, and for what? To be eaten by a man-eating magical plant, and it's all your fault!"

"Stop it! We'll be fine," said Finn.

"Stop it? Sure. Just as the bile burns through our skin and eats us outside-in! This is totally a time to be calm!"

"Will you just stop talking? We're almost out!" he lied. The fluid started filling up more, burning through the bottoms of their clothes and any loose objects near their hips. *I can't give up!* He kept telling himself. *She doesn't deserve this! I won't let her die!*

Tiny squeals came from the outside of the plant. The plant let out a blood-curdling scream and began shaking. It twisted its bloom, trying to finish off its prey. The sound of metal slashing through the plant echoed around Eva and Finn. Above them, light shined, as a figure rushed past, slicing the plant's tip off in a single strike. The plant screamed again, green blood flooding it from all sides. A man stood in a tree above the plant with grace. He knelt, reaching his gloved hand to help the two out. Finn helped move Eva upward as she reached out her hand. The man pulled her up, sitting her beside him on the branch. Finn followed.

The man hopped down and took his sword, stabbing it through the center of the plant. A high pitch squeal rang from the plant, and it went limp. He grabbed the dagger from the bottom of the plant, wiping the fluid off with a handkerchief. The blade gleamed smoothly and without blemish.

Finn hopped down from the tree, assisting Eva on her way down.

“Are you okay?” he asked. “Does it hurt anywhere?”

“My leg hurts a little bit, but I think I’m okay," she said, more startled than anything.

“Let me check it out. Can you walk?”

“I-I think so," Eva said, flushing.

Finn sat Eva down on a large rock near a tree. He pushed her ragged dress up to her knee. The plant's acidic bile bore holes through her boots, now barely wearable. He gently pulled the boot off her foot. Her skin reddened with blisters where the boot holes laid. Finn’s clothing was in a similar fate.

“Thee best hast that checked out," the blonde man spoke. “If thee allow it t’ sit, it will fester.”

Eva looked at the man, wondering who he could be. Lanky and thin, the man towered before them, his icy blue eyes full of cynicism. His long pale face appeared rigid and pristine, as if age resisted him. With his lengthy ears pointing out of his hair, Eva knew immediately he was an elf.

“Eva, this is Ijaïh. He's the one I was talking about before.”

“Thank you, for saving our lives.”

Ijaïh pointed his attention at Finn, not giving any thought to Eva’s remark. “This is what thy secret plan is about? I will not be a part o’ it,” he said in disgust.

“Ijaïh here me out," Finn requested, quickly standing up to walk towards him.

“Nay! If King Valdof finds out, we will be in worser fates! I will not hast mine village torn apart because o’ some human girl!”

“If he gets a hold of her, all of lives will be at stake! Not just you, or yours or mine village. The whole kingdom. Please, help me.”

“Nay.”

“Don't be like that Ijaïh. Let's talk it out. I promise it's worth it. This could finally make this land whole again. The way it used to be.”

Ijaïh took a second to think about Finn’s offer. “It puts too much at risk,” he said and then started to walk off.

“Well at least let us come to your village! As you said, Eva needs medical attention! We both do!”

“Fine, but then thee leave.”

Finn sighed, knowing that Ijaïh’s mind wouldn't change. He turned back to face Eva, with a soft smile, and helped her up.

“Did I insult him in some way?” she asked, feeling guilty for his lack of aid.

“No. Ijaïh is just particular to who he helps. He'll come around; he always does...usually.” he said calmly, keeping Eva close in case she stumbled, as they set off to Ijaïh’s homeland.

Chapter 6

The Elvish Culture

Entering the new village, the elves welcomed Ijaïh with high grace, each of the village elves nodding their heads with respect when he passed them. Ijaïh walked with pride, not glancing at anyone who greeted him. The people started to whisper in an olden tongue amongst themselves. The villagers kept their hands close to their weapons, glaring at Finn and Eva as they approached.

"Why are they speaking in Old English?" Eva whispered to Finn.

"Old English? You must be mistaken. That's Native Aloncian. It's the oldest and most formal way of speaking."

"I've read enough Shakespeare to know what Old English sounds like, and that is it."

"It is not- Oh I understand. That's quite interesting. I never thought of how that would've affected you. Grant it, I never did try that spell on anyone but tribe members. That's truly fascinating!"

"What spell?"

"The Polyglot Spell. See I knew you wouldn't understand what we would be saying here, so I decided to make things easier for you. I never thought it worked quite like this though. It's intriguing. Normally when I cast the spell, people can speak, read, and hear the languages they couldn't understand before. Languages can be deciphered easier, but it's not always clear. The Elnaïrians take pride in speaking Aloncian's native tongue. While I hear their natural way of speaking, you hear Old English, which I assume is the closest version of a native language you know."

"You mean, I'm speaking another language?"

"Yes. Isn't it great?" Finn said, excitement filling his eyes.

"Very."

Woodwind music could be heard throughout the enchanting tranquil village that stood in a meadow within the woods. Small huts made of woven leaves and wood lined the edges where the trees remained. The men and women's long, flowy hair danced delicately across their fair skin. The men worked on crafting weapons, fixing the huts, and practicing their fighting skills while the womenfolk were caring for the young, preparing food for the whole village, and a select few aiding in the combat practices.

Ijaïh led Finn and Eva to one of the huts where a few elves were sewing bits of fabric for clothing. "Sujïno, take Miss Eva and Sir Barrett t' the recovery center. They hast come t' encounter wi' a spritser. Be sure t' give them whatever they need and allow them t' cleanse in mine own lavatory while thee tend t' their robes."

"Aye," the elf said, curtsying in his presence. She looked at Finn and Eva then continued. "Follow me. Marrethi and I shalt aid thy wounds."

~:~

In the recovery center, Sujïno and Marrethi examined Finn and Eva's wounds. "What wast thee doing in that area o' the forest? Thou must know 'tis filled wi' spritsers. There wast a mad infestation this past month," Sujïno said noticing the burns on Eva's legs.

"We were on our way to meet Ijaïh. I have some important information I must talk about with him," Finn said. "I've been gone for the past three months and just got back yesterday. If I would've known about the spritsers, I would have entered a different area."

"I see... Thou art quite lucky. The venom hath not exceeded the infected area. Not the pleasant of burns, but t'will be simple t' cure. Any longer and thee would hast t' balm the toxins. Merrethi, draw a bath in Lavatories One and Four. I suggest thee add some epsom salts. Add lavender t' Lavatory Four. Miss Eva hath need extra treatment. Hie."

"Aye, Ma'am." Merrethi nodded then headed out of the room.

Moments later, the baths were drawn, and the elves took Finn and Eva their separate ways. Entering Lavatory Four, a strong gust of lavender filled the air. Sujïno excused herself while Eva undressed and stepped into the bath. The water came to Eva's neck. Its warm touch soothed her. Eva could feel the burns on her legs ease, releasing the spritser's venom out of her pores. She dunked her head under for a moment, cleaning the green slime and dirt off her face. Time in Aloncia seemed to be moving so fast; it felt like forever since Eva last took a bath. Sujïno reentered the room to grab Eva's clothes.

"'Tis a fair jewel," she said, holding up the necklace.

Eva turned her head to face her, eyes wide. "Oh, please don't take that! A dear friend of mine gave it to me. I didn't want it to get wet. It's very special."

"'Tis alright. I shall leave it here," Sujïno said, taking a closer look at the gem "'Tis peculiar though. I hast not seen a jewel like this in quite some time. Orange quartz 'tis not?"

"Yes."

"A valorous stone t' keep on thee. Wearing orange quartz will keep hence negativity and heal the soul. Thee should become more in tune wi' thyself. There is a wondrous power within this stone. Best keep it safe," she continued, handing the stone to Eva. "Now, I shall crisp and mend thy robes. I will be back momentarily and bring thee new boots."

"This contains wondrous powers?" Eva said, leaning her arm on the edge of the stone bath, looking at her necklace. "I wonder what she meant by that."

~:~

Meanwhile, in Lavatory One, Finn just finished washing up, and put on his, now mended, clothes. He laced the strings through the holes of his vest, tightening it until it was snug against his shirt and body. He left the lavatory and walked out to the main part of the village to find Ijaïh. Finn found him sitting on an aged tree trunk, whittling a spruce block into an arrow, out in the far end of the village where few people roamed.

"I am not interested in joining thee on thy quest," Ijaïh said, focused on his whittling. His hand gripped into the wood, with each wooden flake relieving him of a distasteful thought about the proposal.

"Look I get it alright. You're learning how to become a strong leader now and must fend for your people, but at least give me a chance to explain why this isn't any normal quest."

"Thee may speak, but thee will not convert mine decision."

"Eva…she's not like other humans," Finn sighed. "There's something about her I can't quite place my finger on it. You must've noticed."

"Iwis," he said, "but the lady is none o' mine concern."

"Damnit Ijaïh! Can't you see that if Valdof gets his hands on her, he'll kill her in an instant, just like all the others! Once he does that something bad is going to happen! I felt it in my gut ever since that night at Valdof's castle!"

"Then what is thy plan?"

"To keep Eva as safe as possible, take her where Valdof will never find her."

"Thy knavery is rude. Tell me the truth," Ijaïh said angrily, standing up.

Finn stood there in silence.

~:~

Eva walked out of the lavatories, looking as if she had never encountered that horrific plant. Sujïno dried and braided her hair. She hid her necklace in one of the pockets in her bag, deciding it best to keep it out of sight until she found out what Sujïno meant by it having power. She figured Finn remained inside cleaning up, so she stayed nearby the building looking around the village.

A stone wall sat next to the recovery center. An elf pulled up the rope of the water-filled bucket, placing it on a wooden pole to carry double the amount. She carried them over to a large tin pot, which she filled with water. Three elves washed their clothes around the pot. Behind them stood another elf hanging up the wet cloth to dry.

A small rustling noise came from behind her. Eva quickly turned around, noticing the bush beside the hut moving. She walked to the bush, only to hear another rustling sound coming from nearby. She looked around until she spotted a shrub next to the elves doing laundry. By the time she got over to the elves she caught a glimpse of something large scurrying into another bush a few yards away. She sneakily pushed away its thick leafy branches to see a bare spot. She looked at it perplexed, wondering where the creature went.

"Good morrow, fair maiden!" a voice came from behind.

There stood a young boy with a big mischievous smile crawled upon his face as his pointed ears perked up. A blackened mark rode up the right side of his neck. His hair laid short and jagged as if it were recently cut. He wore a baggy shirt, that reached well below his hips, tied with a thick rope at the waist. Silver embroidery danced symbols along his boots which resembled that of Ijaïh's.

"Wast you looking for me?" he said, with his hands behind his back and leaning forward toward her. Curiosity filled his pale blue eyes.

"Why yes! Was it you, hiding in the bushes making that noise?" Eva smiled mirroring his actions.

The boy looked at her in shock that she even talked to him. Unaware as of why the boy looked so surprised, she stood up straight and slightly tilted her head, wondering his sudden change in attitude. The boy looked at her with great seriousness, grabbed her hand and pulled her down to be at face level with her. "Canst you keep a secret?" he whispered in her ear.

Eva overheard some of the elves doing laundry. They looked at her and the boy in disgust. "Hath she no shame?" the one elf said.

"What a fool. What err she hath done, fainly speaking to that knave," another said.

Eva narrowed her eyes at the elves and then smiled softly at the young boy and gave a nod. He smiled greatly and clenched her hand pulling her further into the wooded area surrounding the village. They ran for a while before coming into a small valley full of flowers. Even the trees filled themselves with various colored blooms. Eva looked around in awe. The petals layered the blooms, some in tool-like rows, others with small humanoid figures matching the vibrant colors of the stems. One bloom shined bright violet and its thin petals spread out like a tutu with a sepal bent into a position that made it look like a ballerina. Eva bent down to take a closer look.

"What a peculiar flower," she said, placing a finger upon the petal. The flower started to spin into the air. All the flowers followed, bursts of bright light encasing their petals. As the light dissipated, small humans with translucent wings hovered in the air.

"They're fairies!" Eva exclaimed. She giggled as the fairies flew around her. A few put real flowers in her hair, making her braid prominent with small daisies and baby's breath.

A fairy whispered something into the young boy's ear, making him laugh.

"What?" Eva asked.

"Oh, 'tis nothing. She just said you look like a frog. Hast you ne'er seen a fairy 'ere."

"No, I can't say I have."

"They live everywhere!" he said, astounded. "Thou art not from around here, art you?"

"No."

"Well, that makes more sense as t' why you treated me so earlier. Most would pay no attention t' me."

"Why is that?" Eva asked, sitting down next to him.

"I am different from the other elves here. Kind of a tarnish rapier in a way," he said, twiddling his thumbs.

"I see. I'm not like many here, myself. Where I'm from, very few folk talk to me. I guess you can say we're alike," she smiled.

The boy stared at her as if no one had spoken to him in years, then grinned. "That so! My name is Datorajï Tàileach, but you can call me Dator," he said holding out his hand.

Eva shook his hand. "Well Dator, my name's Eva Dawkins. It is a pleasure to make your acquaintance."

A fairy landed on the skirt of Eva's dress. Eva held out her hand, and the fairy climbed into her palm. Humanoid in appearance, she glowed that of a rose, enchantment lining her large purple eyes. Her dress appeared to be made of woven green silk layered with deep blue petals. Her delicate wings shined in the light, expressing their translucent and delicate design. "You're very beautiful," Eva said in a soft voice. The fairy's whole body turned a shade of pink when she said this.

A small munching sound came from behind a tree. The fairy looked at the source of the sound with slight fear. She signaled with a whistle then flew off in the opposite direction, all the fairies following.

"What was that about?"

"They sense a drawrble," Dator said, standing up.

"What's a drawrble?"

"That," he said as a three-foot tall creature stepped out from behind the tree. Its fur had a blend of white and brown that led down from its head all the way to its diamond-shaped tail. Ram-like horns, wrapped in vines, rose above its short snout. In between the horns sprouted a yellow flower with five round petals, its long thin tongue trying to capture the remains of the prey it just caught. Dator walked up to the creature with ease and began to pet it. "Come. It won't bite. Just don't touch the flower on his head."

Eva slowly walked to the odd animal. She reached her hand out for it to smell. As it did, Dator chuckled, grabbing her hand gently and bringing it to rest on the drawrble's back. She ran her fingers through its coarse fur. The drawrble nudged Eva playfully as she scratched its back.

"They are quite peaceful creatures, drawrbles are," Dator said. "They feast mainly on insects and occasionally fairies, which is why they flew away in haste. Most fairies know o' its fake flower at this point, but the unlucky few get caught occasionally."

"It must be hard on the fairies."

"Aye, but they can be very shrewd when they want t'. Mind thee, ne'er take anything from the fairies, or you shall regret it. Mischievous beasts they be."

"They seem so gentle though."

"That's what they want you t' believe."

"I see," Eva said continuing to stroke the drawrble's back. "This drawrble kind of reminds me of a goat."

"'Twas one. We took species from the human world years ago. We roamed with hundreds of goats and one o' them accidentally ate a fairy as it went to graze the fields for flowers. The fairy's magic roamed through the goat, allowing it t' use the power, and thus transformed into a similar figure as this. The goat survived longer than the rest, as its new powers increased its ability t' fend against disease and allowed it t' produce more young. The idea has come t' be known as the theory o' transformation. I suggest you not speak o' it, for many doth not like the idea, calling it a mere coincidence."

"Fascinating."

The drawrble licked Eva and Dator's face before running off after a butterfly that passed through. They rubbed their cheeks to rid themselves of the slimy essence that remained.

"I feel like I could stay out here for hours, but I should probably head back," Eva said, as she stood up and dusted off her dress.

"Thou art going back t' Finn and Ijaïh, art you not?"

"How did you-"

"I saw you come with them. What business doth you hast with him?"

"Well, Finn and I were hoping he'd help us on our journey."

"A quest! Oh, what excitement!" Dator said jumping to his feet. "Thou must know, Ijaïh will only accept with good reason."

"That's our problem. We need his help. Finn seems quite adamant about it. Finn says this quest can change everything."

"I can help there."

"How so?"

"I shall wend t' father. He always praises mine brother so."

"Wait a minute. Ijaïh is your brother?"

"Aye."

"And you're just willingly going to help me?" Eva asked. "Why?"

"No reason," he grinned.

Eva's eyes narrowed. "What's the catch?"

"No catch. Just an act of kindness for you."

"I don't know."

"He will ne'er agree if you deny mine offer."

He says he knows how to persuade his brother, but this could be a big risk...What if he's lying? Finn could get angry. But what if he's right? This could be our only hope.

She sighed. "If you fail…"

"I won't. Thou hast mine word. Father will be most excited t' hear Ijaïh hath accepted a quest."

"Okay, but you better be right."

Dator and Eva headed back to the village. In the middle of the village stood a tall, robust man whose withering face held stories of long ago, from a time that most could not reveal. He gazed upon the village, making sure everything was at peace and as it should be.

"Father! Father!"

"Not now."

"I hast great news."

"Canst thee see I am busy? I must attend t' the village."

"But 'tis about Ijaïh. He hath accepted a quest that shall make our world better!"

"A quest? 'Tis most exciting! I must speak with him at once!"

The elderly man rushed over to where Ijaïh and Finn stood arguing; Eva and Dator followed behind.

"Come on Ijaïh, you must help me," Finn said, at whit's end.

"Out wi' thee! I say nay! I will not continue t' listen t' thy foolish requests!" Ijaïh yelled, beginning to walk away.

"Ijaïh, my boy! Thy brother hath told me o' thine great quest! I am most proud!" the man said with mirth. Ijaïh glared at Dator with a look of pure hatred.

"Father, thou art- "

"Art verily pleased mine son hath accepted a noble journey t' help thine village. I shalt prepare for thy leave," he said, and with that the man left to gather supplies.

Finn stood there in shock.

"Thou hadst no right!" Ijaïh spat. Dator smiled smugly, knowing he angered him.

"Thee wilt march ov'r to father and tell him o' thy knavery!"

Dator turned away from his brother, with his hand behind his head. "'Tis too bad. Father wilt be most disappointed that his *noble* kin declined a wondrous quest. Especially now that thee art t' be the new vaward come autumn."

Ijaïh sneered.

"Of course, if thee wast t' partake in this journey, the whole village will know of thy *bravery* and praise thee for thy *honorable* and *selfless* deed."

"Thou wretched little imp! Thou will regret this!" Ijaïh growled between his teeth.

Dator turned to face him with a sly grin.

The elderly elf made his way back to Ijaïh and the others. "Ijaïh, my son, the village hast decided t' prepare a grand feast for thee and thy companions before thy departure," he smiled. "Come, let us prepare. I must speak t' thee in private."

As Ijaïh and his father walked away towards the village, Finn looked at Dator. "That was amazing! If I knew it would be that simple, I wouldn't waste my time bickering with him."

"'Tis nothing. Thou ought t' thank Miss Eva, for she is the true reason for mine actions."

Finn looked at Eva, who smiled modestly.

"Right," he said awkwardly. "Oh, I almost forgot, here," Finn continued, handing Eva her dagger. "Ijaïh found it when he killed that spritser back there."

"Thanks," she said, placing it back into its leather holder.

"Don't drop it next time," he said.

"I won't."

~:~

Ijaïh followed his father into their home. The elderly man locked the door behind him, then lit the lantern that hung near the door.

"Ijaïh, I know thee wish not t' be a part o' such a travel."

"Father, I-"

"I wish thee would go forth on this journey. Thou art strong and full o' valor. Thou make me proud, but thou hast t' think o' what 'tis best for thine village."

"But father, if I shall venture towards this task and fail, our village shall perish."

"Then doth not fail." Ijaïh's father pulled out a small object from his pocket, placing it into his son's hand. "Take this. 'Twas what thine mother gave t' me before the war broke out. It shall bring thee the hope and courage t' persevere. Follow its wisdom and thou shalt find thy path o' righteousness."

Ijaïh looked down upon the round object. The talisman bore symbols for hope, courage, wisdom, and perseverance, within the sun-shaped carving. Ijaïh closed his hand around it, thankful for his father's gift.

“The symbols will glow bright and grow hot when thou hast gone against thy destiny. Follow thy path, until the end o’ thy journey.”

“Aye.”

“Oh, and one more thing," he said handing his son a bow with a quiver filled with feathered arrows and sack full of medicine, food, and charms. “Take thine brother with thee.”

“What? How shall I succumb t’ take that vile creature! He hath destroyed his pride and has brought dishonor t’ our family! He is a disgrace t’ the Elnaïrian culture!”

“He needs guidance; thine guidance. Thou have grown distant from one another, and I am ashamed I must treat him in such a manner, but ‘tis mine duty t’ keep this village strong. Laws art laws, and there is at each moment punishment when broken. He hath lost his way and although he hath brought dishonor t’ us, he can repent for his errs. ‘Tis rare t’ see him around the village often. This journey hath lightened his curiosity. Guide him back t’ us. Teach him o’ the importance o’ our ways and provide him with pride and honor. Make him see his true potential.”

“Thou must reconsider,” Ijaïh suggested, but his father just stared at him intently. Ijaïh sighed, “I shall do as thou request.”

Chapter 7

The Quest

"Alright, so here's the plan," Finn said, rolling out a rather large map of Aloncia upon a handcrafted table. "We're here in Elnaïr. Originally, I figured we could travel east through the Cedarina Woodlands, but due to the spritser infestation, we should head south towards the border. Ijaïh where did they invade?"

"The spritsers hast taken refuge from which thee came, however, I hast seen them further north as well. I hast been clearing the land o' those vile plants as they make their territory. If we head south twenty-seven miles, we should be past their path."

Using a divider, Finn traced the path of which they would take. "Then, at this point here, we would travel eastward, escaping the plants' range. From there, it should be about a four-day journey until we reach Tiltin Hollow. Then we head south towards Vîgarie."

"Would it not be best t' travel by teleportation? The fairies doth owe me for their protection from the drawrbles," Dator said.

"What hast thee doing wi' the fairies?" Ijaïh grimaced.

"Never mind that! That wouldn't work."

"No?" Dator said.

"No. We must keep our magic usage to a minimum. If we teleport to Vîgarie, Valdof will find us in an instant! He knows Eva is here, and by transporting her there by magic, it will send out an alarm. He will notice the massive amount of power immediately, and all of this will be of waste. We must stay quiet," Finn said.

"Then why hasn't he found us now? If he can track such magic, as you say, shouldn't he have noticed when we came here, or at the very least, our movements?" Eva asked.

"No. After the crash I set a barrier around us to hide my magic and your presence. There's no way he could've tracked our travel back. The barrier should protect all of us from Valdof and his guards, but it will leave me practically useless except for a few simple spells and combat."

"Mine skills should aid if any danger come forth so long as thee doth not cause much ado," Ijaïh said referring to his brother.

"I don't plan on making a fuss. It's not like I chose to be here anyway," Eva smirked.

"Ugh, not thee!"

"Let's not argue about this! Everyone will behave and get along with one another, got it?" Finn said.

Eva crossed her arms. "Fine with me."

"Ijaïh?"

"Aye. Just stay out o' mine way," he scoffed, leaving the hut.

"Jeez, is he always like this?" Eva asked.

"Most of the time," Dator said.

"Ijaïh's dealt with a lot these past few years. It's just his way of handling it, that's all,"

Finn said. "He'll warm up eventually."

"Yeah...probably."

The three exited the hut to see a large feast upon the ground for everyone to enjoy. A roasted pheasant with sage, mushrooms and herbs, and an array of fruits and vegetables in separate wooden dishes lay across the table. Everyone encircled the meal, sitting down after Ijaïh and his father took their place. His father raised a wooden cup full of wine.

"Thank you, your Majesty," Eva said with a curtsey.

Ijaïh's father laughed heartily. "Mine child, thou honor me too highly."

"She meant nothing by it, Sotoverra! She's…well she's-" Finn stuttered.

He held up his hand and Finn became silent. "Thou art a peculiar child. T' not know thy rulers rank is quite insulting. Tis almost as if thou are not from 'ere."

"Not from here?" Eva gulped. "Nonsense, I come from Laurik!"

"Father, we best be going forth if we wish to pass the spritsers' range by nightfall," Ijaïh said. "Doth not worry o' simpletons like her."

"Ah, thou art right, mine son. I see thou brother is on his way. Doth not fail me."

Dator came running up to them holding out a small sac of fruit. "Take this upon thy journey. I desire thee will hast safe travels."

"Keep thine offer," Ijaïh said coldly.

"But-" Dator said with a sorrowful look.

"We will not be needing such items as thee will be coming wi' us. Thee can carry 't wi' thine other belongings."

Dator looked at his brother in shock. "Thee wish for me t' be a part of thine group?"

"Didst thee not hear mine request?"

"Y-Yes!" Dator said quickly, smiling ear to ear. He placed the sac of fruit in his pack. "This will be most exciting!"

"That it will be," Eva laughed. She smiled at him, hoping this quest would do him well. *Perhaps this is what he needs to prove his loyalty to the Elnaïrians.*

~:~

The trail remained quaint, with birds chirping and the occasional animal running by. Ijaïh brushed off spritser stems and petals from his shoulder. Green bile lay upon his cheek, simmering.

"Ijaïh, here, take my cloth to clean your face before the bile burns you," Eva said.

"Doth not insult me, petty human," he said, smacking her hand away. He wiped his cheek on his sleeve and pushed past her.

Dator quickly picked up Eva's handkerchief and gave it to her. "Pay him no mind," he said grabbing her hand. "Besides, I shall keep you safe! Anyone or anything that tries to snatch you will have to go through me!"

"Thank you, Dator," she said.

They walked for what seemed like hours until before them stood a soft patch of land. A long day's travel soon came to an end as the two moons made their way up the blackened sky. Finn collected eight stones and with a snap of his fingers, they formed a circle large enough to set up camp within. A green ring connected them, creating a barrier.

"Alright. We'll stay here for the night," Finn said, throwing his pouch to the ground.

Eva let her legs give in. "Thank goodness! I've never walked so long in my entire life."

"Well, there's more to come. We still have a long way to go."

"Hmph. Quite feeble doth thee not think?" Ijaïh asked, rhetorically.

"Hey! What's that supposed to mean?"

"T' be weary ere the fall o' a single day is merely pitiful," he said, striking a piece of flint against a few stone-encircled twigs.

"Are you calling me weak?" Eva snapped.

"Perhaps thee doth hast more wits than a boar."

Eva clenched her fist.

"W-What Ijaïh m-meant t' say is that everyone struggles at first!" Dator said quickly.

"All of you stop bickering! There's no use in fighting over silly matters such as these! It is late, and all of us are tired. Let's just set up camp and be done with it," Finn said. He waved his hand over his satchel and a thin, leathery material slithered out. It rose into the air, fanning out before wooden pegs pinned the ends down forming a marquee tent.

Eva looked at the tent in amazement as it came together, moving poetically into place. As the tent settled itself, a small snicker arose.

"What's so funny?"

"You," Finn sniggered. "You look so awestruck by me setting up the tent."

"That's because you made it so much easier. Back home it would've taken at least ten minutes to put it up," she gawked.

"You sure do get joy out of the simplest of things don't you."

"Well, my mother always told me 'simple pleasures are the best.'"

"Then you'll be delighted by everything here. We simpletons always make the best of things," he joked.

Eva chuckled, letting her shoulders ease. "Can I take a look?"

"Sure," Finn said. He lifted the flap to let her through. Its inside looked larger than what its outer presented. Eva patted the soft woolen blankets folded up by the door, yawning knowing they would prove warm during the cold night's air. "You look tired. You should probably get some rest."

"But what about you and the others?"

"Ijaïh and I will be taking shifts guarding the camp, so we'll be staying outside for the time being. Dator may come in to rest later, but he seems to be enjoying the warm fire," he said. "I'll bring over some fruit in case you get hungry later."

"Okay," she said. Finn exited the tent, leaving her alone within the fabric cocoon. Eva wrapped herself in a blanket and curled up on the hard ground. She held tight to her orange quartz necklace.

Oh Maddie...what am I doing here? I can't wait to get home. You, Mom and Dad, and Rina must all be so worried...at least I have this to remember you. I just don't know what to think anymore. This place...Aloncia...it's all so weird and yet, beautiful. Is it odd that I feel like I've been here before? I recognize this place. It's silly, really.

I don't know what to do about the others. Ijaïh seems to hate everything about me for whatever reason. I'll be lucky if he doesn't kill me before we reach the safe zone. Dator...I don't know, he's just a little kid. He doesn't seem to be of any harm, but maybe that's a sign. I mean, there are all those horror films about evil kids and all...No, NO, there's no way he's like that...I hope...

Finn seems nice. Huh...ain't that a weird thing to say about my kidnapper? Oh, forgive me, 'protector.' One thing's for sure, he's smart, but he's hiding something. Not that I should pry, but it feels important. Maybe I'm overthinking this...I tend to do that a lot anyway. That's probably what's making my stomach knot up. I don't know what this Valdof guy has in store. If he's as bad as Finn makes him out to be, I don't even want to think about what might happen if or when he finds us. Finn seems to be really determined to stick this mission through though.

"Hey Eva? I brought some fruit for you," Finn said.

Eva jumped, startled by his sudden appearance. She hid the necklace under the blanket. "T-Thank you." she stuttered.

"You're welcome. Sorry for scaring you."

"Oh, it's okay, really," she said, sitting up and pulling her knees close.

"You must really miss your home, huh?" he said. Eva nodded. "You know, you don't have to be afraid of us. We won't harm you. I guess that seems hard to believe coming from me."

"Maybe. I'm sorry for being so tense. You all have been so nice to me...well most of you anyway. I may have been a bit too on edge."

"No. It's to be expected. I mean you've never been here before and coming the way you did for the reasons you had to, didn't exactly help. If anything, sleep it off and take it easy. We'll be there to protect you at all costs."

"You make it sound like I'm royalty," she said.

"Well, that's my job," he teased. "But now, milady, I must bid you goodnight. Fear not of the ways our travel may be and let not the words of that overbearing elf worry your little head. For now, sleep well."

Eva meekly smiled and wished him well. She rested her head upon a soft patch of grass and looked at the necklace once more. *You know, for someone who could've easily caused me harm, he's very sweet. Maybe he isn't really as bad as I think. Perhaps I owe him and the others a second chance... I'm sure things will get better, and even though you're not here, I got a feeling things will work out.*

Goodnight Maddie. Please, be safe.

Maddie jolted up grasping her chest. Her heavy gasps hastened as she looked around. Muddied stones with hints of blood surrounded her as thick iron bars caged her in. A smell of rot and decay filled the air.

"You've finally awakened," a soft voice echoed.

"Who's there? Where am I?"

"Hush, you will stir the King," the voice said. A pale hand covered in bruises shakily held out half an orange. "Eat."

As Maddie grabbed the orange, the hand grasped her wrist. She gasped, trying to pull free. Her eyes widened at the beaten woman's lashed body and cloth covered face.

"Listen to me very closely. Eva is in trouble. You must survive for her to live. The King will use you to get to her. You must obey everything he commands or else the plan will fail. Disobey, and he will beat you. You must not fail."

"What do you mean? Where's Eva?"

The woman let go of Maddie and stiffened. "The King stirs! I have said too much."

"Please, tell me where Eva is! I have to find her!"

"Hush!"

"Then at least tell me your name!"

"Call me Verona."

Darkness filled the room as King Valdof entered. "Ah, my little doll has awakened." He opened the cage door. "Come, Maddie, let me have a look at you."

Maddie glanced at Verona, then took a few steps forward until the chains pulled her legs tight. "Where's Eva?" she said.

"Now, now, you will see your friend in due time. I have many plans for you," King Valdof said, stroking her cheek.

"Don't you touch me," Maddie said, snapping at his fingers.

King Valdof slapped her with a sneer. "A feisty young sprite. Mind your tongue when in the presence of royalty."

Maddie held her cheek. "F-Forgive me," she said in disgust.

"That's better," he said. Juice ran down Maddie's arm from a now pulped orange. "No, no, that will not do. That is much too tart for you. It will spoil you." Valdof snapped his fingers, and the orange was gone. Maddie stepped back, her heart racing. "You humor me, sprite. Take this. It will be deliciously good for you," he said placing an apple in her palm.

The cage doors slammed shut before her. "What are you doing? You can't just leave us in here!" Maddie screamed.

"Perhaps a few days in here will teach you to respect your elders, sprite," he hissed. "I give you food and shelter, and I can take that away with a flick of the wrist. You will listen to me, or your little friend will perish. Understand?"

Maddie pursed her lips.

"Good, sprite. Now, I best continue my search. Odd to think the pure one would mingle with a human spitfire. I see there is much to learn. Very much indeed."

Chapter 8

Practice Makes Perfect

Eva woke up to a strong hand nudging her shoulder. Finn knelt beside her and placed a finger to his lips. She sat up, collecting herself for another day's worth of travel. She grabbed her satchel and wiped the sleep from her eyes. The slight smell of smoke floated through the air from the remains of last night's campfire. Finn signaled her to follow him into the woods. Dator slept next to the fire pit, while Ijaïh sat nearby, tending the fire with a stick. He paid no attention to Eva and Finn as they walked past him into the eastward side of the woods.

"What time is it?" Eva yawned.

"Just after daybreak."

"Where are we going?"

"Not too far. Just over that hill there," Finn pointed.

They climbed up a small hill and into the valley beyond. Few trees surrounded the area, allowing for weeds to grow amongst the grass. Standing in the middle of the field, Finn waved his hand slowly in front of him. A green bubble appeared around the valley, slowly becoming opaque. He walked towards Eva.

"What are you doing?" she asked.

"Take out your dagger."

Eva did so. Finn waved his hand across the blade and did the same to his own dagger. "I'm creating a force field around the valley, so that we can stay hidden. No one will be able to see or hear us here, let alone penetrate the barrier. I'm going to teach you how to fight. I put a magical shield around yours and mine daggers so that they can't cut us. Of course, if you hit me across the head with the blade or handle, it still would hurt," he ended with a chuckle.

“What about Ijaïh and Dator? Won’t they worry if they can’t find us?”

“Nah, I told Ijaïh we were heading out this way last night. He and Dator are going to hunt for some food for us. I figured you probably wouldn’t like doing that, so instead, I shall teach you the ways of the dagger," he smiled, giving a dramatic wave of his weapon, before placing his dagger in his sheath. Eva giggled.

“First rule is to hold a tight grip on your dagger," he said, tightening Eva’s hand around the handle. “You can’t be letting go of it when you’re in a fight.”

“That was one time," she smirked, knowing he’d probably never let that incident slide. Her legs shook and she strained a smile.

“Don’t be afraid of it. If you use it right, it shouldn’t hurt you. You need to be prepared for the worst. If Ijaïh, Dator, or I aren’t there to save you in a situation, you must fend for yourself.”

Eva nodded, looking down at the dagger, hands trembling.

“Watch how I maneuver my dagger and try to copy it. You always hold your dagger in your dominant hand. There are two ways of holding the dagger: forward or reverse," he said showing her with his own knife, the blade facing above his hand, then below. “I personally like the reverse grip better, as it tends to be more effective in most situations.”

Eva copied his movements.

“Now, keeping the blade facing downward, move your arm, so the front of your forearm faces me. The blade should lay flat against your arm. Protect yourself like this,” he said, then fixed her arm to make it sturdier. “If someone comes at you with a weapon or certain magic, move your arm towards their attack, and the dagger will block it," he placed his dagger against hers, so she could get a feel of what it would be like.

“If you push your arm forward, it will then push your opponent back as well, but watch out that they don’t use their other arm to grab you from your underarm, for this will lock your arm, making it easy for the attacker to force you to drop your knife," he hooked her arm with his, his elbow locking the arm at her shoulder. As he forced her arm up, he used his other hand to gently knock the dagger out of her hand, and then let her go. “Now you try.”

Eva tried to mimic Finn’s actions.

“Your grip is loose.”

She tightened her arm and pushed the dagger out of his hand.

“There. That’s right," he said as she released him. “You can also defend yourself by holding the handle and the blade of your dagger to push away stronger fighters.” Finn placed Eva’s hands on her dagger properly, then placed his dagger against hers, applying more force than the time before. She pushed back, causing him to back off. “Good.”

Eva gave a small smile.

“When you hold your dagger in reverse, you can hit your attacker in many areas. In the front, around the collar and chest, under their arms, and if you bring them down, you can stab them in the back. Always keep your arm at the level of your eye, facing your opponent. It will make it easier for you to keep a hold of your weapon. I am going to show you an attack. Let’s say I am coming at you like this," he said moving his dagger towards her chest before halting it. “You must put up a defense. What do you do?”

Eva put her arm in front of the dagger, holding her dagger against her forearm.

“Good. That would work if this weren’t a trap. Any attacker will make you believe.

they're coming at you, but if they lock your arm, they can slice the side of your waist," he said showing her the attack tactic. Eva tried the tactic, performing it perfectly.

A couple hours passed, and Eva learned many attacks and their defenses against them.

"Alright. Do you feel ready to attempt some one-to-one combat?" Finn said seriously.

"I guess. Just go easy on me, okay?" Eva said.

"Of course," he said with a smile. "Get ready. On the count of three. One. Two. Three."

The two went at each other. Finn went for a direct attack. Eva pushed away his arm, tilting her dominant hand to the side. At that moment, Finn grabbed her wrist pulling her down as he placed the point of his dagger in the center of her back before letting her go.

"Try again."

Eva ran towards Finn, aiming for his gut. Finn grabbed her forearm, twisting it as he kicked the back of her leg, causing her to fall, allowing him to grab her dagger and place both points to her neck, with her arm pinned down gently by his foot. "You're not thinking! If you expect to survive, you got to do better than that," he said releasing her and dropping her dagger beside her.

Eva glared at him before picking herself up, dusting away the dirt on her skirt. She picked up her dagger and pointed it toward Finn. A grin grew upon her face. Finn launched an attack at her that Eva blocked, pushing him backward. She went for his shoulder, but he slapped her arm away. She jumped back, her knife at eye level, contemplating what to do next. Finn came at her aiming for Eva's head. She blocked the attack, twisting his wrist backward, and in response he pulled her other arm back, causing both to release one another. She shoved him, causing him to stumble backward. He gave a menacing look. Adrenaline rushing, Finn ran at Eva, thrusting her into a tree. She shivered as pain trickled down her back.

"Got you," he whispered with pride as he held his knife to her throat.

"Aha, so you think," she countered with a sly smile, as she pressed the dulled blade on his stomach.

Finn, a little shocked, let her escape his hold. She went for his arm. Finn moved away before she could hit him, allowing him access to stab her side. Eva blocked the punch and went for his head. As Finn went to block the dagger, their arms locked, their daggers pointing at each other. They looked at each other for a slight moment, both panting.

"You're a lot stronger than you look," Finn commented.

"Never doubt my abilities," she said with a laugh.

They released their guard, placing their daggers back in their sheaths and sat down next to one another to catch their breath. "We ought to do this more often," Eva continued.

"We can if you want. If we practice like this once or twice a day, you'll be able to fight on your own in no time."

"I think I hold out pretty well," Eva said, acting all high and mighty.

Finn snickered. "That you do, milady, that you do."

They sat there for a moment, glancing around the area. Finn looked up to the sky. "It's almost midday. We better head back," he said, standing up.

Finn held out his hand down. Her burning limbs gave in as she hit a rock stepping forward. She fell forward into Finn, who tumbled with her. Eva felt the pulsing beat of his heart as her head touched his chest. She lifted herself up, flustered, and their eyes locked. Finn's freckled face reddened. For a split second, the world around them stopped. Snapping to her senses, Eva quickly picked herself up, apologizing for the incident. Finn stood up, equally embarrassed.

"We should, um, we should go," he said, clearing his throat as he started walking back towards the camp. Eva followed bashfully, her stomach twisting as her heart fluttered. Images of Finn's face and breathless lips filled her thoughts. She shook her head and clenched her fists. *This is no time to be romantic. There's nothing between you. But maybe, perhaps- NO! Goodness Eva, get ahold of yourself.*

The trip back remained awkwardly silent.

~:~

Ijaïh sat sharpening his knives for the preparation of his prey. Beside him rested a brown woven sack that appeared to be lumpy at the bottom. He noticed Eva and Finn enter the campsite, and by their tension, knew something occupied their minds. Ijaïh kept quiet.

"How'd hunting go?" Finn asked.

"'Well, we would hast hads't more, but the little imp decided t' take things int' his own hands," he replied with a smirk.

"What did he do?" Finn asked.

"He got in the way o' mine capture o' a blue crane. its plump body would hast fed us for days."

"A blue crane? Aren't they a threatened species though?" Eva interjected.

"Nay. In fact, they're quite invasive here. 'Tis been that way since they hast been brought t' this wretched place. Beside the point I managed to gather a few rabbits. Therefore, we hast about a day and a half's worth o' food t' share."

"Well, I'm sure we can scrounge up something on the way," Finn said, trying to lighten the mood. At that moment Dator ran in from the forest, carrying a small sack in his hands that appeared to be full.

"Ijaïh! Ijaïh! Behold my findings! I hast found a large supply o' jubi berries just yonder riverbank!" Dator smiled excitedly, opening the sack to reveal dime-sized berries in shades of violet. "We can boil them down t' make a sweet water and-"

Ijaïh slapped the bag from Dator's hands, causing the berries to spill out onto the ground.

"Thou art a fool! Doth thee not know jubi berries art poisonous t' humans!" he scolded.

His brother's harsh words left Dator confused. "But Eva doesn't seem t' be human!"

"Then thee wish t' test t' view the effects o' thy precious berries on her? I assure thou hast no more brains than the dirt which thee trail!"

Dator took off into the woods.

"Dator, wait!" Eva yelled, running after him.

"Eva!" Finn called out, but she refused to listen to him, and kept going. He crossed his arms and looked at Ijaïh with a scowl. "Nice. Very nice Ijaïh. You just had to chase him away didn't you."

Ijaïh turned his head away from Finn, in disgust, and made his way to a nearby tree.

~:~

Eva continued to run until she could no more. She lost track of Dator moments before. *Dang, that kid is fast*, she said to herself as she caught her breath. She looked around her. Everything looked the same as did most of the forest.

"Dator! Where are you?" she shouted.

She heard no response.

"Come on, Dator, don't be that way! Answer me!" she continued, walking further into the woods.

She could hear the sound of water rushing nearby. As she came closer, Eva heard a soft *plopping* sound. Dator threw rocks and large twigs he snapped into the river.

"Dator?" she said softly in a calm voice, so as not to provoke him any further.

"What art you doing here?" he returned in angst, avoiding eye contact.

"I figured you'd need someone to talk to. Are you okay?" she continued as she approached him.

"I'm fine. Just leave me be."

"You shouldn't run off like that! You made everyone worried!"

"No one wouldst worry about me."

"I did. Ijaïh had no right to treat you like that."

"Ijaïh, Ijaïh, Ijaïh! It's always about him!" he bellowed, throwing a large rock into the river before standing still, facing the ground. "...and never about me," Dator's voice grew soft and he sat down, pulling his knees to his chest. He fiddled with a rock beside him. Eva looked at him with sympathy and sat down beside him.

"He always gets all the praise. Everyone in the village adores him and treats him like royalty just because he's father's favorite! The '*soon to be vaward of the village*.' So what? Now he will hast a huge league under his control and if he make one mistake, no one will even notice! I used t' love playing in the village with all the other young elves. We would hast the most pleasant o' times making bows and arrows, or catching fish from the lake... Then one day, I made one mistake, and everyone hates me."

"Oh Dator, I'm sure they don't hate you."

"Really? Then how doth you explain why no one talks to me! They look at me as if I'm some evil being, and no one says a word t' me unless 'tis to rid me o' their presence! Even mine own father doth not speak my name!"

Eva looked at him with saddened eyes. "Well, let me tell you a story," she said, giving him a small smile in hopes it might cheer him up. "Once upon a time, a tiny doe roamed through the forest. She was different from all the rest of the animals in the forest, for she was the only one of her kind besides her parents. She had long slender legs and tiny white spots on her back. The forest homed many other species: flocks of owls, herds of cattle, sounders of swine, a variety of insects, and many more. One day, she walked through the forest and came across a large group of animals. They seemed to be having a good time talking to one another, and so she decided that it might be a good way to make friends. As she approached the group, they all became silent and stared at the doe.

"All the animals laughed at the small doe, making fun of the way she looked. She went home to her parents, who comforted her. The next day, the little doe went back into the forest. As she passed a burrow, she curiously stuck her nose in and a five-clawed creature of black and white scratched her. The badger scolded the doe for her actions, and she went on her way in hopes of finding a friend.

"She heard a rustling in the trees and then something hard bounced off her head. Shaking off the sudden pain, she looked down to see an acorn. Two squirrels laughed in the trees above. The little doe began running as they threw acorns at her, leading her deep within the forest. It took most of the night just to find the way back to her home.

"The little doe, so scared of the outside world, stayed with her mother until she could no more. The doe set out, knowing she'd have to find another place to stay from now on. The animals in the forest never changed their ways and continued to mock the doe whenever they came across her path. She kept her tail between her legs and held her head low, worrying about what else might happen.

"Eventually, she came to a beautiful meadow filled with dandelions and high grass. She frolicked in glee, spreading the tiny seeds into the air. The quail, hidden in the grass, started to laugh at the doe's dance, questioning its absurdity. The doe, ashamed for her happiness, walked away. She came to a part of the forest she had never been to before. The canopies shaded the ground. The wind blew hard, rustling the trees and bushes, signaling that a storm approached.

"She heard a hissing noise coming from the bush beside her and a large green viper poked its head out, calling for her to come closer. The doe, so frightened, backed up, ready to run, but the moment she turned around the snake struck her leg, tightening around it. She fell to the ground, scraping at the dirt to pull herself free. She cried for help, and the animals in the forest came. They saw her and laughed. Those who remained in silence despised the doe, as they believed her to be unworthy to be in the forest. They made a pact with the serpent to rid of the doe so that they could feel in control of the forest. They thought by making fun of others, whom they feared, they could make themselves look better. If they rid those who they envied or were different, they believed they could feel better about themselves."

"What did the doe do?" Dator gasped.

"Well, she became so upset that she considered giving in. If everyone saw her differently, then she might as well accept her fate. At that very moment, a crack of thunder rang through the sky and all the animals, except for the snake, jumped and ran off. The doe took her chance to kick the snake and escape from his grasp. She scrambled to stand and ran until she could no more. Fear raced through her as her leg bled from the snake's bite. She felt alone in the world. She limped her way to a nearby cave she found on the way. She knelt to the damp ground and licked her wounds. A growl came from the end of the cave, and she perked up. A large shadow cast upon the wall and it seemed to be coming closer. Too weak and scared to run off, she kept quiet, hoping it would go away. A giant grizzly bear shook the cave floor as she came to see the suspicious creature that entered her home. The bear noticed the doe, who cowered believing she soon would become a midday snack to the large creature. The bear sniffed the doe, noticing the snake bite on her hoof and grimaced.

"To much of her surprise, the bear took the doe in and cared for her wounds. The bear had heard of the rumors of the doe, which she found disgusting. For you see, the bear believed everyone deserved to live in the forest, regardless of where they came from or what they did. The doe never heard such kind words from anyone before and cried in relief that she found a friend who would truly care for her.

"Time passed and the bear and doe learned more about each other. The bear spent day in and day out helping the doe recover by bringing her food and water, and within three-days' time, the doe recovered. Grateful of the bear's kindness, the doe decided to find some honey and berries for her. She walked through the woods and found a large berry bush filled with the sweetest raspberries. Just as she was about to leave with a leaf full of berries, the forest animals approached her. They began making fun of her, as usual. The doe begged them to leave her alone. A loud growl came from behind, and soon the bear approached them, striking fear within the hearts of all the forest animals. The bear criticized their behavior, pointing out their hypocrisy and proving the goodness within the doe's heart.

"With that, the bear and the doe left. The bear's words shocked the animals. They realized how awful they truly had been. Some apologized to the doe, and those who didn't rarely showed their face in the forest. Until the end of their days, the doe and bear lived happily together. And all was at peace."

Eva looked at Dator with a smile. "Don't ever let anyone tell you that you're unworthy or less of a person because you're different from them. You're worth more being who you are. I know it's hard right now, but life will get better. I don't know what mistake you made to cause your village to stop speaking to you, and even though we barely know each other, I can tell you're a great person inside, and more people should get to know you. Good people deserve happiness, so never let someone take that away from you. I guess what I'm trying to say is, be proud for who you are! Don't let your mistakes or differences get you down. Let people know the real you, and if they don't accept you, then they don't deserve to be your friend. You're worth more than you know Dator, so don't let them get you down!"

Dator looked at Eva, his eyes the size of sunflowers, trying ever so desperately to hide his quivering lip. In a sudden movement, his arm wrapped around her waist. He buried his face in her chest. Eva smiled softly down at Dator, rubbing his back. She took a moment before releasing him. "How about we go back to the others, okay? Before they start thinking we got into some trouble," she said standing up. Right as she started to head back, Dator grabbed her hand.

"Thou know…you remind me o' her…" he said. He held his head down low, avoiding eye contact, so she would not see the sorrow on his face.

Eva looked at him, slightly confused, but mainly concerned. "Of whom?"

"Mine mother."

She sat back down beside him as he released her hand.

"She was most optimistic and liked t' tell me stories, just like thee. Wise, gentle, and kind. Never once didst anyone say a negative word about her. She was looked upon with the highest degree by the entire Elnaïrian village. We had a close bond between us, for she understood me. We shared the same heart, mind, and spirit. Although I was most mischievous and tended t' get in trouble, she protected me at every moment. I remember the days we used t' spend creating wild stories. Some humorous, others full of mystery, but each one contained a hidden meaning. She used t' wake me early t' see the sun rise, and by night, she taught me the ways o' the stars. She adored animals, but her most loved creature o' all was the blue crane. I think… she truly wished t' be free from it all and be one with nature."

"What do you mean?"

Dator sighed. "The village folk would often come t' her for advice. O' course, she was quite fond o' helping everyone, but her love for them took a toll on her. She wouldst go out t' the woods, far away from everyone. T' a place where no one could find her. One day, I decided t' follow her. 'Twas very deep within the forest, where I hath ne'er walked before. We passed many twists and turns before we came upon a hidden hole in the mountain near the village. Once on the other side, the sight 'twas more beautiful than you couldst believe. A lake stood at the end o' the pasture filled with at least a hundred fish, that fed the flock o' blue cranes resting in the area. Trees, with dangling moss wrapped around their branches, jittered with the music from songbirds and little critters. And t' top it all, thousands o' flowers flooded the pasture floor. I could not help but gawk at the wonderful sight. Mother knew instantly that I had followed her."

"Was she mad?"

Dator shook his head. "No…in fact, she seemed pleased. It became our little hideout. We would stay for hours upon hours. Ne'er did we share an unhappy moment. All that changed when King Valdof took the throne three years ago. He believed it best to keep species with their own kind, so he devised a plan t' separate everyone. He sent his armies t' each village for relocation. He segregated them into their own set o' land, and anyone caught living in another's village wouldst be killed on the spot to raise terror. However, if it be true that one wished t' travel through a village for supplies, they could without issue."

"What happened to her?"

"Mother became tired and ill. She spoke little other than our secret place. Staying so long from there weakened her soul. I hath decided t' find a way t' bring her back to her land without father or Ijaïh finding out. I made a deal with the fairies t' transport us t' our hideaway. Mother was thrilled, although she would be displeased t' know o' the deal. I assumed I could manage the fairies request when they wished t' be repaid. I was wrong in doing so, for King Valdof's guards hath found us there shortly after. We hath broken the rules. My mother hath kept yelling at me t' run hence, as she held the guards back. I ran and ran until I came across my village. The guards followed and announced to the village of our betrayal. The leader of the guard threw down mine mother's floral crown, reddened with her blood. I knew my actions were in vain and that I would ne'er see my mother again. With my tribe filled with anger and my father with shame, I hath left for the woods within my village's range. 'Twas there where I cut my hair. 'Tis o' only good nature and high honor that Elvish hair is worth. I was neither, and I deserved my punishment," he said. And with that, Dator headed back to camp.

Chapter 9
Stick to the Path

By the end of their second day's journey, Eva was just about fed up with the unsettling silence that lurked around the group. Tension filled the air between Dator and Ijaïh. Occasionally, Eva would hear a mumble from Finn as he was trying to figure out which way to go, but other than that, it was quiet. Eva's stomach turned and her mind raced with worries on how the group would get along. She hoped that she could get away for a couple minutes to destress from their unnerving demeanor.

The night fell and Finn began setting up camp. He placed a few logs onto the ground and sent a couple green sparks beneath it until it inflamed. Soon the smell of the rabbit's meat rose into the air. It was the second time rabbit roasted that day. Eva sat near the fire, watching the flames dance around the wood. Her queasy stomach resented the smell.

"It will be about an hour before they're finished," Finn said, rotating the skewed rabbits.

"I expect 'twill be finer than the amiss from this morn," Ijaïh scoffed.

"If you're going to act like that, how about I skip your share and you can cook it yourself?"

"I did my dole. 'Tis not mine place t' pass-"

"Then I suggest you don't complain. Unless, of course, you would like to eat in the dirt where you belong."

"How dare-"

"Can you two just cut it out! I'm so sick of everyone being at each other's throats all the time! Can't we just enjoy a peaceful evening for once?" Eva interjected.

"You're right. I'm sorry. I shouldn't let him get the best of me," Finn said.

Ijaïh scoffed, mumbling contumelious remarks.

"Why don't you tell us a tale, Finn?" Dator asked.

Finn smiled. "That's a great idea. What are you thinking?"

"Oh, tell an exciting one! One with fights and valour!"

"Then let me tell you the tale of Wulfric Alon: King of all!"

"Sounds like a wonderful story!" Eva said.

"'Tis only the most virtuous story o' all time!" Dator said with excitement.

Finn cleared his throat. "As you know, the Humans had taken a turn against us. Darkness grew stronger and all hope seemed to have been lost. Many were caged, beaten, and left to rot. Our blood boiled in rage. One way, or another, we were going to find a way out. One evening, a man, by the name Wulfric Alon, escaped."

~:~

Amidst the Battlefield, 1349

Wulfric stood upon the bodies of the men who fell around them, drenched in their blood. He threw his sword to the ground and looked upon his friends. "How many have been lost?"

"Just three," Elias panted. "The rest were either captured or found their way to the hideaway north of here."

Wulfric came upon the three magic folk mangled in the mud. A child rested in his mother's arms next to their vanquished protector. He gently closed their eyes. "A grave loss, it is, to lose a child. Let your souls find rest in the afterlife."

"What happened to the demon?"

"I lost track of him. He's wounded, but still very much alive. I can only hope that the loss of his arm will keep him at bay."

"Son of a bunkaroo."

"Calm yourself, Elias. We must find the others."

Wulfric pulled him up, helping him walk as Elias guided him to the hideaway. The magic folk gasped as the cave door opened. They cheered upon their fellow leaders who survived. Healers came and mended everyone's wounds as thoughts of worry lingered.

"My fellow friends, I know you all are exhausted and cannot fathom the idea of fighting again. These are trying times, but we must prevail in order to save not only ourselves, but our future generations. Tomorrow, we will fight. We must."

The folks grew quiet.

"By dawn, we will make our ways to the Valley of Jade, where Man has caged our friends and family. Once we free them, I will create a portal for us to escape."

"A portal? Wulfric, if thee do this, thee will surely-" Elias muttered.

Wulfric stared at him sternly. "I will create a portal which will take us to a place of freedom. A place where Man will never find us. I know thee are scared, as you should. All our lives are at stake. There will be hardships thee may face: torture; injuries; and wort of all death. If we do not act now, Man would rule over us forever. Are thee with me?"

Everyone looked at each other.

"I am with thee" Elias said, standing.

"Aye," a woman said cradling her broken arm.

Soon everyone stood up in agreement.

"Then we leave at dawn. Mediums and psychics, send the word. "Everyone else, let us rest," he said and laid against the cave door.

Dawn approached and Wulfric led his warriors to the Valley of Jade. The magic folk rustled with excitement as their locks were picked. Wulfric tried to keep the silence, as Man approached. Cage by cage, the doors opened, and Wulfric's dread became reality. Hundreds of men surrounded them.

"Wulfric, what shall we do?" Elias gulped.

"The only thing we can. Warriors, assemble. Today, we bring freedom!"

The cages were opened, and war broke out between man and magical folk. Blades clashed and blood spilled across the grassy plains. Throats slit, bodies gouged, limbs severed. Even the best magical tactics from a drained folk were no match to a well-rested man and his weapon. One-by-one bodies were slain.

By mid-battle, Wulfric found himself against the demon who led the men. Blue flames surrounded the demon. "Flames? You're such a weakling," the demon spat. They lunged for each other, magic and blades swirling around them, and Wulfric knew his time was near. The demon pinned him to the ground.

"Well, well, well, Alon. Looks like our playtime is up. Why don't we end this now, Wulfric? I'd hate for you to spoil. Any last requests?"

"As it may be, let me know the name of mine conquer."

"Is that all?" The demon pressed a blade into Wulfric's arm, twisting it as he lowered his head. "My name, sweet Alon, is Zabaolres."

"Then, my dear Zabaolres, I banish thee to hell!" Wulfric blew blue flames into the demon's face, stunning him long enough to plunge his dagger into the demon's chest. He chanted and a golden blue formed him. Zabaolres screamed in agony and lunged for Wulfric. As his hand touched the aura, his body faded into dust.

Wulfric turned to his people. "Flee my warriors, our time has come!" he commanded, opening the portals. The magic folk ran to safety, dragging the injured with them. Elias ran to Wulfric, tears streaming down his face.

"Please, Wulfric, come with us before it's too late."

“My dearest friend, please go and save thyself. I’m afraid, I can only hold the portals for a few minutes more,” he said lowly.

“I won’t leave you!”

“Elias, forgive me,” he said before using his magic to tie him up and throw him into the portal. “Take care of our friends. I know thou will do what’s right.”

A man with an Elvish sword, that he tore from the hands of a fallen soldier, stabbed Alon from behind. Alon crumpled to the ground, too weak to perform any magic. The man stabbed him again and again, until finally forced enough energy to throw the man upward thirty feet. The man’s neck cracked as he hit the ground, killing him instantly. The Elvish sword stood straight up through Alon’s chest, pinning him to the ground. His blood seeped into the already bloodied soil. He gazed up at the sky.

“Let it be that no man shall remember our presence. Our worlds shall never meet again!” and with the last of his energy, Wulfric sealed the portals and wiped the memory of all humans.

~:~

“Many lost their lives that night, but none were as sorrowful as Alon’s. Everyone heard of his brave act. In this new world, he created for them, our ancestors formed agreements to never amend their ties with humans. They started a kingdom, naming it after our lost leader, who never gave up. And thus, became that of Aloncia.”

“To Wulfric Alon!” Dator said, placing his fist on his chest. “The most valorous, aweless, and powerful King of all time.”

“To Wulfric Alon,” Finn and Eva said.

“How’s that rabbit coming? I’m starving.”

Finn began poking the rabbit. “Should be any minute.”

Eva glanced at him; his rosy freckled cheeks radiated in the fire’s glow. *Wow...*

Finn looked at her, and Eva quickly evaded his eyes, putting her fist to her lips, her face completely red.

Stop thinking about this Eva! There's absolutely nothing between you and him. Right now, you must focus on keeping safe and finding a way home. Home! Oh dear...mom and dad must be so worried. I hope Maddie and Rina are okay.

"Eva, are you okay?" Finn asked.

"Hmm?" she said looking at him wide eyed. "Yeah, I'm fine. Just thinking," she laughed nervously, brushing her fingers through her hair.

"Are you sure? You seem flustered? Maybe I should make you some tea?"

Eva cusped her cheeks. She pointed at the closest item between them. "Oh, look at that! You're low on firewood. I think I will just go out and find some more for you."

"Well, let me come with you," he said lifting himself up.

"NO!" Eva yelled, standing up quickly. She paused for a moment. "I mean, no. Thank you. I should be fine out on my own."

"O-okay… Don't go too far. There's a trail of lights on the path. Just be sure to follow them," Finn said. With a snap of his fingers, small spherical green lights formed a line down the eastern part of the forest.

Eva followed the path hastily, as her thoughts filled her with emotions of rage and self-doubt. *Eva you idiot! He's going to be suspicious now! Did you see the way he looked at you? He probably thinks I've lost my mind!*

She walked along the path for a good five minutes and came to a fork. "Great. What do I do now?" Both paths were led by green lights. The one to the right traveled into the darker portion of the woods and the left one led into a brighter side. "Well, at least it may be easier to find twigs and branches with more light. To the left it is."

Eva headed down the lit path and started looking for some twigs. She picked up a dozen or so when she noticed a pile of splintered wood. "I guess a tree must have fallen," she went to grab a couple of the pieces of wood when she noticed a small round object on the ground.

It was a pumpkin. Confused about its whereabouts, she examined it, thinking of all the types of food Finn could make. Her stomach growled. She placed the wood down and reached for the pumpkin.

As soon as her hand touched the rubbery flesh, the ground shook beneath her feet. A slender branch shot from the ground and grasped Eva's ankle with its finger-like twigs. The pumpkin began to shake, and a jagged blackened smile crept upon the base of the face, followed by a high-pitched laughter. Its eyes opened pointing inward as if a nonexistent brow furrowed in evil success. Its sunken eyes appeared hollow except for the two yellow gleams of light that flickered like candles in the back of its fruitful skull.

The creature gripped both of its hands-on Eva's legs, clawing at the outside of her skirt. Eva tried pushing it away. The creature raised its two wooden feet from the ground, and slithered itself around her, restraining her arms. Humanoid in shape, the creature wore the remains of an old woven sack tied around by a tassel at the waist. Raggedy black fabric lay upon the outfit. Eva struggled under its grasp, which only tightened with every movement.

"My, my, what have we here? A human no less! Oh my, you are a long way from home. How did you end up all the way here, I wonder," the creature chuckled in a high-pitched voice. "No matter, you foolish creatures always follow my lights. I can mimic any light that I want you to see, and you'll always follow them. It's the curiosity that killed the human, I always say."

Eva continued to struggle, broke free one arm and grasped the dagger from its sheath. She thrust it toward the creature harshly.

"Oh, ho, ho, a feisty one! I *love* it when they're angry," he grinned. The creature snapped its fingers and more twigs wrapped around Eva like chains, binding her from her ankles all the way up to her shoulders, causing her to fall. "Now, now, stop struggling, or it will be more painful. Then again, all the more fun for me," the creature laughed, watching the twigs tighten. "Let's see, what would be better? Strangulation? Asphyxiation? Oh no, you're much too good for that my dear," the creature said licking its lips with its pulpy, blackened, tongue. "You seem special. Hmm, I know! A long *smoldering* roast should do the trick. Hu, hu, hu," the creature said, as he grasped her by the hair and dragged her further into the forest. Eva let out a scream and struggled between the branches, unable to move her blade to cut the twigs. She envisioned the terror that would befall upon her if she didn't find a way out of there soon.

Within a split second, a loud thud came from behind her. He released her hair. The branches wrapped around her were cut in a single slash of an almost invisible blade. Eva quickly rose to her feet only to notice a cloaked figure hovering over the twig-like creature. The figure had the creature pinned down.

"Heh, heh, you think you can stop me? You foolish being. I'll have you and the little human for dessert," the creature laughed, then spat a sizzling orange fluid at the cloaked person. They stumbled backward rubbing the fluid from their face. The creature rose to its feet and launched an attack against the figure, who jumped back and pulled out another blade. The figure ran toward the creature, thrusting the blades at the pumpkin's head. The creature darted the attacks. The figure misguided the creature, coming behind it. The creature snarled, and with the figure's high kick attack, found itself on the ground. The creature squirmed in pain as his smile split to his chin.

The hooded person ran toward Eva, grabbing her wrist, and began to run back through the forged path. Eva felt the branched fingers wrapped around her left wrist as they were about to flee. The creature gleamed at her with soulless sunken eyes.

“You will not escape me!” it growled with an evil grin, as it dug its claws into Eva’s skin.

The cloaked figure took its blade and slashed through the creature’s arm. The creature released Eva. They continued running, and the person whistled. A sound like nails upon a chalkboard rang through the air followed by the ripping and snapping of wood and fruity flesh. The figure brought Eva back to the forked road and threw her forward. The person’s face remained covered. Its hourglass figure stood stiff beneath the cloak.

“Who are you?” Eva said, but the figure disappeared into the darkness.

Eva stood there in disbelief. She jumped at the sound of a distant growl and hurried herself to the camp. Ijaïh, who had been sitting by the fire eating what remained of his rabbit meal, looked up at Eva with disgust. Dator and Finn looked back with slight concern.

“I thought you were bringing wood,” Finn stated.

“Ah, you see," Eva said nervously, hiding her wrist behind her back, “I-I couldn’t find any! Oh well, it seems we will just have to go to bed and search tomorrow!”

“Are you sure you’re okay?”

“Aye Eva, you look pale. Eat some rabbit, ‘tis good!” Dator offered.

“No, no, I’m fine! I’m just a little tired. It’s been a long day you know, ha, ha. I think…I think I’ll just head to bed early.”

“Aren’t you hungry?”

“No, I think I’ve had enough rabbit for one day," Eva said, swiftly making her way to the tent. “Goodnight!”

She grabbed a woolen blanket, hiding beneath its wraps. She realized the markings where the creature grasped her were starting to turn black. Her body started to shake as an overwhelming tangent of possible outcomes raced through her head. *Oh God! It’s getting worse! Maybe I should tell Finn...but if I tell him, he’ll never let me be alone again! What to do? What to do? Ah! The ointment! Yes, that ought to work!* Eva took some ointment from her bag and rubbed it over the markings before wrapping it with some linen.

From afar, the hooded figure sat within a tree, gazing at the campsite. A long scaly creature, the color of night, returned spitting the remains of the pumpkin creature into the figure’s gloved hand.

“In due time, my sweet. In due time.”

Chapter 10
A Wondrous Sound

The sound of chirping awoke Eva. She peeked outside where everyone was occupied with cleaning up camp. She gently unraveled the bandage of her throbbing arm. The wound sank in further, widening the holes. The blackish skin was now a deeper shade than before. Ambiguously, there was no blood. The skin itself burned to a hollow crispy crust. Eva bit her lower lip and looked around the tent for anything that could possibly help. She noticed a small bucket of water next to a bowl of fruit.

Finn must have put this here last night. She moved closer. Eva plucked one of the sweet grapes and plopped it in her mouth. She looked at her reflection through the small bucket. *Ugh...I'm a mess.* Eva dipped her hands into the water, splashing it onto her face. She scrubbed the dirt off her cheeks and out of her hair.

"Okay, now for the hard part…" she whispered. She held out her arm and gently poured some of the water over the wound. A gasp escaped from her lips. The wound sizzled, sprouting small bubbles within the punctured skin. She quickly dried it off and added more of the ointment before wrapping it again. She pulled down her sleeve. Eva ate a few more grapes and a pear before placing the rest of the fruit in her bag. She then collected her items and exited the tent. Green orbs circled around it, compressing the tent and flying it into Finn's satchel.

"There she is. I was about to wake you up myself," Finn said with a grin.

Eva paused, her cheeks reddening as she twiddled her thumbs. "I wanted to thank you for the bowl of fruit you left in the tent. It was most generous of you."

"Ah, it was nothing. I figured you would be hungry by morning. You seemed out of sorts last night. You look much

better this morning. Better hurry, we'll be heading out here in a bit. Ijaïh and Dator already made a head start."

Eva helped Finn gather the remaining supplies from the camp and they started into the forest after the other two.

~:~

The sun rose high as they continued their quest, keeping firm on the trail.

Eva's arm began to burn. She clenched her fist, rubbing her wrist gently. *The pain, it's becoming unbearable. I have to tell him…*

"F-Finn?" Eva quietly stuttered.

Ijaïh came to a sudden halt, standing perfectly still. A silence filled the air.

"Hey, Ijaïh, everything al-"

"Sush!" he said. "Doth thy hear that?" he whispered.

Eva listened closely, hearing only the slight wind rustling the leaves of the trees.

"Yeah, I do…it's so beautiful." Finn commented, taking a step forward.

"Like a lark raising the morning sun," Dator murmured.

A sudden shiver ran down Eva's spine. A high pitch echo ran through her ears, chilling the air surrounding them. Unsure of what presence lurked within the trees, she gently tugged on Finn's sleeve. "Maybe we should move on. This doesn't feel right."

Finn jerked his arm from Eva's grasp and headed towards the invisible sound. "I must see where it comes from." Ijaïh and Dator followed behind him.

Eva quickly grabbed Finn's hand. "What happened to sticking to the path? You said we never can go off the path or we'll be in danger, right?" Finn forced Eva's hand off his and continued. She blocked Ijaïh's path. "Come on Ijaïh, you have to talk some sense into him!"

"Move out o' mine way," he said sternly, moving past her.

"What's gotten into you guys? This isn't like you!"

The three of them continued into the wooded area, going further away from the path. Eva followed swiftly behind them; an uneasy feeling tightened her stomach. As they continued, the sound of high-pitched screeching rang through Eva's ears again. The sound was almost deafening. An immense pain ran through her head, like a hot knife through butter.

I think I'm going to be sick!

Finn, Dator, and Ijaïh continued forward, enchanted by the sound. Brushing past a vinery veil revealed darkened cave like area with trees everywhere. Small teal lights floated like Christmas lights strung around the rocks and trees. In the center of the grotto sat a lake with six women bathing. Their taloned fingers swept through their long-disheveled hair. Their voices rang through the air, sharp and precise.

"Sirens!" Eva gasped.

At that very moment the words left her lips, the women looked directly at the men, glimmering in glee that they had arrived. They bared their razor-like teeth in bitter excitement. Finn and Ijaïh walked forth in a daze. Eva grabbed Dator, lifting him off his feet as he attempted to step forward.

"LET ME GO!" he screamed, thrashing in her arms. "LET ME GO, I SAY!" but her grip only tightened.

"Dator, listen to me! They're not what you think they are! They're dangerous!"

"I DOTH NOT CARE! LET ME GO!"

From the trees dropped more women with leathery wings sprouting from their back. Short soft fur covered parts of their torsos, accentuating their breasts. They huddled towards Ijaïh, caressing his chin and silky locks.

Thinking quickly, Eva pulled out a bit of linen from her bag and shoved it into Dator's ears. Within seconds, he stopped and looked up at her. "Eva?" he questioned. "Wha-"

"There's no time Dator, we got to help the others!" she said.

Dator ran towards his brother. "I'll get Ijaïh, you help Finn!"

Two of the winged women stood next to Finn, cooing at him with their high-pitched voices. He chuckled gently, as he ran his hand down the one's face. Eva cautiously walked towards them. One of the women noticed her and hissed, clenching to him tightly. Her snake-like tongue slithered rapidly, warning her to stay back. She threw her head to the side and the other flew behind Eva.

Eva ran away from the woman, and towards a nearby tree. As she approached her, Eva glanced up. A thick vine hung from the highest branch that she could see. She jumped up towards the lowest branch, holding onto the thick oak. Her feet slipped a couple times and pulled herself up. The woman came closer, clasping her hands around Eva's ankle. Eva yelped and thrust her foot into the woman's face until she let go. The woman screamed in fury, and Eva darted up the tree. The rough branches scraped her hands, but little pain could be felt.

As she grabbed the final branch, her dress caught onto a twig. She jerked her leg upward, cinching the fabric. The winged siren below sunk her nails into the tree and scurried up its trunk. Eva tugged on the material until she could hear it tear. She pulled herself onto the last branch and scooted herself towards the vine. The sound of hissing lurked behind her, coming closer and closer. She stood up, her hands shaking as she grasped the withered vine.

I hope this works...

She glanced down below. Finn stood beneath her with that wretched winged creature fondling him. A loud scream sounded from behind as the woman clutched the branch, crawling onto it, her body disfigured and crooked as if every joint in her body was dislocated. Eva flinched and looked down, shaking with fear. *It's now or never.* The woman screamed again, launching towards her. Eva stepped off the branch, holding onto dear life, narrowly missing the woman's grasp.

Eva let out a scream, closing her eyes tightly as the air rushed past her. She swung in a circular motion, and soon met a hard mass. Letting go of the vine, she tumbled to the ground. She shook her head and looked up, noticing she had knocked the woman off Finn. Her body lay frozen upon the ground. Finn, too, was face flat. He pulled himself up and started dragging himself towards the lake. Eva got up and jumped onto Finn, pinning him down. He thrashed beneath her, screaming and grunting. She loosened the seam upon the torn section of her dress, trying to tear off a small piece. Suddenly, Finn threw her off his back. She hit the ground with a loud thud. Finn held her down, his eyes hued in white. The sirens screeched with joy with his actions, cooing him on. He wrapped his hands around Eva's neck. She gasped under his constricting grip.

"F-Finn...p-please," she stifled. His hands trembled ever so slightly. The sirens squawked softly, and the white hue deepened in Finn's eyes, leaving only the limbus visible. Eva's vision blurred and she gasped for air, pulling at his hands. She spotted a patch of moss nearby. She reached out her hand, which came just shy of the patch. *Please! Just a bit further!* She begged silently. She felt the soft moist moss beneath her fingertips and dug her nails into it, ripping off as much as she could. She shoved the moss and dirt into Finn's ears and pushed him backward with all her force. Eva coughed rigorously. Finn stumbled backward, grasping his head as he came too. He noticed Eva and moved to her side.

"Eva! Oh my god, I'm so sorry! Are you okay?" he panicked.

She coughed for a moment and replied in a raspy voice. "I-I'm fine. We need to help Ijaïh. D-Dator ran after him."

The women screamed, dashing towards their morning meal. Finn quickly pulled Eva up and away from the women. He threw a green orb towards them, sending four of them flying into the lake. The sirens squealed as the water splashed upon them. Dator yelled for Ijaïh, as the women pulled him into their grasps. Ijaïh inched closer to the lake's murky water.

"Dammit! If he enters the water, they'll drown him for sure!" Finn spat. He sent out a couple green flames towards the sirens swimming near Ijaïh. They shrieked, diving back into the water. Finn grabbed his knife and flung it forward. It hit a tree, separating Dator from the winged wretches. A green line strung from the back of the knife. The women launched forward.

"DATOR RUN!" Finn yelled, as he tugged on the other end of the string. With a swift release, the magical rope rebounded, wrapping itself around the four women and piercing through their wings. They screeched as the rope tightened and shocked them. The knife flung back, like a boomerang, returning gracefully into Finn's hand.

Dator ran towards Ijaïh, finally grasping onto his cloak, pulling him back. Eva and Finn followed, green bursts of light shooting towards any of the women who approached them. One of the sirens latched onto Ijaïh's hand, dragging him forward. His cloak gave way, and Ijaïh fell forward into the water.

"IJAÏH!" Dator screamed.

"Shit!" Finn said, dashing towards the lake. He took off his leather vest and satchel and threw it back at Eva. He dived into the water after Ijaïh. Dator gripped the edge of the shore. Eva quickly pulled him up.

"Don't! I won't let you get pulled in too!" she said.

The siren wrapped her silver tail around Ijaïh, clutching his face as she dragged him further down. She locked her lips with his, forcing water down his throat. Ijaïh struggled, feeling the slimy muddy water rush down his lungs. Suddenly, a spear the shade of lime ran into the side of the siren. Her voice gurgled with a squeal as her body convulsed backward. Ijaïh's body sank further into the depths of the water. Finn swam toward him, wrapping his arm around him.

Above the shore, Eva had grabbed a large branch from the ground for defense.

I'm not strong enough to fend them all, but maybe if I keep them at a distance...

She kept Dator close behind her, making sure that none of them would be able to grab him. A few of the winged beasts came forward and Eva thrashed the branch at their heads, knocking them down. They bared their fangs, sending fear through Eva as she backed away. One came from behind and she swung the branch around, and then thrashed it downward multiple times upon the fallen woman. Eva heard a splash of water. She turned around to see Finn breaking the surface. She ran towards the shore with Dator, helping him pull Ijaïh from the lake. Finn sent out a green wave thrusting all the women backward. Eva noticed a shimmer beneath the water heading towards them.

"Finn, watch out!" she cried. He was jerked downward. Eva grabbed his arm tightly, refusing to let him go under again. Her arms were pulled down into the icy water, which sent a soaring pain through her arm. She could feel her wound sizzling like acid on metal. She hissed in pain and took what strength she had left to pull Finn forward. Finn glanced at the siren beneath, and with his free hand sent flames of electricity toward her. The siren screamed and released Finn. He reached his hand out to grasp the land above and with Eva's help, safely pulled himself out of the water.

Dator successfully dragged Ijaïh away from the lake, helping him come to. The half-drowned Ijaïh could barely stand. Finn quickly pulled him up, wrapping his arm under Ijaïh's shoulders. "We have to move now!" he said. The four of them moved swiftly towards the exit, but the women only followed, creeping closer by the second.

"Eva, look in your bag for the silver spherical object! It will produce a bright light of immense power! They cower in the light as it blinds them from their prey! We'll have to move fast for it only lasts a few seconds! And whatever you do, don't look back!"

Eva dug her hand into her satchel, grasping the small object. She hastily threw it behind her. The object bounced twice before shattering upon impact, releasing a bright light. Screams echoed upon one another, increasing in agony.

The four rushed past the veil of vines and kept forth until they reached the path. They fell to their knees. "We made it," Eva panted. "I thought we were goners."

"Are you okay?" Finn asked, worried.

Eva touched her neck softly. "Yeah, I'm okay. How are you?"

"I could be better. How are you doing Ijaïh, Dator?" Finn asked.

Dator nodded, still catching his breath. Ijaïh grunted, turning his head.

"You know you could at least say 'thank you' since we saved your ass!"

"Go to! I didst not need thine help," he said.

"Oh sure, I guess we should have just let you drown," he spat sarcastically. "Maybe then you'd learn to show some common courtesy."

Ijaïh's face reddened. "I will not be ridiculed for such motley-minded actions," he stood up swiftly and headed along the path. "Come. We will lose precious time if we doth not keep hence."

"He'll never learn, will he?" Eva sighed, pulling herself to her feet. Her head still hurt from all the jagged screams, and her arm felt as though it was hanging on only by a thin tendon.

"Give him time. Ijaïh's stubborn, but he means well. This is quite a mortifying moment for him. If others found out of this, his reputation could falter, and with his coronation to become leader for his village warriors, it'd be best not to mention this to anyone," Finn whispered.

"I see."

They followed Ijaïh down the path, distancing themselves from his fuming rage. Eva noticed the water dripping from Finn's hair. She pulled out the woolen blanket from her satchel and handed it to him, along with his vest and sac.

"Here, you'll catch cold if you don't stay warm."

Finn smiled, placing his vest in his bag, and wrapping the blanket around him. She looked at him, wondering what would have happened if she hadn't stopped them. Her thoughts dwindled about those wicked women.

"Since when did sirens have wings with a full human figure? I thought they were supposed to be half woman and half bird or fish."

"Half bird? Where did you hear that?" Finn asked.

"There's a book called *The Odyssey* and, well, it's a long story."

"Well, there's nothing like that around here, although you are right about the half fish part. The others were succubi. They're wretched creatures that dwell the night to steal the souls of men through their disgusting seducing ways."

"Oh. I guess it's a good thing I was there then," she laughed nervously.

“Ha, ha, yeah. Thank you…for keeping hold of me back there. I owe you one.”

“No problem,” Eva blushed.

They walked for what felt like hours, even though it had been but half. Eva gazed at the ground. Her head filled with pain as though her brain rammed itself into her skull, throbbing with every rebound. Her vision started to blur as her heart quickened. She stopped for a moment, grasping her head, squinting to lessen the strain.

“Eva? What’s wrong?” Dator asked.

Finn looked back, noticing her pale face. He came by her side and rested a hand on her shoulder. “Eva?” Noticing a black substance dripping down her arm, he quickly grasped it, pulling up the stained sleeve to reveal her wound. “Where did you get this?” Finn said.

“I-I um-” she stuttered weakly. Her heart throbbed and her body felt heavy, as if it was weighed by bricks. Finn swiftly caught her as she fell into him, pulling her limp body close.

“Eva! Ah, she’s burning up! Ijaïh! We need to find safe ground! Eva, hold on.”

Chapter 11
The Cloaked Figure Returns

You'll never be good enough, you know. You're weak and useless and will never amount to anything. You will always be alone, for no one will ever want to be your friend. You waste their time and are a worthless excuse for a person. You know it's true. Just accept it.

You Are Nothing.

~:~

Eva awoke abruptly under a stack of three woolen blankets. Her body felt hot and clammy. She felt warm fluid drip from her temple. Giving a soft groan, she gently brushed her hand against her face, pulling away the wet cloth that was once cold. Sitting up, she gazed around the area. She was in the tent again.

"It was only a dream," she sighed.

A warm lantern lit the room, flickering gently along the cotton drapes. Dator slept on the other side of the tent, all curled up. Salty stains ran down his face. Her heart sank.

A soft pitter-patter splattered across the ground, arousing the soft scent of petrichor. A soft wooded sound echoed across the damp winds, complementing the dancing droplets. Two voices could be heard in mere mumbles, swallowed by the storm.

Eva's head throbbed as she rose to her feet. She swayed a moment, holding onto one of the wooden beams for balance. She looked at the entrance to the tent, noticing the darkened sky and soft droplets falling to the ground. The night had settled; a whole day's voyage wasted. Eva glanced down at her arm. She gently pushed her sleeve up. The bandage remained intact from the morning. It reeked of rotten eggs.

I should probably tell Finn about the other night...

She gazed out the entrance. Across the small patch of land stood a smaller tent. A light shined from within, forming two shadows upon its woolen cover. Ijaïh sat in a tree near the tent, playing his pan flute, keeping dry beneath the leaves of an old beech.

Eva grabbed one of the blankets and draped it over herself. She stepped out into the rain, its icy touch sending shivers down her spine. The closer she got, the louder the voices became, one of which sounded awfully familiar.

"How could you let her wander off like that?" the voice yelled.

"I told her to follow the path. It's not my fault she didn't listen to me," countered Finn.

"You had one job, Finn! One. Job. And you can't even do that right!"

"Hey, I'm doing my best here!"

"Uh-huh, sure you are! First you get her into a car crash-"

"That crash was an accident, and you know it!"

"Then, let her wander off into the woods to *collect firewood*, and today you practically get her killed by freaking sirens nonetheless!"

"We got out alright. Everyone was fine until-"

"Until she collapsed! Dammit Finn! You're such a dingus! I bet you don't even know what the hell is wrong with her, do you?"

"Dingus?" Eva breathed. Feeling a sense of familiarity, she peeked into the tent. A tall, slender figure stood in front of a stuttering Finn. Her black cloak swayed as she slapped him upside the head.

"You're such an idiot! I knew I shouldn't have left this up to you! At this rate, you'll get her killed before you reach the safe zone!"

That voice... She glanced again. Through her distorted vision, she noticed the short dark hair covering the woman's caramel-colored skin.

Within a moment, a quick-footed black creature jumped out at Eva, knocking her down into a muddy puddle. The long scaly creature growled, baring its teeth as it pinned her down. A sudden silence came from within the tent. The woman lifted the flap to the tent's doorway, glaring down at Eva.

"Rina?"

"Hello Eva," she said. She glanced at the creature. "Krimm. Away," she said sternly. The creature leapt from Eva and decreased in size as it twisted its way up Rina's skirt and into her satchel, keeping only its tail outside the bag. Rina pulled Eva from the ground and into the tent. "What are you doing out there in the rain? Do you want to catch your death?"

"I-I was just-"

"Eva! You're awake!" Finn said. "You should stay in bed where it's warm! You're still so pale and-"

"Shut it, Finn," Rina snapped.

Eva looked back and forth between the two of them. Her cheeks were warm with fever. "Wait, Rina? What are you doing here? How are you here? And what are you wearing? That outfit…" she rambled.

She wore a tight-fitting dress made of leather and black scales. The high-collared V-neck surcoat matched nicely to her center-slit skirt that detached at the waist. Scales striped the skirt and lined the collar. Sacs and weapons held snug against her belts. Stockings and knee length boots could be seen beneath the skirt. Her thick leather gloves were cuffed by scaly armor that reached to her forearms.

"It was you? You were the one who saved me from that-that thing in the woods the other night!"

Rina looked away shyly. "Yes."

“Why didn’t you tell me? I-I would have understood! I would have been grateful! I-” Eva said, holding her arms forward; her wounded arm shaking ever so slightly.

“Hold on a minute. What thing in the woods? That’s where you got that wound, isn’t it?” Finn intervened.

Rina’s eyes glanced down at Eva’s arm, and with a swift movement, grasped it making her flinch. She pulled the sleeve up to reveal the bandage. She tore its remains from her arm, grimacing at the blackened markings that lay upon her wrist. Her skin blistered beneath the crusty skin, practically raw. “The jack-o-lantern," she said grinding her teeth.

“A jack-o-lantern? That’s why you’re sick! Damn that creature! He must have secreted toxins into your skin! Why didn’t you tell me?” he said.

Eva shook a bit, feeling like a struck child. “I-I’m sorry. I didn’t want to be a bother to you or Ijaïh and Dator. I thought I could treat it w-with that ointment you gave me before our travels, but it didn’t work and cleaning it only made it worse and-”

“That ointment is for minor injuries! Do you realize what could have happened if we hadn’t found out? You’re lucky you’re not-”

“That’s enough, Finn," Rina said. “Leave her alone. Can’t you see she’s already been through a lot?” Rina wrapped an arm around Eva’s shoulder, covering her with her cloak. “Come on. I’ll fix that up for you. You’ll be better faster than you can say bunkaroo.”

Exiting the tent stood Dator, who had been peering into the tent shortly after Eva woke.

“Eva” he said softly. Finn rested his hand upon Dator’s shoulder.

“Let them talk. We shall sleep here for the night.”

~:~

Rina took Eva back to the tent. She sat Eva down beside the lantern and looked at her arm. The toxins had already begun to spread, blackening the veins under the skin. She dug through her satchel, pulling out a small canteen. She ripped the cork out with her teeth and gently poured the currant-colored fluid over the wound. Eva hissed, for the fluid produced hot steam when it came into contact with her skin. The blackened crust covering the wound melted away and the holes formed back to normal. Rina capped the canteen and returned it into her pouch. She pulled out a small jar filled with a green cream and rubbed it over Eva's wrist before wrapping it with a new bandage.

"Essence of figwort and the water from the head of a kappa will do the trick. Neem and burdock root cream should remove any extra toxins. As for your fever, it should be gone by morning," Rina said, wrapping a blanket around her frigid friend.

"Thank you," Eva said softly, hanging her head. "I'm sorry. I should have mentioned it to Finn. It really isn't his fault, so please don't be too hard on him."

"Yeah, you should of, and he deserves to get some sense knocked into him too, but I'll ease up for now. He got off easy…this time."

"How do you two know each other?"

"We met a couple years ago. We became buddies fast as we enjoyed many of the same things, like training. Plus, he knows how to bake, so he's an easy source for food. That's beside the point. The most important thing is that we made an agreement to protect you at all costs."

"But why me? Finn mentioned that King Valdof is chasing me, but why? Why am I so important? What business does he have to come after someone like me?"

Rina looked at Eva, eyes widened grimly. She gritted her teeth before turning away. "It's not my place to say."

Eva pursed her lips. "Not your place? Rina, you're one of my best friends! You, of all people, have the right to tell me! What's going on?"

"I can't tell you. It's best you don't know, for everyone's sake. Please, just trust me," she said, staring into her eyes. Beneath those hardened eyes, Rina feared what would become of this travel. Knowing she wouldn't budge, Eva sighed.

A small silence lingered around them for a moment.

"It all makes sense now," Eva said.

"What does?"

"You're reaction that day. You rode off so quickly after I mentioned Finn's eyes. I knew something was off. It all adds up. Why didn't you tell me?"

"Because I knew how you'd react. You'd get angry and upset, and even though I knew it would pass, would you really believe me if I told you about Aloncia?"

Eva smirked. "I guess not. I'm not mad. In fact, I'm just happy to know I have someone I know here."

"Me too, pal."

"So, I guess you've never lived in Algeria or Nevada huh?"

"Nah, I mean I've visited those places to gather supplies, but other than that, I've been here my whole life. It was only when you came around that Finn and I began to search for you. Once we did, well, you know the story."

Eva's face lit up. She stared at Rina with serious eyes, miserably hiding her excitement. "So, if you've lived here your whole life, does that mean you have powers?"

"Well, duh."

Eva squealed happily, shaking her fists up and down.

"Woah calm down! You'll make yourself dizzy," Rina said, placing her hands-on Eva's shoulders.

"I knew it! I knew it! You must tell me! No, let me guess! You have the ability to become invisible whenever you want!"

"No."

"You can transform into any animate object?"

"Not even close," Rina laughed.

"Then what?"

Rina solemnly held out her hand. "I can summon a death curse on anyone with the wave of my hand. And if anyone dares to attack me, they will come to meet a most painful experience through my blades of wrath."

Eva's face paled and her eyes widened.

Rina snickered before bursting out in laughter. "Wow, you should've seen your face! I can't believe how gullible you are!"

Eva blushed, giving a nervous laugh. "You really had me going there."

"No seriously, though. I can read the minds of anyone and change their emotions when I feel the need to, and if they are willing to," she said, grabbing some roots and shrubs from her bag. Placing them in a mortar, she began to grind them into a fine powder.

"Really?"

Rina nodded. "Yup. I can even foretell what someone will do within moments, so if I need to protect myself, I will know what the enemy has in mind."

"That's so cool!" Eva smiled. "You must show me!"

"What?" she said, dropping her pestle. Dust scattered across the tent floor. She quickly scooped up the power with her blade, placing it back in the bowl.

"Come on Rina! You can't obviously think I'm going to let you slide with just a simple explanation, do you? I want proof."

"Oh please, you already believe me anyway. You believed my lie in a heartbeat."

"Aha, but you see, because of that lie, I have become skeptical. Prove to me that you're not just tricking me again. What am I thinking right now?"

Rina rolled her eyes, pouring the powdered mixture into a small metal bottle before placing it in her bag. She leaned back, smirking. "You're thinking of how you're 'so lucky to have a friend like me.'"

"Anyone could tell me that," Eva scoffed.

"Alright. You're wondering 'how I know about everything that's happened to you during these past couple days.' Did you seriously think I wouldn't watch out for my friend? I've been looking out for you since the beginning of our friendship. More so recently than other times, but still. Note, the cloak does mysterious things," she retorted, lifting the cloak to cover half her face.

"You're smart enough to guess that though. If you truly have powers, you'll be able to guess something I've never told anyone."

Rina sat up straight. She stared at Eva for a moment, then smiled. "That's very poetic. As the mind of a true dreamer once said, 'when the moon rises over the starry night sky, I enjoy sitting in my windowsill, making up stories and questioning the wonders of the world.'"

Eva sat there, gaping. "You truly are a mind reader!"

"Intellect."

"What?"

"We call ourselves the Intellects."

"Well, then I guess that makes you a really good *intellectual," Eva* smiled, laughing at her own bad joke.

"Wow…that's even worse than when you started reading pun jokes off the internet in precalculus," Rina sighed, giving a look of disgust.

"Oh, come on, you know you love me."

"Yeah, even though you're a total prissy princess, whose naivety and oddball intelligence are too much for her own good, you're still my friend, and that will never change."

"You're so sweet. So, you said you can change emotions, right? Can you change their overall feelings or is it temporarily?"

"Depends on the willingness of the person."

"Really? Try me!"

"Ha, ha. I think it's time you went to bed, *your highness*," Rina said, grabbing Eva's hand and pulling her up, and taking her towards her bed.

"Aw, please?"

"No ma'am! You need your rest. I think that fever is getting to you," she continued, forcing Eva down to the bed and covering her with blankets.

"I'm feeling much better."

"I'm sure you are. That's why rest is the most important thing now. Besides, you have a long journey ahead of you," Rina said with a smile.

"You're right," Eva sighed.

"Sweet dreams," she said softly before turning away.

Eva reached out and grabbed Rina's hand, holding her back. "Please stay with us. Join the group. I don't want you to hide anymore."

Rina looked back at her friend and sat down beside her in defeat. "I'm not going anywhere. It will be much easier saving your butt if I do, especially with those dopes."

Eva laughed, and with a yawn thanked Rina. Rina blew out the lantern and draped her cape over herself as she lay down near Eva's bed.

"Psst. Hey Rina. If you can see the immediate future, did you know all of this was going to happen?"

Rina groaned. "Goodnight Eva."

Chapter 12
A Nearby Village

Eva woke up bright and early, full of joy. Her fever had broken during the night, and it was as though all her worries had disappeared. Sitting up, she noticed Rina still beside her, fast asleep with Krimm wrapped around her, holding her head up like a pillow. Noticing the tear on the bottom of her chemise, she searched through her bag to find a needle and thread. She patched the fabric and looked at the rest of her dress. Crisp dirt stretched across her gown. Rubbing away the flakes proved to be insufficient as the stains remained. Eva gently ran her fingers through her hair to separate any knots and smooth out what she could before braiding it and leaving the tent.

A slight snoring rose from the small tent across from her own. Ijaïh had slept up in the tree and based on his sunken in eyes, stayed up most the night, sticking to his guard duties.

Everyone's been so nice these past few days. I wish I could do something for them.

A couple feet from the tent sat a bush filled with blackberries. She remembered eating wild berries as a child when her parents took her to the woods. The memories brought her a bitter-sweet feeling, but she pushed the saddened thoughts aside and tried to focus on the positive.

"I'm sure these blackberries would go nice with the apples from yesterday. I wonder if I could find any eggs…"

As she finished picking the blackberries, she heard a slight huff behind her. Eva turned around to see Krimm. She took a step back. She threw him a blackberry to which he gulped in one swallow. He walked over to her and gently nudged her leg, as if thanking her. Eva smiled and gently patted his head.

"You're not so bad after all, are you Krimm?" The creature gave a playful growl as she fed him another blackberry.

"Say, do you think you could help me out?" The creature looked at her with sly eyes. "I want to do something nice for the others. You think you can get me some bird eggs? I'm sure Rina would be most grateful," she said. He looked back to the tent where Rina slept with slightly worried eyes, and then back at Eva. He huffed again before scurrying off into the woods.

She laid the berries down on a large piece of bark that had fallen off during the storm. She then encircled a small dirt patch in some stones and placed a couple of twigs and some leaves in the center. She grabbed a match from her bag and lit the leaves, which smoldered under the heat. She gently blew on the leaves until the twigs started burning.

Eva pulled out the remains of the sourdough loaf she received from Finn's village and cut it into thin slices. Its whitened insides gently toasted upon the stone covering the fire. A sweetened steam filled the air as the berries cooked. A loud thump came from her side. Krimm had returned with five rather large eggs. Eva threw him a couple more blackberries. Krimm leaped with glee. He nudged stones to Eva. She chuckled, patting his head. She dusted the stones off and placed the blackberry and apple toasted bread upon them. She then turned back to the fire and cracked the eggs. The smell filled the whole camp yard.

"What you got there?" a voice yawned.

"Breakfast. I just figured I'd thank you and everyone else for caring for me last night. I hope I wasn't too much of a burden," she said flipping the eggs with her dagger.

Finn sat down beside her. "You were nothing of the sort! I'm just glad you're doing better today," he said. "Although, I wish you would have told me about what happened, but I understand why you didn't," he picked up one of the pieces of toast and took a bite out of it. "Not bad. Where'd you learn to cook like this?"

“Well, I was a Girl Scout when I was young, and we’d go camping every now and then. I enjoyed it so much that my parents started taking me camping every couple of months. I learned how to differentiate fruits that were safe and poisonous, and even how to cook a bit. I know it’s not the best, but with a limited supply, there’s not much to go upon.”

“I think it’s pretty good, but, what’s a Girl Scout?”

Rina awoke shortly thereafter. She heard Eva and Finn laughing together.

“Aren’t you two gettin’ real close?” Rina smiled with sarcasm. She plopped herself down across from them, stretching her arms to the sky. “Watch out, Eva, or lover-boy here will get you. Unless, of course, you want him to. You’ll catch more bees with your sappy look.”

“Rina!” Eva said blushing. Finn practically choked on his food with Rina’s remark. “I made some eggs and toast," she said handing her the stone plate. “Even Krimm helped. He’s such a sweetie.”

“My Krimm helped you out?” she said looking at the scaly beast. He found a twig, ripping it from a tree. He rolled around the ground, gnawing on its bark. “What a goofball," she said.

Eva looked at the creature. He stood about three and a half feet tall and had a broad chest and slender build. His black scales were smooth, and his tail was layered with thick spines that rose above one another, connecting in the center like stacked cups. Two wings laid flat across his back. Krimm had wrapped himself around the large wooden branch, twisting his body and tail around it. His beady yellow eyes enlarged as he snapped it in two.

“Krimm’s not exactly what I expected a dragon to look like," Eva said. “He seems much more snake like than I imagined.”

“That’s because he’s only part dragon," Rina said. “Most dragons here are stouter unless you’re looking at the water dragons. His father's an armadillo lizard and his mother, a black dragon."

A tree branch rustled behind them as a short-tailed weasel dropped to the ground. Krimm's head perked up at the sound. He hid behind a bush, shrinking to the size of a rabbit. He scurried out from the bush, enticing the weasel. Wide-eyed, the weasel began dancing, jumping around, and doing flips to gain his prey's attention. Krimm sat silently, staring at the weasel. The weasel went for the kill, but as soon as he came close, Krimm tackled him to the ground, pinning him down by the scruff. The weasel growled, twisting its body, and biting at Krimm's feet. The two wrestled one another, throwing leaves and grass into the air. A loud squeal arose as Krimm bit down upon the weasel's shoulder. The weasel's body seized, becoming still behind its breaths, completely paralyzed. Krimm pounced, and the weasel went limp.

Eva gasped, turning away from Krimm as he returned to his normal size and picked the weasel up. Blood trickled down his lip as he tore the body apart.

"No need to look so nervous. It's just nature," Rina said.

"I know," Eva said. "I feel bad for the weasel though, but then again, it tried to eat Krimm too."

"Exactly. Technically, I could have saved it with just a drop of this night lily's tea as it counters Krimm's venom, but even if I did, it was likely to die from the bite anyway."

"Natural selection at its finest."

"Yep. And with what it's worth, Krimm's been treated well. He's smaller than most dragons. Probably the runt of his litter, but I found him to be the strongest and quickest learner." She snapped her fingers and Krimm hopped over, nudging his two-horned head against her arm until she pet him. "Plus, he's the cutest and fiercest of the group. Ain't that right Krimm?" The creature growled and huffed then laid its head on her lap, gently moving his tail back and forth.

Dator and Ijaïh came towards the group moments later. Dator smiled brightly at Eva, throwing himself at her in an embrace.

"I was so very worried about thee last night Eva. I am glad thou art feeling well today."

"Thanks, Dator."

He sat down and ate the berry toast, while Ijaïh sat across from them, eating from his sac of berries. The group sneered at his action, but decided to put it beside them, figuring it best not to mention it.

"Oh, by the way, Finn, I looked at the map last night. I figured we could stop by Mildora today for supplies. I've been meaning to get some more hydra blood for future defense. I also need some ground yarrow root just in case we get into any trouble."

"Well, cutting through the village would save time," Finn pondered. "I guess we can go. We can pick up some food there as well."

"Great. Then it's settled," Rina said.

~:~

The group set off for Mildora, which lay three miles ahead. The woods shined brightly, light bursting through the leaves. Ijaïh lagged behind the group. Finn stood in the front, looking at his map from time to time, with Dator by his side. Eva walked beside Rina, glancing around at the light that shined through the trees.

"How are you liking it here?" Rina asked.

"Oh, it's very lovely. The woods are so beautiful, and much fuller than the ones at home. Not to mention how amazing it is to be around magical folk. I can't wait to get to Mildora. I'd love to learn more about the culture here. This whole place…it's so surreal. It's like a fairytale."

Rina snickered. “You really are a funny girl. I was sure you’d be freaking out by now. Especially with all those frightful moments with the sirens and that jack-o-lantern. I still don’t know how you all got out of that one.”

“Oh Rina, you should have seen it! They were everywhere! I had to climb this tree and-” Eva continued to tell the story from the previous day. “I’ve never been so scared and excited in my whole life!”

“Are you sure you’re Eva? The Eva I know couldn’t even hurt a fly, let alone take down a succubi," Rina said with a half-smile, half-smirk.

Eva giggled, shoving Rina playfully. “If I hadn’t, who knows what could have happened. Finn’s been teaching me to use my dagger, so I guess you can say I’ve been learning fast these past few days.”

“She’s not half bad," Finn interrupted. “She actually matched me at my lowest defense.”

“Well look at you, miss feisty one! And here, I thought you’d stay a damsel in distress your whole life.”

Eva blushed stubbornly. “There’s nothing wrong with being a damsel, and if she be in distress, then at least there’s a chance for her to be rescued.”

Rina sighed. “You really are a Disney princess, aren’t you?”

“Well at least I’m not a loner," she retorted.

“I’d rather be a loner than a clutz like you," Rina said smiling deviously.

“What!” Eva gasped.

“Hey Finn!” Rina said. “Did you know that last year Eva walked right into a pillar standing in the lunch hall at school?”

Finn looked at Rina, and with a soft snicker, looked back at Eva, whose face was red. “Really now?”

"Oh yeah! We were just talking about how awful derivatives were and *BAM* she hit the pillar face forward." They both chuckled.

"Oh yeah! Well, Rina fell asleep in class once and the teacher had to slam a book on her desk to wake her up!" Eva said.

"Oh please, you can't embarrass me. You flipped your desk trying to reach a pencil," Rina smirked.

Eva tackled Rina from behind, clasping her hand over her mouth. Her face was as red as a tomato. She raised her hands up and Eva dropped her hand. She bashfully walked behind them. Finn glanced at Eva, still stifling his laugh. Rina looked at him with disgust.

"Now, now, Finn, show some courtesy. We all know you have some embarrassing moments too. How rude of me not to share, when I've told some of Eva's."

"You wouldn't dare," he said, his face turning pale.

Rina wrapped an arm around Eva's shoulder. "I found out the secret to why people joke about his love life!" Rina whispered into her ear.

"Really?"

"Apparently, as his village folk say, Finn fell for a woman and would sneak letters into her basket when she wasn't looking. The whole village knew her, except for him since he had been on one of his travels for a while. When she found out who he was, she returned his letters one by one. Confused, he set out for her, only to find out she was a sister of the cloth."

"No!" Eva gasped.

"YOU LITTLE RAT!" Finn yelled.

Rina dove behind Eva. "You wouldn't hurt a defenseless girl like me, would you?"

Finn's lips tightened. "Defenseless my ass! Rina tried altering the emotions of a pig for fun, and it went terribly wrong!

The pig became obsessed with her and followed her around for days!"

"She did what?" Eva exclaimed.

"Okay-Okay! I'll stop! Please just don't say anymore!" Rina said.

"Promise?" Finn and Eva said in unison.

"Promise!"

Blood dripped down her face as the pain sunk in. Her body quivered from the lashing she had received. She breathed heavily, which only made her injuries worse.

"Are we ready to play nicely now?"

She nodded, shaking uncontrollably. It took all her strength to keep from collapsing. "She travels with four others. You will find her hidden within the mass of crowds of Mildora."

"Perfect," King Valdof grinned.

He turned to his henchman.

"Ready the guards. It seems we have some festivities to attend to."

Valdof turned to Maddie. "Do you understand now, little sprite? You ought not mess with me if you wish to survive. This waste of flesh is only useful when obedient."

Maddie glanced at Verona's crumpled body and back at Valdof. "You're a monster."

"Mind your tongue," he said with a hiss. Maddie's mouth became sealed with a tar-like substance. Valdof yanked her arm. "Or I may have to punish you like this impertinent fool." He unlocked her chains and ran his fingers through her hair. Maddie pulled away, yelling at him tight lipped. "Ah, ah, ah! You're such a beautiful treat. Full of zest. I'm here to help you, my little sprite. You've become so dirty down here. You must be properly cleaned."

Maddie glared at him.

"You must look your best for the party tonight. You are the guest of honor, of course," he said releasing her from her silence.

Chapter 13

The Golden Moon Festival

"So, what's Mildora like?" Eva asked.

"Mildora is a large village most known for their leather and hides, but also theatrical arts" Finn replied.

"Aye, and they also make the best stews!" Dator said. "I can't wait t' try their beet and scallop stew! I can already taste the spicy and earthy broth now!"

"Oh, and their rooster and cumin noodle stew with carrot and potato dumplings!" Rina said licking her lips.

"How can you two be hungry? We just had breakfast," Eva laughed.

"What can I say? I am a growing boy!" said Dator.

"I'm just always hungry," Rina said straightforward.

"Look guys! We made it!" Dator shouted when he reached the top of the hill.

"Hey, wait up!" Eva said chasing after him, followed behind Finn and Rina. Ijaïh kept his pace.

Over the hill lay a village filled with hundreds of people. Teal and purple streamers were being wrapped around the lamp posts, and banners hung between the village entrance. Violets and morning glories decorated the borders of houses and booths that sat upon the cobbled stone pathway. The booths were filled with different foods and handcrafted trinkets. From the center of the village rose a beautiful sound of horns, woodwinds, and string instruments, playing a happy tune. Their music flew into the air like leaves in a gust of wind.

Eva gazed around the wondrous sight. Tiny birds flew around the area, creating a blur of tweeting colors.

"Welcome to Mildora! Travelers, I presume? Come! Enjoy yourselves and celebrate this blessed day!" a man said popping in front of the group. His black hair curled around his pale skin complimenting his plum attire.

"Excuse me sir, but what is it that we ought to be celebrating?" Eva asked.

"What ought you celebrate?" he said in surprise. "Why today is the Golden Moon Festival! It is our annual celebration of when our two moons pass in front of one another, sending a day of peace and tranquility across the land, restoring the powers, of all us sprites, to full capacity with its golden-silver beams. It is a night of beauty and joyous activities to welcome the new morning in and spreading our hopes and wishes to others."

"That sounds wonderful!" Eva exclaimed.

"As a token for your arrival, please take this flyer for a free charm available from any of our lovely booths. Be warned that it may only be used once, and any trickery will lead to an immediate curse of tomfoolery to act upon you until the end of the festival at the stroke of midnight." The man handed everyone a cloth flyer. "Now be on your way and have a splendid time!" the man concluded, snapping his fingers, and burst into smoke.

"What a strange man. I wonder what he meant by a 'curse of tomfoolery.'" Eva said, imagining jesters goofing around. She giggled then looked at the others. "Should we cash them in?"

"Nay. We came here for supplies lest I be mistaken. A sheer moment o' knavery is merely foolish," Ijaïh said.

"Oh, come on, Ijaïh! It will be fun!" Eva pleaded. She looked at Finn. "Can't we stay just until the festival is over?"

"I don't know…we already lost time from yesterday," he said rubbing the back of his neck.

"What harm will come if we're a day or two off schedule? You said passing through shortens the way, right? Why not spare a little time for some fun?" Rina said nudging Finn's side.

"Aye, please Finn?" Dator intervened.

Finn paused. “Well, it would be fun. I guess we can spare one more day’s travel.”

“YES!” Rina, Eva, and Dator shouted in unison.

“This is going to be so great!” said Eva.

“I can’t wait t’ eat the food!” Dator said rubbing his hands together.

“Maybe they’ll have kerploples," Finn said.

“What a wretched day this will be," Ijaïh sighed.

“I hope they forged some fancy weapons! But first!” Rina smiled linking her arm into Eva’s. “We’re getting you a new outfit!”

“A new outfit? What’s wrong with this one?” Eva said, a little flustered.

“Have you looked in a mirror lately? It’s practically shredded!” Rina dramatized, looking at the slightly torn and dirty dress. “Plus, this outfit is terrible for travel. I’ll get you something much more fitting. Consider it my birthday gift to you!”

“O-okay.”

“Hey Finn, we’ll be back in a bit! We’re going to Jacob’s.”

“Alright! Stick together. Look for me afterward. I’ll be near Macken!” he yelled as they ran off.

~:~

As Eva and Rina entered the small shop, a strong whiff of leather surrounded them. The scent made them dizzy. Around them were many dresses, vests, and other clothing articles. Dim candles lit the room gently, making the iron suit of armor in the corner glimmer.

“Welcome! I’m Maudy Jacob. How may I be of service to you?” said a middle-aged woman. She was a plump woman with olive skin and thick curly greying hair. She wore a long, short-sleeved dress with a leather corset cusped around her waist. The long royal blue skirt laid beautifully across her hips, and the white bodice fitted against her figure.

"We came to find my friend here a new dress. Preferably one for traveling," Rina said, pulling Eva forward.

"My poor dear. You've been traveling in that? Why it's a wonder it's still in one piece!" the woman exclaimed and walked around her and examined her. "You see this is a common gown. One to wear in the village or at home. It may be nice for a stroll, but it's terrible for defense and is likely to catch on anything with how dangerous the forests have become." The woman looked at a rack nearby and pulled off a tight leather dress with metal shoulder pads that wrapped around the chest, which would reveal much skin, even with tights. "How about this one?"

"Umm…maybe something a little more modest," Eva said feeling slightly uncomfortable even thinking of trying something like that on.

The woman searched and came back with a mid-length gown made of hide and lined with fur. Its sleeves held loose, cinching at the wrists.

"This one seems nice," Eva said, eased by the conservative design.

"Oh please, poufy sleeves and hide? You'll be burning up out there. No offense, Miss Jacob," Rina interjected.

"None taken."

Rina looked around for a moment and then quickly pulled out a gown. "This one will do," she said before grabbing a white blouse and some cotton tights and shoes. "Go on, try it on," Rina badgered, shoving them into Eva's arms, and pushing her into the dressing room.

Eva looked at the outfit. "Are you sure? I mean-"

"Just try it on before I come in there and put it on for you!"

Eva took a deep breath and quickly dressed herself in the new outfit. She looked at herself in the mirror. The white blouse formed to her body, with sleeves cuffed at her elbows. She pulled the collar out from under the dark brown leather dress. With little strain, she tightened the corseted back and buttoned the buttons that rested on her midriff. The skirt fell to the middle of her thigh, pleating around her hips. Eva blushed at the way the dress flattered her body, as her chest became prominent, and it hugged her body in all its natural curves and bends. Her matching tights and calf-high leather boots pulled the outfit together. Eva took her leather belt that held her dagger from her other dress and buckled it around her waist where it lay gently on her hip.

"I don't know Rina. It's kind of short. It barely reaches my hips," Eva said. She heard a small snicker from outside the door.

"You're wearing tights! It's fine," she said.

Eva sighed and grabbed her satchel before exiting the room. She looked to the ground, twiddling her thumbs. "What do you think?"

Rina and Maudy smiled. "It looks great!" Rina said.

"Very elegant." Maudy replied.

"You think so?" Eva said, her face now a shade of pink.

"Mm-hm, but it's missing one thing," she answered. Maudy ran over to one of the mannequins and pulled off a cloak. Bringing it over to Eva, she gently buckled it around her collar, and laid its burgundy heavy linen material upon her shoulders. "There. That's perfect."

Eva held the cloak close.

"Now don't be sheepish. Show off your outfit. You should! You know I used to look like you when I was your age. Oh, those were the days." Maudy said. "Now if only we can fix this hair," she said pulling up a couple strands of Eva's hair.

She pulled Eva off to the side and sat her down in a chair. She brushed her hair with a wooden comb, releasing any knots within its rats. Maudy added some oils, making it silky to the touch. She put up part of her hair, letting the rest lay flat. Its waves gently accented the braided bun.

"You're ready to go. Oh, and here. You can keep the brush. Compliments on your purchase. A woman's hair is one of her most precious treasures, you know," she said. Eva looked at herself in the mirror and blushed. A different figure stared back at her, one with confidence, maturity, and elegance. Everything she yearned for.

Rina paid Maudy and dragged Eva out of the shop. Eva kept the cloak close.

"Will you stop that! You're fine! Everyone here wears clothing like that when they travel. You look weird by not showing it off," Rina scolded her.

"I don't know Rina. It just feels abnormal."

"Then why don't we see what Finn thinks?" she said pointing at him. He fidgeted with some small items in front of the Macken's Novelty Shop.

Eva grabbed Rina's hand with her own. "Oh no, please don't! He'll laugh at me!" she begged.

"No, he won't! Stop being such a bumblesnatch!" she said pulling her hand from Eva's and walked toward Finn. "Oi! Finn!" she yelled. She dragged him over to Eva. "What do you think? Doesn't she look wonderful?"

Finn looked at Eva and blinked a couple times. "Wow…" he gulped. It was all he could say before he, too, blushed. "You…ahem…you really did a good job Rina. It's very suiting," he continued, unable to look away. Eva's eyes went wide as she hid her face.

"Right." Rina said slowly, placing her palm on her face. She nudged Finn with her elbow playfully. "Hey Finn, why don't we go check out those charms now? We get them for free anyway."

"Gr-great idea," he said turning around and heading towards the booths. Eva came up to Rina and they followed behind Finn. Eva twiddled her fingers through her hair, giving a small smile.

They arrived at the booth moments later. Eva examined the table which had tons of little charms made of metal, wood, or gemstones. Each one of them had a symbol she could not read.

"Wow they're so beautiful," she said softly, in awe.

"Ah, I see you have the fliers. You may choose from anything on the table," the merchant said noticing the three crowd the table.

Finn looked for a moment and grabbed the smooth grey stone with a swirl encased in a square whose borders pinwheeled around the center.

"The sign of loyalty and perseverance. A trait dear to those you care about. With that, nothing can stop you from accomplishing your deepest desires."

Rina quickly chose hers with barely any glance at the other charms. Her wooden piece had a carving of a straight line with two lines forming a v at the center.

"Vitality. A great hold for the hands of a warrior."

Eva looked at the charms for quite some time. She contemplated between the thin metal and the pale blue crystal. As if drawn to it, she gently held the crystal, stroking her fingers over the symbol which represented that of an unwound treble clef.

"Now that, my dear, is quite a rare one indeed. So surprising that you should choose the celestite with its symbol of hope and determination, when you, yourself, hold such a pleasure. 'Tis a harmonious stone that will bring peace and balance the nature of those around you as well as yourself. Best to keep it safe."

Eva nodded, holding the stone close.

"Look at all the charms, Ijaïh!" Dator said. He gazed upon the charms with wandering eyes. Just as he was about to choose a charm, Ijaïh snatched the cloth flier from his hand. "Hey, give that back!"

"I will not let thou practice in such foolish acts," he scoffed. "Meaningless charms. A squander o' thine precious time." The cloth burst into purple flames, turning to smoke instantly. He looked at his now empty hand, confused.

Suddenly, an acorn bounced off his head. Ijaïh glanced up noticing a squirrel glaring down upon him from atop the booth. He quickly leaned toward the small animal to scare it off, but it only flicked its tail. Within seconds a dozen squirrels came behind their leader and with a squeak, launched themselves at Ijaïh. He danced around the scurrying rodents. Laughter rose from the people in the village who gazed upon his predicament. Ijaïh brushed the squirrels off and drew his blade. A gasp came from the villagers.

"Damn vermin!"

"Ijaïh don't!" Finn yelled holding out his hand. Ijaïh swung his blade hitting the squirrels in one stroke. He looked at them wide-eyed as none of them were hurt. The sword had phased right through them. The crowd roared in laughter.

"What a fool!" one of them shouted.

"Doesn't he know that you can't hurt a single soul during the Golden Moon Festival?" another called out.

Ijaïh looked at his blade in confusion before thrusting it back into its sleeve. He turned around and walked off, acorns from the other squirrels bouncing off him as he pushed through the mass of people.

"Shouldn't we go after him?" Eva asked.

"No, just leave him. He brought it on himself. Maybe he'll lighten up for a change," Finn laughed.

"It's not funny."

"Oh, don't be such a sourpuss. Come on, let's get some food," Finn said, wrapping his arm around Eva's shoulder. Rina looked at Dator.

"Hey shortstop, are you coming?"

"Uh…aye. Sure," he replied looking back and forth between Rina and the charms.

"Courage, my boy," the merchant said, holding out the charm Dator wanted. "Find it within. On the house."

~:~

A large wooden stand stood in the middle of the booths resting fifteen pots filled with a variety of stews. Besides the pots were loaves of sliced bread and ales. Steam rose from each of the stews, blending the scents together into a wonderful combination.

"Wow! It smells so good!" Eva said.

"Yeah, and they all taste good too!" Finn said, chuckling at Eva's child-like reaction. "Any ideas on what you want?"

"Oh, I don't know. There are so many choices! Why don't you decide for me?" she asked. Finn smiled, and ordered two bowls of different stews, picking up a loaf of white bread and a couple bottles of ale. Rina and Dator ordered theirs as well, and the four of them walked over to a table. Dator wasted no time slurping down the hot stew, while Rina took her time with her own meal, breaking off bread to dip into the spicy dish.

Eva looked down at her bowl, eyes full of hunger and excitement. Its rusty orange broth was filled with different vegetables, red and white meat, and lentils. It smelled strongly of rosemary, thyme, and garlic, making Eva's mouth water. She took a scoop and tasted the stew. Her eyes widened. "This is amazing! What is it?"

"Perpetual Stew, or as I like to call it, the never-ending pot," he smiled, taking a spoonful from his own bowl. "Probably one of the best ones out there. No matter how much you eat, the pot will never empty because you can always refill it to get the same effect. It has just about everything you can think of beans, parsnips, venison, pheasant, turnips, cabbage, you name it."

"I think it's wonderful! Much better than my mom's beef stew, and that's one of my favorites! It has so much flavor and the meat is so tender!"

Finn laughed. "I'm glad you like it," he said pulling out a bottle of ale and placing it in front of her. "Tastes even better with this. Go on, try it."

Eva shook her hand. "Oh, no. I don't drink. I'm not of age."

"Not of age? Ha, ha. That's the silliest thing I've ever heard! I've been drinking this stuff since I was twelve! Everyone here drinks. It's about the only good thing to drink anymore."

"You see Finn, Eva's not like most people. She doesn't go for such 'scandalous' antics," Rina smirked, taking a drink from her bottle of wine. "She's what you call, a 'rule binder.' Never wanting to follow the crowd, but rather following the rules to the utmost priority."

"Well, aren't you a stick in the mud?" Finn teased. "We ought to get you to be more relaxed. Have some fun!"

"I'm perfectly fine being a *stick in the mud*, thank you very much. It's improper to partake in such drinking habits," Eva said as she patted her lips with a napkin.

"Okay *your highness*," Finn snickered, pulling out his canteen. "You can have this then. Don't worry, it's safe."

Eva hesitated before taking it. She looked at the fluid which appeared to be clear, and then took a small sip. Her face scrunched up. A sweet honey flavor faded the odd taste in her mouth, which filled her with anger. Finn practically fell out of his chair laughing.

“You’re such an ass, Finn!” Rina said, snatching the bottle from Eva’s hand. “But I have to admit, seeing your face when you took that sip: pure comedy!” she continued, sniggering.

“You should have seen your face! Oh man, you were so sure of it too! I figured mead would have been perfect for your *proper* ways!”

Eva sat herself straight, pursing her lips. She glanced at the crazy buffoon, and with a forceful shove, pushed him off his chair. Finn hit the ground with a thud. Eva continued eating her stew. Dator snickered, then turned still as Finn sent magical sparks at him, making his hair stick up and click with static. Rina burst out laughing, leading Dator to respond by throwing a small two-inch orb at her. The orb burst, spewing golden glitter all over her. Rina let out a scream, her brow furrowed deeply. Eva about choked on her food as she saw Rina’s new *glamorous* look. Rina, feeling cunning, threw the rest of her loaf of bread towards her. Eva ducked out of the way and the loaf hit the back of a rather large bald man. Rina’s eyes went wide as the man glared back at them and formed a ball of water, sending it her way. Rina dodged the water, which hit a pixie passing by, causing it to fall to the ground, dripping with mud. Almost instantly, a fight broke out amongst all the people in the mess hall. Magical sparks of all colors flew in every direction, as did food and bottles.

Eva dropped to the ground. She glanced around the room as everyone began relinquishing their competitive nature. She gasped as Finn pulled her back. Crouched beneath the table, they watched in awe of the fight they created.

“This is great!” Finn smiled.

“No, it isn’t you dimwit! How are we going to get out of here without getting hit?” She scolded him.

“Oh, lighten up miss prissy prat! You need to learn to put yourself out there and go wild!” he said as he started to tickle her sides.

"N-no! St-stop it!" she said between uncontrollable laughs.

"Oi, love birds! Sorry to impose on your budding romance, but we got to go. Baldy over there still seems angry with me," Rina smirked.

The two crawled out from under the table and snuck out from behind the tent drapes with Rina and Dator. A small sneeze came from Rina's satchel and glitter puffed into the air. Krimm popped his head out, shaking away the golden flakes that covered his head.

"Poor Krimm," Rina said, then glared at Dator. "I ought to knock you silly," she said, glitter still pouring off her.

The others snickered. "'Tis hard t' take thee seriously with you looking so pretty. You look just like a princess," Dator gleamed.

Rina shoved him to the side. "I told you never to call me that."

"Oh, my apologies, *your grace*. I wouldn't want t' offend your *high status*."

"What are you talking about?" Eva said confused.

"Didn't thee know, Eva? Rina's-" Dator started only for Rina to shove a rag into his mouth.

"Nothing. I'm just simple old me," she said sternly, looking slightly perturbed.

"No. What? Tell me!" Eva said.

Finn cupped his hands over her ear and whispered, "She's the daughter of the ruler of her tribe."

Eva's eyes went wide and looked at Rina. "You're a princess?" she yelled.

Rina looked at Finn, enraged. "I'm going to kill you!" she screamed, running after him as he escaped into the crowd. "You get back here! Do you know how long I'm going to have to hear this from her now? You're going to be sorry, Finn Barrett! Just wait until I get my hands on you! I'm going to tear you into shreds and beat you so hard, your grandchildren will feel it!"

"Gotta catch me first!" Finn laughed, running.

Eva and Dator watched as the two ran around the village, wondering how long it'd be until they saw them again.

"You think they'll come back?" Eva asked, tickled by Rina's harmless threats.

"Who cares? Let's go see what's going on over yonder!" Dator said, pointing across the other side of the village where the people congregated. He grabbed her hand and excitedly pulled her to the edge of the crowd.

"Gather round, everyone and witness the mystical acts of our lovely cast! We have fire breathers and contortionists, glass blowers, and aerials! See the newest, never before seen performances provided by Martilora, Forte, and Zula!"

As the announcer said each of the entertainers' names, they appeared in a colorful burst of smoke. Martilora, whose creamy-yellow skin, shimmered in her periwinkle leotard that elongated her naturally thin and curved bodice; her long black hair tied up in braids, reaching to her hips. Forte stood beside her in a berry-blue attire. White stripes twisted around his tights, making a dizzying illusion of silent movement. His darkened complexion was lined with silver facial paint. Zula completed the group wearing nothing but a wine-colored bodysuit that glistened with gold and silver sparkles. Her mid-length strawberry blonde hair flowed smoothly back and forth across her pink-hued skin.

"Now without further ado, let the show begin!"

The three performers jumped into the air, striking a pose, as swirls of blue, silver, and purple magical dust surrounded them, allowing them to hover. Forte raised his hand to his mouth and blew golden flames at the girls, turning them into dust before dropping to the ground, sending a ripple of flames around the stage. With a snap, he released a flame from his hand, shaping it into that of a three-tailed fox, letting it run around toward the crowd. Its movements left behind a trail of prints that simmered and turned into floating glass shards. He twisted his hand forward, sending out a fire pixie and unicorn, each the size of their natural live forms. They sent sparks around the crowd, which turned into streamers. By the end of their little celebration, the three creatures brought the trail of glass they left behind to their creator before coming together and bursting into a giant flame. Forte raised his hands to the shredded glass, bringing it to his mouth. The people gasped as he swallowed the handful of glass shards followed by the flames, for no one had attempted an act such as that before. With a moment of intense silence, he rose his hand into the air and released the flame. As the flames extinguished, a solid piece of glass sat in his hand, in the shape of a phoenix. Forte handed the glass bird to a little girl from the crowd, who admired the figurine. With a spin, he turned into smoke, only leaving a pile of ash beneath where he stood, and in his place stood Martilora.

A symbol sounded from behind and she bent her body into an odd position. Her feet rose above her head as she knelt down. Her body now round as a ball, she lifted a leg up pulling up her braids along with it. She rolled herself back, jumping into the air only to hold herself up by one finger touching the ground. She spread her legs and bent them in opposite directions, and with a quick whistle, two golden orbs formed on her feet. She twitched her feet upward and downward, juggling the two balls. She whistled again and pushed herself into the air, and with a flick of her hair, held onto a matching golden hoop to which she wrapped her body around in ways that to any normal person would be impossible. Dator's jaw dropped in awe. Seeing Martilora bend her body in unnatural positions made Eva feel uncomfortable. A sudden gust of wind passed by her, and someone grabbed her from behind, making her jump.

"Woah, hey, it's just me!" Finn said, coming in front of Eva.

"You scared the crud out of me!" she scolded softly. "What are you doing?"

"I need a hiding place! Rina's still after me and fuming!"

"You brought this on yourself, but why do you need a hiding place? You aren't *scared,* are you?" she teased.

"What? No! I just don't want her to find me."

"Uh-huh. You're totally scared," she said, looking around. She noticed Rina stomping around. She looked back and forth and walked past them to the other side of the crowd. "I think you're safe now," she whispered.

Finn stood up, looking over Eva's shoulders. "Thanks Eva. You're a lifesaver," he said patting her shoulder.

"There you are!" Rina glared.

"Well, gotta go!" Finn shouted, running off in the opposite direction.

The crowd clapped at the end of the second act. Within seconds, two dark blue translucent draperies, as fine as silk, fell from the sky, attached to nothing but the air. Zula spun down the magical material, halting in the middle, hanging only by her arms. She walked through the air, swinging herself around the stage to appear as though she was as light as a bird in flight. After the third time around the stage, she wrapped her right leg through the material multiple times, then let herself fall, coming to a standstill three feet from the ground. She struck a pose, releasing hundreds of tiny glittering butterflies from her hands. Wrapping her arm in the second drape, she twirled herself up and let go as she reached the top. She spun rapidly and as she was about to hit the ground, the material wrapped around her like a cocoon and released itself to reveal her disappearance.

A small whistle rang from behind the crowd and there stood Zula with Martilora, Forte, and the announcer, balancing themselves on top of a tented booth. They bowed thanking the audience for their attendance before turning into dust, leaving everyone in awe.

“That was amazing!” Dator exclaimed.

“It sure was! Did you see how that woman disappeared at the end of her silk?”

“Aye! Or the man who swallowed the glass! How did he do that?”

“I have no idea, but it’s impressive!”

“I’ll say! Breathing fire is hard t’ begin with and swallowing the glass t’ mold it; ‘tis pure genius!”

“I’m glad you enjoyed it. Let’s go see if we can find Finn before Rina clobbers him.”

Chapter 14
Rina's Pursuit of Vanquish

Eva and Dator escaped to a nearby clearing to search for their missing friends. Dator climbed one of the metal lamp posts.

"Do you see them?" she asked.

"No," he said. Across the village stood many people having a great time, enjoying the shows held in different portions of the town. Sword throwers, magical rarity auctions, and various other acts lined the edges, forming a puzzling contraption for seeking two individuals out. "Wait, I see something!" Dator said excitedly. "'Tis Ijaïh! He looks quite annoyed and OH! He just got hit with a berry pie! Ha, ha! He's absolutely covered in its juices and crème!" Dator laughed.

"Poor Ijaïh." Eva said, shaking her head. "Now's not the time for that. Do you see Finn or Rina anywhere?"

Dator's ears perked up at a swift movement. "There!" he pointed. "I see them! They are right beside the fighting rink yonder past the charm booth!"

"Great! Let's go!" she said. Dator slid down the post and they ran off towards the booth where they received their charms.

Rina chased after Finn, who seemed exhausted after the long run. He hid within the crowd, panting heavily.

"Phew, I think I lost her," he said. As soon as he turned around, Rina appeared in front of him, and grasped his collar, pulling him close.

"Don't you ever reveal a-"

"You, there! Young woman in the scaled leather! Come forth!" a man yelled from the middle of the rink. "I got a bean to pick with you!" he growled. "Or shall I say bread?"

The surrounding faces awaited her response.

"There you two are! We've been wondering when you'd show up," Eva said between breaths. "What are you doing, Rina? Put him down!"

Rina rolled her eyes and dropped Finn. "Come on, let's leave," she said sternly, placing a hand on Finn and Eva's backs.

"Turning away, are you?" the man threatened. "Just like you did in the mess hall! What, is *little miss pretty* scared of getting her dress dirty?"

The crowd laughed, enjoying the foul humor the man proclaimed. Rina's fist clenched and she headed towards him. Eva grabbed her hand, pulling her back.

"Rina, you can't seriously think of fighting this guy! He's over twice your size and could easily crush you with one grasp!" she said, her words filled with dread.

"Trust me, he's no match," she said in a calm manner, then faced the man. "You're just some pintsized cyclops whose brain is too small for your fat, bald head!"

A silence formed amongst the crowd followed by a wave of tension questioning the man's capabilities.

Rina broke free of Eva's grasp, handing her satchel, with Krimm, to her. He stood ten feet tall and looked as though he could break any object, live or inanimate, with a swing of his fist. His build was that of a fully trained warrior, one of which had rippling pectorals and biceps the size of watermelons. Rina grinned keenly.

"I'm gonna crush you like a bug," the man growled.

"Then let's make a bet."

"Alright. If I win, I get to keep your puny dragon hybrid."

"And if I win, you hand over that nice-looking combat knife of yours. The one made of the horn of a chimera and doused in its venom."

The man clutched his knife, knowing of its power. "Then it's a-"

"I'm not finished yet. And on top of that, you have to tell everyone here that you're a cowardice pig who lost to a girl who's four times smaller than you."

The crowd oohed followed by soft murmurs of the intensity of the bet.

"What is she doing?" Eva whispered, heart racing.

"I don't know, but I sure hope she does," Finn said.

"You really think you have a chance to beat me? You with your big words and petty apparel," the man hissed.

"You're right. I don't have a chance to beat you," she said with a flick of her hair. "I have a chance to destroy you," she said curling her lips upward and slammed her fist into his face.

The man stumbled backward, unexpected of the sudden force that came upon him. Rina threw her sword to the ground. The man charged at her, head front. Rina dodged his attack, not a single ounce of fear residing in her eyes. She ran her knee into his gut as he continued running. He collapsed to the ground in pain. He grabbed her fist and flipped her, slamming her into the ground. He jumped into the air, elbow faced down, but Rina's quick movements were no match for his technique. She unbuckled her overskirt and jumped on the man's back, pulling its rough material against the fat of his neck. The man roared in anger, thrashing back and forth, but Rina's hold only tightened.

Suddenly, red sparks surrounded her face, temporarily blinding her. Rina let out a cry. Opportunity at hand, he grabbed her single handedly, and threw her into the dirt. He fell on top of her, crushing her.

"Rina!" Eva screamed.

The man chortled at his short-lived victory. His body vibrated for a moment before he was thrust upward. Rina, a little scuffed up, rose to her feet. She buckled her skirt and waited for the man to fall before pinning him down, sending punches one after another into his somewhat swollen face.

The man punched her straight in the gut, sending her high into the air. Rina hit the ground hard, but quickly pulled herself up. She spat at the ground with fury. The man caressed his jaw. Rina jumped into the air and just as the sole of her heeled boot inched towards his face, the man swung her like a discus, throwing her as far as his strength would allow.

Eva gasped, grabbing Finn's hand. His hand tightened against hers, easing the shakiness of her clammy palms.

Rina tumbled to the ground, dust forming around her from the fall. She quickly grasped her trick wire from her boot and tied it to one of the posts of the rink before running around the man. He turned around, throwing his fists to the ground, but Rina somersaulted between his legs. She kicked his back, which only made his blood boil more. He swung his fists, but no matter what attack the man attempted to use, he could not touch her. Rina was too fast and in no time had the whole court wrapped in thin wire. Frantic, the man froze, for the trap before him would lead him to tumble. Hopping along the filamented path, Rina took a leap of faith upon the tension filled wire, flipping backward as she dug the cap of her shoe into the man's jowl. Midair, she tugged upon the wires, binding the man's arms, sweeping him off his feet as she landed. She stood gracefully upon the wire and with a second leap, rammed her fist into the back of the man's head, forcing it into the mud below. He was defeated, his body limp and severely bruised. The crowd roared at Rina's victory, amazed by her agility and powerful tactics. She grabbed her sword, and yanked the combat knife from his belt, attaching it to her own. She passed the crowd, wiping away the blood that stained her lip.

"Rina, that was incredible!" Eva exclaimed.

"Yeah, you really showed him!" Dator said.

"I'm so glad you're okay!" Eva said, hugging her friend. "How did you do that? I thought for certain you were a goner when he tackled you!"

"I told you, he's no match for me. Besides, that was easy. The blubbering idiot couldn't even control his own temper long enough to block his thoughts. I saw practically every move he intended to make," she smirked, secretly proud of her victory.

"Great job, Rina! You're getting about as good as me!" Finn laughed.

"Says the one I had to teach everything to!" she spat. They all laughed at their friend's amazing performance until a man pushed through the crowd to the group. His eyes filled with exhilaration. His short silver hair laid flat against his tanned face, with a few wisps shadowing his brow. His ears were as pointed as his nose which lengthened his face, making his transparent eyes and thick lips ever so elegant. He wore a blue tunic with bronze buckles and a satchel made of hide around his waist that matched his boots. His white sleeves cuffed at his elbows revealing the symbol of spirit on his left wrist.

"Wow! I mean, just wow! You're absolutely amazing! The way you flew into the air and slammed that guy down was beautiful! I've never seen such precise movements! You must teach me!" he said before turning a shade of orange. "O-or that is…I'd like you to."

"Sorry, kid, I have better things to do," she said with a smirk.

"Oh, please reconsider! I'm a great fighter, and quick too! I even took down a whole army of grindylows that were trying to snatch the children from our village a couple of years ago. I'd be on my best behavior and even pay you-"

Rina thrust her blade past his face. It phased right through his skull, as she knew it would. The man fell back to the ground. "Heh, you're not so fast as you say you are. You didn't even see my blade. Face it, you need a lot of training, and honestly, I care little for money. Unfortunately for you, I don't have the time to train you. Like I said, I've better things to do than to babysit."

The man sat paralyzed as Rina beckoned the others to follow. They obliged, too nervous to say anything.

"Then at least give me your name and I shall prove myself worthy for your training!" he continued, stumbling to his feet.

"Oh, come on, tell him. He deserves that much," Eva whispered, nudging her side.

His reddened face lusted with hope. She sighed and turned away. "Rina," she said in a cold tone. The man's heart filled with admiration as the group of four left the rink.

~:~

"That was very rude of you back there, Rina," Eva scolded. "He seemed very eager to learn from you. And he's cute too!" she continued, knowing her goal of finding someone for Rina would not occur anytime soon.

"Please. He's a wimp. I doubt he even beat one grindylow, let alone a whole heard of them. Besides you're my main mission. I can't waste time training some pipsqueak who can't even dash a blade."

"He was just excited," Finn stated.

"Excitement leads to disaster in the field of battle. You, of all people, should know that. Let's just forget it and go on. I'm sick of hearing this conversation."

Chapter 15
Ijaïh's Past

The sun had set, and four empty plates lay across the wooden table. A big chicken dinner had filled them to the brim.

"Hey Eva, look at this!" Finn said, handing her a golden ball with three rings floating around it.

"What is it?" she asked, admiring the spinning rings.

"It's called a kerplople. Go ahead, try it! Just connect the three rings."

Eva studied the object and gently brought the three rings together. A small hiss came from the object before it opened, and a gush of wind flew into her face. The other three laughed at her befuddled state as the wind stopped.

"What is it?" she asked. Out of the corner of her eye, blue shimmering waves drifted by. She pulled up a strand of her hair which was now a deep blue color and tightly curled. "H-How?"

"Wow, it's so bouncy too!" Finn said playing with her hair. Eva playfully smacked his hand away.

Rina grabbed the golden ball and opened it, only to receive a squirt of water to the face. She brushed the water into her hair, which highlighted her dark wisps in pink. Dator snatched the kerplople and his hair steamed into green spikes. He threw it at Finn who opened it, and with a flash of light, his hair turned a golden shade that draped over his right eye.

Everyone laughed at their ridiculous appearances.

"I'll be right back," Dator said running off to a nearby booth. He came back with a small purple sac. The other three stood around him, questioning its contents. He opened the bag. Each of them pulled out a coin-sized candy of a different color.

"These aren't normal, are they?" Eva said, suspicious of the small silver candy.

"'Tis Blazing Medlars! They art only the best sweets for celebration! They give bursts of magic with each piece having a different effect!" Dator smiled. He plopped a black one into his mouth and black smoke surrounded him. When it dissipated, he became transparent. "See!"

Eva's jaw dropped, and in excitement to experience magic, bit into the candy. The creamy shell revealed a sweetened puree like that of an apple. A surge of energy ran through her body, and she felt something grow out of her head. She rolled her eyes upward. Two large fluffy ears lay upon her head and a matching grey tail popped out from her rear.

"Oh my gosh! This is so cool!" Eva squealed, her tail wagging back and forth excitedly. She howled uncontrollably. Eva quickly covered her mouth, surprised by the candy's trickery. Finn, Dator, and Rina guffawed, practically collapsing.

Calming down a bit, Finn threw his red piece in his mouth. Two wings sprouted from his back, and he shrunk to the size of a fairy. He flew up and landed on Rina's shoulder. She flicked him away. He flailed backwards before transforming back into a normal size. He threw a candy her way, hitting the ground by Rina's feet just as she put her yellow candy in her mouth. The candies encased her in purple smoke. Rina coughed waving the smoke away. Her skin was covered in green scales and her eyes had slits in them.

"You idiot! You're not supposed to mix them!" she yelled. Yellow sparks flew out of her mouth with every word. Rina pursed her lips and threw one at Finn. Magenta smoke surrounded him, and matching feathers popped out from his hair like a cockatoo. He squawked and threw another one her way. Rina dodged the candy and it hit Eva straight in the face. Finn gaped, his face paling. Eva brushed away the smoke, surrounded by white sparks that shocked anyone who got too close to her. She looked at her hands and smiled mischievously. She wrapped her arms around Rina, rubbing her fist against her head to which she struggled beneath. By the time she pulled away, her hair stood up. She shocked Finn and Dator as they laughed. The electric field dimmed until no more sparks came around her. There was one medlar left in the bag.

"Who wants it?" Dator asked, holding it out.

"You keep it, Dator. You earned it," Finn said with a grin.

Dator pulled out the small opal candy. A tall slender man came from behind.

"What knavery is this?" he said in a cold voice.

"I-Ijaïh!" Dator said, startled.

The candy flew into the air and landed right at Ijaïh's feet. A transparent smoke rose over him and when it vanished, revealed ram horns on the side of Ijaïh's head. The others gasped. Ijaïh's raged filled eyes stared into Dator's soul. Ijaïh huffed, then flipped his cloak, heading to the forest.

Finn, Rina, and Dator kept still until they could restrain their hysterics no more. Eva felt a painful twang resonate from her chest. As the others laughed about the silliness of the Blazing Medlars, she crept away to the woods.

A small girl appeared, hanging upside down on the young oak. She had curly brown hair and olive-green eyes. She blended in well with the tree, for her attire came from the bark and leaves. She giggled at Eva. "If you're looking for the elf, he went that a way," she said pointing further into the forest. "Although, I must warn you, he seemed quite irate. Seems the fool of the town hast crossed his fate," she giggled.

The girl disappeared before Eva could ask what she meant. Eva shrugged it off. An owl sounded its wary tone throughout the darkening path, making Eva feel uneasy. The further she got the darker it appeared. *It's okay Eva...it's just the sun setting. See even the moons are out.* Eventually, she came across an enormous birch tree. Ijaïh sat upon the lowest branch, with his eyes closed.

"Ijaïh?" Eva said in a warm voice. "What are you doing way out here?"

Ijaïh scoffed and turned away. "'Tis none o' thine concern," he said.

His face hung low with bags under his eyes. His clothes were wrinkled from previously being wet, and his hair slightly stiff from where bits of the pie remained. His horns glistened ever so slightly under the moonlight. He held his throbbing brow.

"Come on Ijaïh, let's go back to the festival. I'm sure everyone will be most exc-"

"I say nay! Allow me t' be in mine own accord! I seek no help from thee."

"Don't be that way. I just want to-"

"LEAVE THIS PLACE!" he yelled.

Startled, Eva stepped back. She thought of heading back to the group then scowled. "What gives you the right to talk to me that way? I come out here on my own, away from the group just to be nice and hope that I can brighten your day a bit, and you yell in my face?" she said, pursing her lips. "You know it's no wonder why your brother is so afraid of you! He's trying to-"

"I WILT NOT ATTEND T' THY MOTLEY-MINDED WORDS! THOU HAST NO BUSINESS-"

"IT IS MY BUSINESS AND YOU WILL LISTEN TO ME!" she screamed. Ijaïh became silent. "Your brother has done nothing but be supportive of the group and try to make everything happier and more fun! Finn is doing the best he can to keep the group in order and only asked you to help him out on the mission and without Dator, you wouldn't have come! Rina came along to protect us all in case any uncontrollable acts befall upon us! I didn't ask to be here anymore than you did, but you should at least provide us with some respect! We saved you from those sirens and you couldn't even thank us! We bust our butts off trying to keep everyone safe and you just act all *high and mighty* like you're better than us! But guess what? YOU'RE NOT! YOU'RE JUST SOME LOW-DOWN SNOBBISH ELF WHO HAS NO RESPECT FOR ANYONE BUT HIMSELF!"

"I will not allow some puny human treat me poorly! 'Tis thy fault we art on this mission t' begin with!"

"My fault?"

"Thee humans always cause problems and care not o' how it harms our kind! From day one humans hast treated mine people like rubbish, some creature for thy t' play with! Doth thee know how many folk thy kind hast vanquished?"

"No, but-" she stuttered. Ijaïh dropped from the tree, his eyes full of detestation.

"Hundreds to thousands o' us hast been slain by the hands o' Man! Elves in quite particular hast been belittled t' an unnerving low! 'Tis thy kind t' blame! The shame o' knowing that an Elven sword destroyed our superior dishonors mine tribe and strengthens mine hatred towards hellish creatures such as thyself!"

Her heart stirred and her jaw grew firm. A heavy lump fell to the bottom of her throat. "I-I know I'm not perfect and t-that h-humans have done terrible things to the people of this world, but times have changed…I couldn't imagine hurting any of you or anyone in this world."

"FOOLISH LIES! HUMANS ART ALL THE SAME! VILE AND CRUEL! DOTH THEE THINK THY ART SPECIAL? THOU ART NAUGHT BUT A FOOLISH WENCH THAT HATH CAUSED DISMAY ACROSS OUR LAND AND IF IT NOT BE FOR MINE PEOPLE, PERDITION ALLOW I WOULD GIVETH THEE T' KING VALDOF MYSELF!" he said. "Now leave me in mine peace!"

"I wish you wouldn't hate me, Ijaïh…not just because I'm human. If you'd see past what I am, and realize me for who I am, maybe-"

"GO T', I SAY! OUT UPON THY WRETCHED WAYS!" he screamed, shoving her to the ground. "Thou vex me with thy petty thoughts! Thou art, but an inferior being; a worthless superfluous piece o' flesh! Thou art nothing!"

Eva hung her head, shaking ever so slightly as to control her emotions from releasing. Tears ran down her face, hitting the ground beneath her. "I thought we could be friends. I figured we could patch ties to make amends from the tension that separated us," she said softly, picking herself up. "...but now I see, your heart is as cold and bitter on the inside as you are on the outside."

Ijaïh's eyes filled with dread at her words of friendship. His hand seared as she wandered off into the woods, west of where she came. He fell to his knee cupping his head in shame. "What hast I done?" he whispered in self-pity.

Chapter 16

The Face Behind the Façade

Eva ran further into the forest, tears streaming down her face. *Thou art nothing...a worthless superfluous piece of flesh...petty...inferior...pitiful...* Each word pounded through her head, each more powerful than the last. Her heart slammed itself against her chest, sending a throbbing pain through her limbs. Her lungs tightened with cold air. Her breath stiffened and she let herself fall to the ground.

"Hoo is it that caused you pain?" a hollow voice called out.

"Who said that?" Eva asked, for around her stood trees and a small pond.

"Look upward, my dear," the voice whistled.

Eva did as it said and up in the trees sat a barn owl, whose big black eyes glistened hazel in the light. He leaned his head forward.

"Far from the festival, I see."

"Y-yes," Eva stuttered nervously, pushing a strand of hair behind her ear. "I-I was just trying to bring back a friend to the festival, but I guess that's improper to say now."

"'Tis he hoo bring you sadness?" the owl said tilting its head over. His head lengthened, bending to a whole half circle.

"Yes, but I'd rather not speak of it," she said, evading his eyes.

"Hoo, hoo," it cooed. "Then think not of it. 'Tis not important."

Eva smirked. *It's easy for him to say.* The owl squinted, standing straight. He spread his wings and flew down, catching a small impish creature. Returning to an adjacent tree, he tore the creature apart, swallowing the pieces whole. He wiped his beak with his talons. Eva gulped.

"Be not scared, for it is an evil dweller upon these woods," he said ruffling his feathers.

Eva nodded with a short sigh in means of calming herself.

The owl sneered at her sternly then spoke again. "There is much for you to attain from your surroundings."

"What do you mean?"

"Seek the truth," he hooted. "*Hooest threaded the needle attempts an action worth pursuing, but only when the spool is through, will one learn to sew.*"

"But I already know how to sew," Eva said.

"Heed my words and you will see. Not everything is what it seems," the owl concluded, and flew off past her. Eva followed until she reached the lake.

"Eva!" Finn yelled from afar. He ran up to her. "I'm so glad you're safe! Why did you run off? We were all worried!" he said. Eva's posture weakened, shaking beneath her cloak. "Hey, what's wrong? Are you hurt?" he asked concerned.

Eva shook her head, wiping away her tears. "I'm fine," she sniffed.

Finn placed two hands on her arms. "You're not fine. What's wrong? What happened?" he asked, sitting her down on a nearby rock.

"I went to talk to Ijaïh. I just wanted to make him feel better and bring him back to the festival to enjoy what was left of it. I guess it was a silly idea," she said with a saddened laugh.

"That bastard. Don't you worry about him. I'll teach him a lesson. You want me to go beat him up because I will. Or maybe I can send sparks at him until he apologizes to you, that sound good?"

"No, it's okay," she said. "Can we just sit out here for a while? I'd rather not have the others see me like this."

"Sure. We can spend the whole night here if you want. Oh, and maybe this will make it better!" Finn said excitedly, sitting next to her. He pulled out a small golden object from his bag. Its cylindrical shape was covered with swirls and stars, reminding Eva of Van Gogh's *Starry Night*. Finn opened the lid, and a bright golden light escaped from it. Tiny golden balls of energy formed into woodland creatures that played with one another and explored their new surroundings.

"They're so pretty," she said. Her fingers passed right through the tiny creatures as she touched them, distorting their shape until she pulled her hand back. "What are they?'

"Lux spirituum. They brighten any space even in pitch darkness. Although they can roam around as they please, once the jar is closed, they return to their resting place. They bring warmth to anyone needing it. Kind of suiting don't you think?" he smiled.

Eva pulled her knees close. She smiled softly, watching the small creatures play. "It's odd, you know? We've only been together for a couple days now, but it seems like I've known you for a long time. I've caused so much trouble for you and the others, so why? Why are you so nice to me?"

"Is it wrong to be nice to someone? It's obvious, isn't it? We all care about you, Eva…I care about you. Look, if it has anything to do with what Ijaïh said, I wouldn't let it bother you. I'm sure he meant no real harm."

"He meant everything he said. Let me ask you this, do you think I'm a burden?"

"Of course not! Is that what he told you?"

She shrugged.

"Eva, you mean more to this group than you think! You could never be a burden! Even if we have to fight hundreds of magical folks, you're still worth it! Burden? Ha! Why, Eva you're about the least bothersome person in this group!"

"So, you don't think I'm worthless?" she asked.

"Why would you ever think such a thing?"

Eva buried her head further into her knees.

"What happened to you? Did Ijaïh-"

"Ijaïh has nothing to do with it! It's all me," she said in a fit of frustration.

"What do you mean?"

Eva sighed, stars shining in her saddened eyes. "About five years ago, I met this really great group of people. We all shared interests and had wonderful times together. We'd go get ice cream, hang out at lunchtime at school, and even go see a movie once in a while. And then, things changed. One day they showed their true faces to me. They said that I'd never amount to anything, that I'd always be alone. No one would ever want to be my friend, and no one would ever be in a relationship with me because I was a nobody. We had been friends for so long, and out of nowhere they said that to me. I-I didn't know what to do. I was distraught. I have never been a popular person in school. It had always been like that, but I thought, for just a moment, they might have been different. They treated me like an equal for three years, and then saying such awful things…" Eva said, hiding her pained face. She dug her hand into the grass, shaking.

"What did you do?" he said, placing his hand over hers. He gently rubbed his thumb across her knuckles.

"Well…" she said softly, laying her chin on her knees. "I cried a little, kept things to myself, and decided I didn't need them anymore. So, the next day, I told them I never wanted to see them again, that our friendship was over, and that I would never come back. They acted so *very apologetic*. They said it was nothing but a *joke* to them, that I took things too *seriously*. The way I see it, if a joke hurts someone deep down like that, and they know those negative thoughts lingered in that person's mind for quite some time, they're not true friends. I could see the seriousness in their eyes as they laughed, and realized, they lied to me…all that time. They pretended to be my friends, and in reality, I had been a joke to them."

She quickly wiped her tears away and pulled her cloak close, trying to hide her face. "I wondered if anyone would notice if I didn't exist. Sometimes, I wished it to. I figured, maybe it was for the best."

"Eva…"

"I feared how my parents would feel, but eventually it just became so bad I couldn't take it anymore. I stopped listening to anyone, stayed in bed as long as I could, but kept to the rules of my home and school, because that's all I was *good* for anymore.

"One day, I started a new cooking class. Everyone required a partner. I sat at a table, just waiting for the teacher to force me with another student. I asked one or two people, and they just laughed saying they had a partner. So, I waited. And then, Maddie came in. I hadn't seen her before. She came up to my table and asked if she could sit down beside me, wondering if I had a partner yet. I was shocked. No one really talked to me in a nice manner, yet alone smile at me, for so long, and she was asking me to be her partner!" Eva said with bitter happiness. "Of course, I said yes. She didn't push me to explain what made me so upset but told me to 'never give up.' Eventually, we started hanging out together outside of class. She told me to 'leap for my dreams,' and that I shouldn't let what other people say bother me. After a while, I opened up to her, and things got better. She taught me to smile again. She made me feel like a human…like I was worth something. If I hadn't met her that day, I don't think I'd be here."

"I had no idea. You always seemed so cheerful. You've kept that in you all this time?"

"Mm-hm," she nodded. "But it's okay. You see from that point on, Maddie and I have been best friends. She saved my life. That's why-"

"Why you keep that necklace in your bag," he said.

"How did you know about that?" she asked.

"I've seen you looking at it when you get worried at night."

Eva pulled out the orange quartz necklace. "It's really beautiful, isn't it?"

"Yes, it is. May I?" he asked holding his hand out. He gently pulled it over her head and tightened the string. "You should keep it on. It suits you," he said.

Eva blushed. A blue light flashed through her eyes.

"Oh, and I got something for you," he said. He pulled out a shimmering object from his bag, presenting it to her. It was a blue orchid. Eva took the flower gently. Its six blue petals were laced with purpling ridges, and a pearl white center, that complemented its silver stem.

"Finn, it's beautiful!" she exclaimed.

"I knew you would like it. It's a rare find these days. They say when the moon hits it just right, it glows, sending out a wonderful scent and spreading its beauty to anyone near it."

"Wow."

"And it will live for a thousand years, even after it's cut."

"It's truly amazing! Thank you, Finn. I shall cherish it always!"

The two moons came closer and closer. Eva rested her head against Finn's shoulder. His warmth soothed her as he pulled her close.

"Do you ever think about it still?"

"Of course. Every day of my life. I'm terrified of going back. I'm always worried that all my happiness is just an illusion, and that one day I'll wake up back in a situation like that again. The one thing I know is that I can never give up. I promised myself I would never go back. I won't experience it again…I can't."

"It's hard to believe that such an experience could happen to you. From a first glance I could never imagine you having such a dark past."

"Sometimes the happiest people hold the greatest sorrow."

"How could anyone treat you so? Why you're one of the greatest people I've met! You're funny, intelligent, shy, and cute. I mean, you're practically perfect!"

"Nobody's perfect," she insisted, smelling the orchid.

"That may be true, but that doesn't mean perfect is only one particular way of doing or being something. People often think perfection must be something without flaws, but the way I see it, perfection is flawed. If you were good at everything, you'd never be happy. You'd be hollow. Being different is what makes us who we are. It's beautiful. Don't let anyone tell you otherwise. Each person has a different look on what is considered perfect to them. For instance, with my raspberry tarts, I prefer them to be nice and crispy, maybe a little burnt on the edges every now and then, but you absolutely loved them when they were a nice golden brown, and soft and chewy on the inside. We'd both consider our favorite style 'perfect,' but they are completely different in their own ways."

"I guess that's true," Eva giggled.

"Look at me," Finn said softly, pulling her chin to face him, his eyes full of sincerity.

"Being yourself, is the most wonderful thing anyone could ask for. You're worth happiness. You deserve everything, and your perfect no matter what. Don't shut yourself away because you're too precious to do so. You are *perfect*, Eva."

Eva's face turned that of a shade of rose. The stars glistened in her eyes. She could feel her heart beating fast, as if it would leap from her chest if she let it. Their eyes met, unable to look away. Finn ran his hand down her cheek. His soft, gentle hand cusped the nape of her neck; he leaned forward, both closing their eyes.

The two moons overlapped into an eclipse, shining a golden-silver glow upon them and their surroundings for a blissful moment. The flower bore a silvery mist, releasing golden spores that smelled of sweetened rain with a hint of vanilla. Just as their lips brushed against each other, a sudden shriek came from afar, breaking the two apart. Flames rose atop the village trees.

"We have to go! NOW!" Finn said, quickly pulling Eva up. Screams and roaring flames echoed through the trees.

"What's happening?"

"The festival is over. Peace and tranquility have vanished."

"But what about Rina, Dator, and Ijaïh? They're still back there!"

"Rina's with Dator. She'll protect him. Ijaïh can help himself! What matters now is that we get you to safety!"

"FINN!" Rina yelled. She carried Dator on her back. Ash covered them. They kept running towards the end of the forest, away from the village.

"What happened?" Finn demanded.

"Valdof! His guards came as soon as the festival ended!" she said.

"Shit! He must have traced us!" he said gritting his teeth.

"There's no way we can outrun them! They've already burnt half the forest!" Eva gasped.

"Krimm!" Rina yelled and within seconds, Krimm jumped from her satchel and enlarged enough to hold the four of them. "Hold on!" she said. Krimm flew up high past the trees, wind gushing past them.

Eva clenched to Finn in fear of Krimm's fast speed.

"Wait, we can't leave Ijaïh!" Dator screamed.

“We’ll have to hurry! Krimm can’t keep this size for too long!” Rina said.

“Rina, can you seek him out?” Finn growled.

“I can try," Rina focused then pointed down to the west near the village. “There! He’s near the pasture! Head that way, Krimm!”

Krimm headed down toward the woods. A glimmer of long blond hair rushed between the trees followed by a large grizzly bear. “I see him! Ijaïh grab hold!” Eva yelled, throwing down a rope. The bear roared beneath him and snatched the rope. Rina grabbed her from behind, keeping her balance.

“What the hell has he gotten himself into?” Rina said.

“Hurry Ijaïh!” Dator screamed. He joined the two and helped pull him upward. The bear shredded the ends of the rope and tugged it.

“LOOK, THERE THEY ARE!” a guard shouted.

“Hurry!” Rina grunted. Ijaïh finally pulled himself onto Krimm’s back. The guards shot arrows into the sky. Black smoke surrounded the bear revealing a hand. The young girl looked at her hands in relief.

“Maddie?” Eva exclaimed.

Maddie looked up at them. “Eva,” she said and reached for the rope.

“Watch out!” Finn yelled as arrows flew past their heads.

“Maddie, hold on! I’ll pull you up,” Eva cried. The rope burned upon her palms as she tugged. “Help me!” The guards surrounded Maddie, reading their arrows.

A loud cry rang through the air as one of the arrows found its way to Krimm’s tail.

“Krimm!” Rina shouted. She pulled herself to his neck gently stroking his head. “It’s okay! Get us to safety!”

Finn grabbed ahold of the rope. “I’m sorry,” he said and cut it. Eva screamed and reached to grab the descending ravels.

Finn pulled her back. “We can’t help her! We have to find safe ground!”

“No! How could you do this? We must turn back!”

“Valdof’s guards already have her! There’s nothing we can do! I promise we’ll get her back,” he said pulling her to his chest. He stroked her hair. “I’m so sorry, Eva.”

Krimm growled in pain through his quickened flight. He huffed, shaking beneath their weight, and toppled down to the ground, sending everyone rolling. Rina jumped up, and quickly went to his side as he shrunk down.

“Krimm, are you okay?” she asked, shushing him as he squirmed. “It’s okay now. Shh, we’re safe. Good boy," she cooed. She gently pulled out the arrow from his tail and used her medicine to mend it before placing a lily near him to let him sleep.

“You alright?” Finn said, lending Eva a hand.

“Don’t touch me,” she said smacking his hand.

“Eva, I’m-,” he said.

“I don’t want to hear it! Just leave me alone,” she said, pushing past him. She sat by Krimm and gently petted him.

“Doth thee think we lost them?” Dator asked.

“For now. We’ll have to keep moving. If they found us then, they will again. We can’t risk them capturing us," Finn said, pulling out his map.

“What the hell were you doing back there? You said your barriers were strong and impenetrable to Valdof’s men! If they catch us off guard again, I can’t promise we’ll make it out!” Rina said sternly.

“I got distracted, okay!”

“Distracted? DISTRACTED? You can’t get distracted during the mission! We’re lucky no one else got injured or killed! You were the one in charge of keeping up the barrier! We need to build a defense before his guards come back!”

"A defense won't mean anything if we can't keep our distance!"

"Screw that! Without that barrier, we're better off just handing ourselves to Valdof!"

"The barrier's back up, so calm down! They won't be able to find us! We need to make distance before they track us down."

"Yeah, for now! What happens if another *distraction* comes around Finn? Huh? What then? We need more protection! They already have Maddie which means we have a whole other issue at hand!"

"Finn's right. We need t' keep hence," Ijaïh said calmly.

"But if we art without defense and they doth come, we will be captured for sure," Dator said.

"Will you stop bickering for just a moment?" Eva yelled. "I don't know what's going on, but I need answers now! All this time you've been pushing off since day one, and I have a right to know!"

"Knowing about this won't help the situation! It may only make it w-" Finn started.

"She's right," Rina interjected, shifting uncomfortably.

"What?"

"She should know the truth, Finn… It's been too long. She deserves to know."

Finn sighed, brushing his hand through his hair. "King Valdof is on a hunt to kill you."

A blue wispy orb escaped from Wulfric's dying breath. It hovered over his body momentarily, absorbing the energy that remained. It wavered over the bodies of those slain. It quivered, as if it were weeping. A white light shined around it, and pools of blood began to soak into the damp ground. The grass and trees reached out and grasped the bodies, absorbing them. Not a trace of war remained.

The orb rushed through the forest, searching for life.

Chapter 17
The Prophecy

"K-Kill me?" Eva stuttered.

"Way to go, Finn. Very subtle," Rina said with snark.

"What do you expect me to do, Rina? She's got to find out one way or another!"

"Yeah well, you could have been a little more sensitive. It's not something you just say out loud you know…"

"I'm sure you would have done it better! Why don't you give it a shot?"

"Oh no. You already worked yourself right here. Better dig yourself out."

"Why would he want to kill me? I don't even know him! I didn't even do anything!" Eva quivered.

"I guess it would be best if I just started from the beginning," Finn sighed, shifting uncomfortably. "When I was young, my father trained me on how to use a sword in case I ever had to use it. It was just fun and games at first, and then I realized I really enjoyed it. I decided that when I grew up, I would be a guard for the royal palace.

~:~

12 years ago

A young boy with curled hair gritted his teeth, holding his withered-baton strong. Sweat dripped from his chin. A straw-stuffed dummy draped in hide lay tattered before him.

"Nice work, son!" the boy's father said, grinning. "You're getting better by the day!"

"Thanks, father! One day, I'm going to become a knight and then I'll be able to take care of you, mom, and the babe."

"I'm sure you will," he said. The clanking of armory sounded rhythmically against the ground as two knights walked through the town, making their rounds. "Hey, look over there."

The young boy lowered his sword and gazed wide-eyed at the knights.

"Supper!" a woman called out to her husband and child.

"Well, we better head in."

"Actually father, I just remembered I had to help Terrowin…uh…finish building his new fireplace. Yeah, I promised him I'd help with the mortar and stone."

"Supper can come first."

The boy ran off. "I'm sorry, father, but I can't. I have to go."

"Be quick then, or your mother will fret!"

"I will!" the boy said.

He snuck behind the guards until he reached the palace training grounds. Hiding behind one of the stacks of straw bales, he watched dozens of men practicing against each other or targets. Metal clashed rapidly, sparking on impact. Arrows whistled through the air, hitting the hay-built targets and the ground below.

A smile rose upon his face as he peaked over the bales. A strong hand clasped upon his shoulder, turning him around.

"Oi, kid! What are you doing here?" a knight said.

'I-I uh," he said clearing his voice as more knights surrounded him. "I want to be a palace guard!"

The guards laughed heartily.

"I'll prove it! I'll challenge any of you! One day, I'm going to be the head guard and lead Aloncia with pride!"

A hushed tone lay across the grounds. A tall man with a blue cape wrapped around his breastplate walked through the crowd to the boy. It was the head guard. The boy paled, and stood firm.

"So, you're the one who has disrupted my troops."

The boy gulped.

"You wish to be a guard?" he asked. He held out his hand to one of his subjects, who handed him a blade. "Then prove yourself."

The boy grasped the sword shakily. His arms hung low and slowly turned towards the wooden post that stood from the ground. The head guard blocked his blade with his own.

"Not the pell. You will fight me."

"Sir Everard, thou canst fight him! He is kin!" one of his subjects said.

"It is the boy's choice! He can choose to fight for his right or run away like a coward. Age is hardly an excuse."

The boy's grip grew strong, courageous anger speeding through his veins. With Sir Everard distracted, the boy took the chance to swing at him. His blade was blocked with little room to escape.

"Striking against a distracted person is a dirty trick," Sir Everard sneered.

"Then don't get distracted," the boy spat.

Their blades clashed over and over, pressure building upon the two's desires. Sweat poured down the boy's face and the head guard's blade pressured against his. Down to one knee, the boy shook, fearing the loss of his one dream. With one opening available, the boy swung his leg, hoping to trip Sir Everard to the ground. Sir Everard stumbled lightly and disarmed the boy. The boy fell back, silently searching for an answer as Sir Everard regained his posture and placed his sword in its sheath.

"What's your name, boy?"

"F-Finn Barrett, Sir!"

"Run home, Barrett."

Finn's jaw dropped and his heart hung low.

"You will need your rest for tomorrow's training. I expect you here by sunrise."

He pushed away a bittersweet tear and smiled. "Yes, Sir!"

~:~

3 Years Ago

Blood dripped down his lengthy-sharp fingers, pitter-pattering along the cobbled floor. Finn and the other guards surrounded him, fearfully appalled at the sight of the fallen King Philos, whose body lay withered and draped in red. The man laughed, licking the blood from his fingers.

"See, here, your fallen ruler! Weak creature he be, but fear no more, for I shall take his place, and you, my sentries, shall bow before me," he said with a slithery voice.

"Hell wilt hath risen before we bow to you!" one of the guards yelled.

"Stand down Zurk," Sir Everard said, blocking him with his blade, keeping note of the sinister shadowy man.

"He hath slain our King!"

"STAND DOWN!"

"You'll do well to listen to your leader. Unless you'd like it best to follow your precious King's path," the man said, running his fingers down the King's recently torn off head.

"YOU MONSTER!"

"ZURK NO!"

The guard pushed passed Sir Everard and swung at the man. Zurk froze and his body twisted unnaturally until an echoing snap made him limp, and he collapsed to the ground. The man chuckled.

"Now you shall see what true power is. Bow before your new King. Valdof, King of all Aloncia. My name shall strike fear amongst those who consider betraying me. Make your decision: follow my lead or end up like the fallen before you."

Sir Everard's face wrinkled in anger. Every part of his being told him to fight, but he knew his power was not strong enough to uphold this power. His men readied themselves for battle, some holding firm, while few vomited upon sight. He grimaced, graciously pointed his sword to the ground, and knelt before Valdof. The guards, wide-eyed, nervously followed.

~:~

9 Months ago

Villages were segregated upon their powers. King Valdof grimaced upon the idea of mixture; a disgusting manner he found confusing. Of course, to keep the people amused, he would allow for travel amongst villages with good reason. Anyone who tried to get out, was to be killed on sight. Lessons must be learned the hard way.

Guarding the Zerath border, Finn came across a stowaway. The woman cowered under her blue woven shawl, pleading for mercy. His hand shook, knowing what he must do. King Valdof approached him urging him to do his bidding. Noticing the fear, Valdof seized the moment and sliced the woman's head off. Blood splattered upon Finn's face as tears began to fill his eyes. He dropped to the ground knowing he had failed to save her. Denounced to the castle guard post, Finn began devising a plan to end this terrifying reign.

Valdof sounded the guards to his throne. His impatience grew strong. As they entered, an unnerving ominous film filled the air. It felt thick and suffocating. A new order had been placed: every girl, from every village that is coming of the age of eighteen, shall be brought to the castle. The guards grew tense, but abided their King regretfully.

Thousands of girls entered the castle, never to leave again. Each day, Valdof became more and more anxious, requesting double the work. The castle guards were sent out to aid the others, pulling in more girls to the impending doom.

Finished with his daily gathering, Finn made his rounds upon the castle grounds. A high pitch screaming rang through the air as he passed the dungeon room. At the bottom of the stairs, he found three girls beaten and drenched in blood. One of which had been from a group of girls he and his fellow guards brought in that morning.

"P-Please! Help us! Don't leave us down here!" one begged.

The sound of a door creaking startled him, and Finn darted behind the walls. One of Valdof's henchmen had come. He unlocked their cell door and dragged each of them by their chained wrists! Finn followed them to the throne room. Valdof looked at the girls and dismissed the guard. Finn hid behind one of the columns as Valdof began to torture them. Not a finger came near them, yet the agonizing screams echoed throughout the room.

"PLEASE! STOP IT! I'LL DO ANYTHING!" they screamed.

Valdof approached each girl, whispering in their ears. They wept, but silently agreed. Suddenly, each of their souls had been ripped from their bodies, in one, single, slash. Their bodies fell into puddles of blood, their faces full of terror.

~:~

"Those girls…t-their blood was on my hands, as were all the girls I had brought in," he continued, his hands shaking. With a staggered breath, he clenched his fists. "I-I should have done something, I…but I didn't. I just ran, making sure I would never be caught because there was no hope for them anymore. Valdof…that Monster…h-he destroyed each of them. He wasn't even satisfied. It was like they were his toys…so I ran. I bumped into Sir Everard. He noticed I was in a panic and asked what happened, but I didn't have the nerve to tell him for fear he, too, would end up like our leader. He punished me, forcing me to clean all the armor for the next two weeks. I couldn't get their screams out of my head… W-what would their families think if they found out. I-I had to do something! I couldn't just sit and let Valdof do anything he wanted!

"One day, after I finished the last of the armor, I headed to my dormitory. I heard whispers. I went up to the tower door. It had a tiny crack just big enough for me to look through. It was Valdof and his henchman. They were in a middle of a conversation."

~:~

4 Months Ago

"The prophecy… What could it mean?' Valdof spat. "It's been months and none of these girls have it!"

"Did you try looking elsewhere sire?" a high squeaky voice questioned.

"Elsewhere? We have practically searched the whole kingdom! Every Girl from Every Village has been dragged into my castle! And not ONE of THEM matches what that little WRETCHED GIRL down in the dungeons mentioned! That doltish seer! I bet she's been lying to me from the start!"

"Oh no, sire! I can tell she is telling the truth. However, she did say it would be only this year to which the girl would become a woman. 'Turn of eighteen,' and it's only been -"

"Shut up you imbecile! We only have 4 lunar cycles left before the end of the year! There must be something…"

"Hmm…what if she isn't in the kingdom?"

"What?"

“You know…the seer girl never said anything about her ‘being’ here you know.”

“You may be onto something. She must be somewhere. If not in the kingdom, then where?” he said slamming his fists upon a table. He paused for a second, then turned around slowly. “Do you…could it be possible…that she may be from the Human Realm?”

The henchman flinched at the mention of the name. “I-It is quite the possibility, sire.”

“A human?” Finn whispered.

“You n-never know sire. She may be there, and with that much power, who knows? She probably would be easy to find.”

“Then we start our search.” Valdof said calmly. He crossed the room to a basin. Greenish black light shined from it. He gazed into it intently. “It shows that there is something. Hell! There must be thousands of them over there!”

“Why not try and see about singling them out a bit? Maybe one of them has a *special* touch perhaps?”

“What do you think I am trying to do?” he glared. “There are some of the magic folk there as well. No matter. I’ll kill every last one of them if I have to!” he said, turning around to head out another exit leading further into the castle. “Come, we must plan our stay in the Human Realm.”

“Yes, sire," the henchman nodded, following him.

“The Human Realm! He’s going to kill the humans!” Finn said startled. “Why?”

~:~

“Nervous that they would come and find me, I decided to do something! I couldn’t let Valdof go to the Human realm! Even though I had no intention on contacting anyone, I couldn’t let innocent people, who knew nothing of our world, be killed because of his dastardly plans. I-I don't know why he's looking for you, but he started searching."

~:~

"Sir. You're not supposed to be here," Verona whispered.

"What did you tell Valdof? WHAT DID YOU TELL HIM?" Finn screamed, clenching his fist around the cell bars.

"I only told him of the prophecy…but why should you matter? It does not concern you."

"He's planning to kill hundreds to thousands of women over in the Human Realm!"

"But why should *you* care?"

"I-I don't know." he said.

The seer girl crawled herself over towards the gate. She grasped his hands, staring intently at him. "A girl… Find a girl of eighteen. Born at the beginning of summer. She will bring greatness to the kingdom… Things will be at one, and if they shall fail…dastardly, Evil beings will roam. Your. Kingdom. Will. Fall," she said in a daze, digging her fingers into his hands before thrusting them away. "Now Go! Save her before things change!"

He trembled from her foretelling and ran for the dungeon stairway.

~:~

"I ran over to Ijaïh's village, knowing that he may know what to do. Ijaïh had been my friend for many years and was someone I could trust. We both knew it would be a dangerous task but were willing to try for the safety of our kingdom. Soon after, I met Rina. We tried so desperately to save as many as we could, but-" Finn said shaking.

Rina placed a hand on his shoulder, sending her energy to calm him down. “Stop. Don’t speak any more of it. It’s okay.”

Finn’s body relaxed and he hung his head low.

“Finn, I-” Eva stepped forward, but Rina just raised her hand and shook her head.

Finn sighed, brushing away Rina’s hand and walked towards the woods. “I’m going to get some firewood. We will camp here for tonight.”

Eva’s stomach turned with the thought of what could become of her and the others.

“Eva? Are you alright?” Rina said.

“Huh?” Eva said, startled. “Yeah-yeah, I’m fine! I’m…uh…I’m just going to…I think I just need some time alone…” she mumbled. She walked to a nearby pond, knowing she should not go far from the group. Picking up a small twig from the ground, she poked it at the water to watch the ripples form.

Was it all a lie? All this time…

“It wasn’t a lie," Rina said a bit perturbed. “You really think that low of us?”

“What am I supposed to think, Rina? If I wasn’t *special* as you all seem to think I am, you would have never even tried to be my friend, and neither would the others! I’m just some pawn to be played with, so as to solve your problems!” she scoffed, feeling uneasy.

“I know you don’t think that," Rina countered. “Admit it. You’re scared.”

“I’m not scared!”

“Liar. Don’t keep these things in. It only hurts you in the end. You have friends who care about you, who want to be there for you, and we can’t do that if you won’t open up to us. I want to help you, Eva. You can trust me.”

"You want me to be honest? Fine. I'm terrified! I'm terrified that this mission will end terribly! I'm terrified that I'll never see my parents or Maddie again! But most of all, I'm scared that all this is just a mission and that this friendship we've built is nothing but a lie!" she said pursing her lips. *And that moment with Finn...*

"WOAH WAIT! WHAT HAPPENED WITH YOU AND FINN?"

"STOP READING MY THOUGHTS!" Eva yelled.

"Look...It may have started out as just a mission, but it's so much more than that now! You're our friend, Eva, and friends stick together."

"So even after this is over, you would still be there for me?"

"Of course," Rina said, playfully nudging her side to try to get a smile. A moment of silence passed. Eva poked a small, wilted flower, understanding its pain as if it were her own. "Feeling better now?"

Eva shrugged. "There's so much going on. I-I don't know if I can handle this mission, Rina. What if-"

"Hey, don't worry about it. That's Finn and mine's job to do. You're safe with us."

"Why did you even decide to help out in this situation?"

"After Valdof burned down my village, I wanted revenge, just like Ijaïh and Finn, so I helped them open a portal to your world," she said.

"Wait. I thought you only had small amounts of power to change the mind," Eva interjected.

"That's true, but because I'm the daughter of the leader of my village, I can transport between the worlds. All leaders' families can, although, it is only used to make sure that the Human Realm and Aloncia never come in contact and that our secret never gets out."

"I see, but why doesn't Ijaïh help out then?"

"His tribe doesn't like the idea of using such power in vain. They consider it an act of treason against the Elven culture. Not only that, but it's extremely hard to perform. Once anyone passes through the portal, it wipes me of my energy. That's why I always slept in class," she smiled, trying to lighten the situation. "We searched many times, and Valdof had killed many girls…which is why you've seen so many missing people reports and talk about serial killers on the news lately. Valdof searched for a long time. He had difficulty finding anyone, so he forced Finn and the other guards to continue their gatherings in Aloncia. We tried protecting them and they never… Let's just say it always failed," she said, glancing back at Ijaïh. "One day, Valdof heard some rumors about the Elnaïrian Village trying to hide the girls…and he burnt the place down. Ijaïh stopped helping us after that, but Finn and I were determined to keep going on. We knew we had to do something. We met with Verona, the seer girl again, and she gave us a location with your description. We headed to your world and soon we found you."

"So that's why you wanted to be my friend and stood by me all this time."

"Yeah…" Rina smirked with guilt. "But I still love being your friend, Eva. I really do!"

"Thanks, Rina," Eva smiled softly. "But 'greatness'? How can I help a place I never knew of before? I mean, I'm not exactly the 'hero' type."

"We'll figure it out together. One step at a time."

"Why me? Why am I so different that he wants to kill me? What have I done?"

"You haven't done anything! I don't know what Valdof wants you for, but if he finds you, he will kill you! He'll take your soul, and if that happens, he'll be unstoppable."

“Then we’ll just have to make sure that doesn’t happen, right? We’ll get to the safe grounds and save Aloncia before Valdof has a chance to get to us," Eva smiled brightly.

“Hell yeah! Now there’s the Eva I know!” she grinned. “And we’re going to be the best protectors you’ll ever have!”

Eva was determined to make things right. As the two headed back to the rest of the group, the wilted flower gently rose, replenishing with life as bits of blue energy twirled around it. With a calm atmosphere, the group slept well that night, ready to face a new day.

Chapter 18

The Dribbling Kelpie

"You ready, Eva?" Rina asked, tossing her blade between her hands.

"Ready as I'll ever be," she replied.

In an instant, the two went at each other, trying to steal a moment to catch the other off guard and win the battle. It had been three hours of training and Eva's defense grew stronger. Out of thirty-one fights, she won twelve. Finn sat a few feet away, keeping an eye on the two, making sure the play stayed fair.

Rina swung her blade forward, just missing Eva's cheek as she leaned back. Eva tried for her gut to no avail. She knew that if she didn't act fast, she would fail again and be forced to battle once more. Her limbs burned like fire upon a raw cut, but she knew she must continue. If she won another time, Rina promised to stop for a break. As Rina thrust her blade down, Eva ducked, quickly darting behind her opponent. She elbowed the center of her back, causing a spasm. In a split second, Rina grabbed Eva's forearm and flipped her to the ground. As she pinned her down, Eva wrapped her legs around hers and pushed herself forward, flipping her in return. With a swift grasp of her dagger, she placed its edge to Rina's neck.

"I win," she panted.

"Good job," Rina said with a smile.

Eva released her friend and let herself fall to the ground in exhaustion. "You're getting better," she said stretching her arms. Rina threw her knife into the ground and sat next to her. "Of course, I could easily tell what moves you were going to make. You never did have a poker face, did you?"

"Showoff," Eva said. "I won fair and square. I deserve my break."

"And a break you shall have. I am a woman of my word, you know."

"Yeah, yeah," she said waving her hand. Finn stared off into the forest. "Hey, Finn, what are you looking at?"

Finn's expression stayed emotionless. Eva tilted her head. She snuck up close to him and gently waved her hand in front of his face. "*Hello*! Earth to Finn," he blinked, slightly alarmed. Eva giggled.

"What's so funny?"

"Just you, silly," she said scooting closer to him and crossing her legs. "You were so dazed; I wondered if you were still on this planet."

"And you call me 'silly'? I'm not the one with dirt on my face," he smirked poking her nose. Eva crossed her eyes, blushing as she rubbed it off.

With a nod of approval, Eva leaned forward. "*So,* what were you thinking about?"

"That's for me to know and you to find out," he teased.

Eva stuck out her tongue, which Finn mimicked.

"Are we having fun?" Rina said, towering over them while tapping her foot. The two shifted away. "Then how about we get back to our training?"

"Actually Rina, I was thinking we'd head back. The safe zone is only about a day's worth away. Might as well get started, don't you think?" Finn said.

"Fine," Rina scoffed. She grabbed her cape and walked off towards the campsite. Eva and Finn followed slowly behind.

"Is it about the festival?" Eva asked, gently nudging him.

"Maybe," he said.

~:~

The journey lasted until nightfall, resulting in each to be thoroughly drained and with sore feet. The moons provided a cold glow along a dirt path that led towards a nearby village. The group came upon an old, rotted tree. Upon the remains hung posts with barely legible symbols on them, pointing in various directions.

East: Forest of Azmir 37.8 mitors

Northeast: Echo Tides 701.4 pillus

South: Vîgarie 344.5 hars

Southeast: Tiltin Hollow 10.2 slyops

Southwest: Mildora 613 ruppets

North: Weeping Peaks 178.6 frugles

"Okay, so if I have this right, Tiltin Hallow should be this way," Finn said pointing in the direction of the post. "It seems fairly close, about two miles. I'm sure we could find an inn or something to spend the night at. If we leave around midday tomorrow, we should be able to arrive in Vîgarie tomorrow at dusk."

"Great! I can't wait to kick back and relax for the night," Rina said.

"Dost thee mean we will be resting in sleep chambers?" Dator asked excitedly.

"That's right!" Finn smiled.

"'Tis wonderful! I doth not recall the last time I slept anywhere but outdoors."

"Thee mean t' tell me, brother, thou hast been sleeping under the stars for three years?" Ijaïh interjected.

"Aye, but not that you would care. 'Tis not lacking valor being under the stars. Makes thee wonder and question the most curious o' thoughts."

"Disgraceful," Ijaïh mumbled to himself.

"Oh, hush up! Leave Dator alone, unless you wish for everyone to know what happened last night," Eva said with a glower.

Ijaïh gritted his teeth.

"Boy someone sure is cranky when she's tired," Rina said.

"What happened last night?" Dator asked.

"Nothing you should worry about. I just want a comfy bed to sleep in!" she said.

Approaching Tiltin Hollow, they found themselves upon a tattered gate, creaking with the gale. The streets were cobbled, with weeds growing between the cracks. Torches hung at each building, lighting the small village. The streets laid bare except for the one or two rats that ran behind the rotting barrels that were scattered across the buildings. The structures held a Germanic style of cobbled brick riding halfway up to reveal creme-painted stones lined with wooden beams. Fog danced around the floor, seeking refuge; not a sound could be heard.

"It seems awfully quiet…" Eva said softly. The chilling air sent shivers down her spine.

"I'm sure everyone's just inside. I think there should be a place over there we can stay," Finn said urging them to move forward.

About halfway through the village came a soft humming sound with stifled mumbles. Lights escaped the windows to the rather large building. A wooden sign dangled from its metal post. A blackened horse with a dripping mane of a tar-like substance was painted upon it with various symbols reading The Dribbling Kelpie Tavern and Inn. Bits of seaweed dangled from the bottom.

"This is it," Finn smiled.

Rina held Eva back. "Just so you know, this isn't exactly a *normal* tavern inn."

"Well of course not. I'm sure there will be some sort of magical play or something," she said, figuring it would be quite fascinating to see the differences.

"No, I mean…uh…well, how do I put this? The people here are a little *unusual*. Just don't stare at them, and whatever you do, don't panic. We won't need any more attention than we'll already be getting."

Confused by her statement, Eva nodded.

Opening the door let out a gush of warmth and a strong smell of mothballs and rum. Large metal chandeliers held hardened candles whose drippings dangled beneath the flames. Eva's eyes widened as she finally understood what Rina meant. Dozens of people, that of half-human nature were conversing with their companions, gambling at tables, or drinking at the bar. A woman with a snake's bottom, wrapped her tail across one of the bar stools that wobbled ever so slightly from her drunken state. A group of individuals sat around an octagon-shaped table, playing some sort of dice game. The satyr sat weeping as a transparent green genie slammed his fists on the table, angered over their losses against the sly fox man who had a luscious orange tail with a white tip.

Across the tavern by the roaring fire stood a small quartet playing an upbeat tune. The man with mangy grey hair with matching dog legs and tail towered over the group, playing his lute. Sitting on a high stool next to him was a grey-skinned fairy. Her long black hair draped over her tattooed body and spiked wings. Her solid black eyes gazed upon Eva as she played her flute. Knelt beside her was a centaur. Her golden hair covering up her bare chest as she moved her fingers gracefully across the harp's strings. A man with brightly colored feathered wings for arms and a raised train with enticing eye-like structures sprawled across his head, danced along to the music. The tavern members hummed, whistled, or tapped their feet with the music.

Eva held close to Rina, avoiding eye contact with those who stared at them. Dator ran off to play a few rounds of dice games as Finn and Ijaïh talked to the tender.

"I am all booked for three-bed chambers for the night, but I do have two doubles to spare," the man clicked.

"That will have to do," Finn said.

The man pulled out a small box and rummaged for two keys. The metal keys were dull and resembled spiderwebs. They looked almost identical, but the tender assured that each were quite different as the webs were crafted in different stitch patterns.

"Ye come from afar, don't ye?"

"We're just passing through."

"I see. Ye best be careful in these parts. I judge ye not myself, but I can't say for the others around here. These are bad times, ye know."

"I understand."

"Ye are welcomed to socialize amongst the crowd and refresh yourselves with mine brews. Just stay out o' trouble."

"Yes sir. For now, I think we'd just like a few drinks. I'll take a dragon flame, Ijaïh what would you like?"

"I will not take part in this action tonight. I will be in the chamber," he said snatching the key from Finn's hand.

"I'll take a whirlwind on ice," Rina said.

"And for you, Miss?" the tender asked, referring to Eva.

"Um…do you by chance have any black-?" she requested timidly.

She'll take a water," he said, then cupped his hand over her ear. "Trust me, you don't want to be drinking tea from this area."

The tender nodded, slightly suspicious of the group. His eight arachnid legs tapped upon the floor as he mixed the drinks. He sent the drinks flying with bits of sticky silk. Eva gulped at the sight of the man's keratinized body. Her hand shook as she picked up the glass of water.

"Is something wrong, Miss?" the man said leaning forward.

"N-No! E-Everything's fine. Thank you," she said backing up a bit and accidentally bumping into the snake woman next to them.

"Watchhh whhhere you're going, girl," the woman hissed.

"Ah, sorry!"

"Seems that one may be some trouble. Best keep an eye on her, mate. That will be five harples," the tender directed towards Finn.

They headed away from the bar to a small table in the corner. "Calm down. You're going to make a scene."

"Sorry. Spiders make me nervous."

"It's fine," he sighed, handing her a small pouch. "I stored some lemon balm in hopes of using it for tomorrow morning before arriving in Vîgarie, but from the looks of it, you'd better have it now."

Eva mixed a few tea leaves in until it turned a golden green color. The minty scent calmed her.

"So, what's the plan?" Rina asked softly, sipping her purple drink.

"We head out tomorrow morning and when we arrive, we'll set up a barrier that Valdof won't be able to break."

"Do you think that's possible to keep up for so long? Don't get me wrong, I know your magic is pretty damn strong, but even you have limits Finn."

"It's a risk we're going to have to take. If Valdof finds us, it's over. All we can do is hide out until he gives in."

"How long will that be?" Eva asked.

"I'm not sure. I'm hoping for no more than a couple days. He's not a patient man."

Eva grimaced, knowing it may be even longer before she would get home, but nodded in agreement.

"It's not much, but it's doable. We'll need more than just a barrier though," Rina said.

"We'll figure all that out tomorrow. For now, let's just relax, and have a good time. Want to teach Eva how to play Dragon Dice with me?"

"I'd love to Finn, but I have some business to attend to. If you need me, I'll be in Eva and mine's room. And Finn, don't stress yourself out tonight," she said, taking the key from the table.

"I wonder what that was about," Eva said.

"It's probably nothing. Here, I'll teach you how to play," Finn opened the small box from the table, taking out a blue and a green seven-sided di. "Each side has a different symbol representing a different species. The spiraled horns represent a drawrble, the eight-pointed star is a spider, the feather portrays a phoenix, the flame depicts the hellhound, the circle is a bumblesnatch, the water droplet is a kelpie, and the eye represents the dragon. Each player rolls one of the di and whoever has the upper hand takes away the number of points the opponent's roll has and keeps the rest. Kelpie, 10 points, beats hellhound, 7 points, which destroys the phoenix, 5 points, who burns the drawrble, 3 points, which eats the spider, 1 point, who ties up the bumblesnatch, 0 points. In other words, if I were to roll a spider and you rolled a phoenix, you would gain 4 points. If the players roll the same symbol, no one gets points, and the next round begins. The first player to reach 40 points wins the game."

"What about the dragon?"

"Oh, that's the best part! If you role a dragon eye, you get double the points of the opposing player's role! You think you got it all?"

"I think so. Seriously though, what's a bumblesnatch?"

"You'll see soon enough," Finn laughed.

~:~

"Yes! Dragon Eyes! I win again!" Eva laughed.

Finn sat there looking blankly at the dice that cost him another game. "How? Twenty-five games and you won twenty! You've never even played before!"

"Oh, don't take it so hard. I guess luck is on my side."

"Or the dice are rigged," he mumbled.

"Rigged dice? Ha! You're just a sore loser, Finn Barrett!" she said proudly. "Why, if we were to put a wager on it, you'd be broke!"

"Is that so?" he countered. He gulped his drink and slammed down his satchel of coins. "Alright then, I bet you twenty harples, three jukes, and thirty-four siltors that you can't win again."

"Finn, I don't want to take your money."

He smirked, taking the coins back. "Then how about the kerplople?"

"You're on."

Suddenly, a loud thunk resonated as a chair flew across the room, followed by the beginnings of a scuffle.

"YOU WRETCHED CHILD!" a man yelled.

Eva and Finn stood up, practically toppling the table over. Their dice fell to the floor, spinning to an unnerving stop. Their faces paled as their fears were confirmed. On the other side of the room, three men were crowding Dator.

"These dice are loaded!" the fox man growled, testing the dice.

"Fulham? Well, I nev'r! Why would-" Dator said in defense.

"LIES! THIEF!" a bullish man snorted.

"You stole our coins." a centipedal man hissed.

"Stole? Thou art nothing but a couple amateurs."

The bull hoisted Dator up by his collar and slammed him to the table, holding his head down. The centipede wrapped his scaly tail around him. "Amateurs, we are not."

"But you won't forget messing with us," the fox scowled. He took the dice and slammed the sharp edges into Dator's hand. "NEVER MESS WITH A GAM-"

"Dator!" Eva yelled, grabbing him, and holding him behind her.

"What have we here?" the fox said, trailing his tail along her side. "What lovely youth."

Eva threw Dator's coin pouch on the table. "Take your money! Come on, Dator. We're leaving."

"Oh, I don't think so. He stole much more than coins can be worth. Dignity is a hard trait to regain, but you could do as payment."

"In your dreams," she said pushing his tail away.

The fox man grew angry and raised a hand.

"HEY!" Finn shouted, pulling the fox back. "Leave her alone!"

"And who are you? Her little *beau*?"

Finn's eyes glowed and wind passed through his hair as he lit a flame in his hand. "Leave now, before anyone gets hurt," he said sinisterly.

The three men flinched at the sight of the green flame and darted away from the table.

"Thank you, Finn."

"What were you thinking? Did you seriously think you could take them on?" he yelled.

"I did what I had to! I'm not going to stand and watch my friends get hurt!"

"But you're willing to get yourself hurt instead?"

"Don't you raise your voice to me, Finn! If you think I'm just going to stand down and leave a friend to get hurt while I stay safe, you've got another thing coming!"

"You shouldn't put yourself in these kinds of situations! You could have been seriously injured!"

"Oh, but it's okay for you to do so! How hypocritical!"

Finn was at a loss for words.

"YOU!" a man screamed from across the room. "You're that knight from the King's palace! I recognize you from that time you came to my village two lunar cycles ago!"

"I don't know what you're talking about," Finn retorted, hiding his face.

"You are! You took my daughter! WHERE DID YOU TAKE HER? WHAT HAVE YOU DONE WITH HER?"

"Sir you must have me confused with someone else."

"NO, I SWEAR IT WAS YOU! YOU BASTARD! YOU TORE MY FAMILY APART! YOU TOOK MY DAUGHTER AND NOW YOU'RE COMING FOR HER AREN'T YOU?"

"GET HIM OUT OF HERE!" the tender screamed. Two of his employees dragged the deranged man to the tavern door.

"THIS ISN'T OVER! I'LL FIND YOU! YOU'LL PAY FOR THIS!"

Finn clenched his fist, shaking with anger.

"Finn, calm down. It's not worth it," Eva said placing a hand on his chest. He smacked it away in fury.

"It would be best if you let me be for the time being. You'll find Rina on the second floor in room fifteen. Take Dator to Ijaïh in room nine. He'll know what to do."

"Finn, I-"

"Just go."

Eva nodded and brought a whimpering Dator close as she took him up the stairs.

Finn sighed and signaled the tender for a hard drink.

A pale woman appeared behind him. Her eyes were covered in faded purple ribbons. "It won't change anything. You can't change what has happened or what's to come," she said softly. She wore a tattered dress stained in blood. Her cloak draped over her head, which showed ragged black locks.

"Verona," Finn gasped.

~:~

Eva rested Dator on the bed and examined his hand. Blood coagulated along the edge. A note lay on the bedside table with a vial, washbasin, and cloth.

Use one drop on the wound and nothing more. - Rina

She gently compressed the wound with the dampened cloth.

"You seem angered at Finn," Dator sniffed.

Eva sighed. "I'm not angry with Finn."

"But-"

"Never you mind about that. What were you thinking gambling with those men?" she said, changing the subject. Removing the cloth, Eva carefully poured one drop of the vial's contents upon the wound.

"I was on a great path."

"Until you got those dice slammed into your hand."

"You should not have interfered."

"And watch them cause more damage to you?"

"'Tis not mine first fight, and t'will not be mine last."

"Where did you even learn such a foul game?"

"One has t' learn a way to earn wage t' keep a crisp slate from thievery."

"There are other ways, safer ways, of collecting money."

"None art as quick and easily earned."

"And none put you in quite as much danger. If Finn and I hadn't been there to help-"

"But all those coins!"

"I'm not sorry you lost them. Gambling is a dirty thing."

"Were thou not t' gamble for Finn's kerplople?"

Eva blushed. "Competition had gotten the better of me. Besides, I would have given it back in the end."

"Then thou art as *hypocritical* as Finn, would you not be?"

"T-That's not the point. There! All finished," she said knotting the bandage. She kissed Dator's forehead and ruffled his hair. "Now, off to bed with you. I'll see you in the morning."

Ijaïh stood outside waiting for her as she exited, ruffling his hair with a towel. He wore a lightly damped linen shirt that covered his braies. "What art thou doing in mine room," he said.

"I was just helping Dator. He got himself hurt. I'm sorry, Ijaïh. It won't happen again," she said, pushing past him.

"Halt," he said. Eva stiffened, waiting for him to scream at her. "Perhaps mine words were too brash. Thou aren't as wretched as one might assume."

"Ijaïh, are you trying to apologize?"

"Doth not think much of it," he puffed, everting his eyes. "However, I thank thee for thine quick action to help me, and in aiding that imp. He means more to me than thou realize."

"Ijaïh…"

"Doth not flatter thyself much, Miss Dawkins. 'Tis merely appropriate to offer gratitude in this instance. 'Tis not an offer of friendship."

"No, of course not," Eva smiled. Ijaïh turned the knob to his room. "And Ijaïh? For what it's worth, I'm sorry for the hurtful things I said before. I think you will be a great vaward someday."

Ijaïh nodded and closed the door behind him.

~:~

Eva entered her and Rina's room, finding it completely dark. "Rina? Why are all the lights off?" she said, trying to find a light switch before realizing how useless that would be. She yelped as the door shut behind her. "Rina, this isn't funny! At least answer me!"

Something landed upon her shoulder. She felt tiny feet crawl up her back. Two large eyes glistened upon the creature that lay upon her shoulder. She quickly lit the candle from the nightstand to reveal a room filled with hundreds of spiders. A hand cupped her face and eyes as she let out a squeal.

"Shh! Don't make a sound," Rina whispered between Eva's muffled cries. She pulled her into the hallway then released her.

"Rina! What in the world are you doing in there? Spiders! Get them off," Eva squeaked, rashly brushing them off.

"Eva, it's okay. They're my friends," she said carefully placing the spiders in her pouch. She opened the door. "Okay, party's over. You'll know where to find me.'"

"What?" she said confused.

Rina lit a few candles in the now spider-free room. She plopped on the bed. "Don't worry. It's safe. I promise."

Eva shakily stepped into the room. "Don't do that again!"

"Oh, come on, Eva. I was taking care of business."

"What business could you possibly have with spiders?"

"I've been sending them to Valdof's castle to mess with him. I meet up with them every now and then, but I promise, they're completely harmless."

"Are you sure?"

"Yes, now can you please sit down and relax?"

Eva sat down upon the silk-lined bed. Comfort filled her as she rested her head on the pillow. "I never thought I'd be so grateful to have a bed."

"They sure do make them fine here. I guess the boys are in the other room?"

"All, but Finn. He seems to be a little tense."

"What do you mean?" Rina asked, sitting up.

"Well, after Dator got in trouble with some of the locals, some guy started yelling at him about him taking his daughter."

"And you left him!"

"He wouldn't let me stay! We had gotten in a fight over stupid things and he told me to go upstairs to find you after I helped Dator, so I didn't know what else to do."

"Shit," Rina whispered under her breath. "We better get him. This is exactly what I was afraid of. He shouldn't be left alone with people who recognize him."

They rushed downstairs to find Finn at the bar. "Another."

"No, mate. I think ye have had enough."

Eva gently laid a hand on his arm. "Finn? It's me. Are you alright?"

Finn held a small white handkerchief in his shaking hand. "Mary…I'm so sorry," he whispered in a voice almost impossible to hear.

"Oh, I shouldn't have left you alone."

"No use, Miss. He's been sitting here blubbering over that thing for quite some time. Best he gets sleep if anything."

"You're right," Eva said. "Rina, give me a hand,"

The two of them headed for the stairs. The young woman with ribbon-covered eyes placed a hand on Eva's shoulder.

"Care for him. Only you can help. Only you can save him and the rest of us. Your destiny awaits," she said softly.

"Verona?" Rina asked startled, but before hearing an answer, she disappeared.

They brought him to the men's chamber, laying upon the empty bed. Eva sat next to him, brushing his hair back with her fingers.

"Mary…" he whispered again, tears escaping from his eyes.

"Shh, it's okay. Everything is going to be alright."

"Forgive me."

"There's nothing to forgive. You've done nothing wrong," she said, gently stroking his head until he fell asleep. Rina stood at the doorway and signaled they should go. They went back to their own room and sat on their beds, staring at the floor. "I feel so awful. If I just stayed with him, this could have been avoided."

"Don't put yourself down. It's his own fault for letting himself get like that."

"He's really upset, Rina. He just kept whispering 'Mary' over and over. Do you have any idea what that could mean?"

"No, Finn never really talked about his personal life with me. I'm starting to get worried. I've never seen him like this before. Whatever that man said must've really set him off."

"Do you think Mary could be related to the kidnappings? Maybe the man's daughter?"

"It's possible. The real question is why Verona is here. The last time I saw her, she was still in Valdof's dungeon."

"She's the one who foretold the prophecy, right?"

"Yeah, but her disappearance confuses me," she said. "There's nothing we can do but wait until tomorrow when he's sober. Perhaps she'll come back sometime tomorrow. Might as well sleep while we still have a chance."

"Yeah. I'm sure he'll be better by then."

Rina blew out the candle lights and covered herself and Krimm with a blanket. Smoke danced upon the exhausted candles. Eva wondered about Verona's words, but most of all Finn. She twiddled the blue orchid, hoping all would he well by morning.

Oh Finn...if only there was some way I could help you. Take this fear and pain from you. I want to see you smile because you want to, not because you don't want others to see you suffering. I want to be there for you just as you are there for me. So please, just let me in.

Verona sat upon the bloodied cobblestone, muttering nonsense.

"Snap out of it! It's been too long! Valdof is sure to come any minute," Maddie whispered.

She gasped and fell to the ground.

"Verona! Are you okay? We're you able to contact them?"

She nodded between pants.

"Where are they?"

"Where are they, indeed," Valdof said. "My, my, seems you two have been troublesome. Contacting our friend are we, little sprite?"

Maddie scurried to the wall.

"Perhaps it is time you tell me more about your friend."

Chapter 19
A Completed Mission

That morning, bright light glistened through the cracks of the wooden shutter that covered the barred windows. Eva opened one of them to let in the morning sun, revealing the tiny dust particles that filled the room. She glanced back at Rina, who was curled up against Krimm. Drool escaped from his lower lip, soaking into the sheets beneath them. She sighed smiling at the village below, watching the magic folk roam. Every now and then she would see one of them begin to glow before turning into their natural, animal-like state and scurry off into the woods while the rest walked about. Unexpectedly, she noticed a familiar face out of the corner of her eye. Finn had just walked out of the tavern and started pacing for a second before walking into the woods. Eva jumped up and headed to the door. Krimm lifted his head, staring intently at her.

"Oh, it's okay Krimm. I'm just going to meet Finn outside," she whispered.

Krimm responded with a look of suspicion.

"I promise I won't be long. If Rina wakes up while I'm gone, tell her where I went."

Eva escaped the room and came to the edge of the village where she last saw Finn. She glanced around trying to see if she could spot him. She kept her dagger close and walked slowly amongst the trees, but still saw no sign of him. She stopped for a moment, unsure as to where to go.

"What are you doing here?" a voice gruffly said as a hand landed on her shoulder.

Eva whipped around, dagger in hand ready to strike.

"Woah! Calm down, it's just me!" Finn said pulling his hands away.

"Jeez! What are you doing sneaking up on me like that? I could've killed you!"

"Not like that you couldn't," he laughed. Eva smirked, putting her dagger back in its sheath. "What are you doing out here anyways?"

"I came to find you. I figured you might need someone nearby. I wanted to apologize for last night."

"Apologize? For what? I should be the one apologizing. I shouldn't have yelled at you. I'm usually not like that. Normally I stop after three drinks. I must have been quite troublesome for you and the others."

"You were no trouble at all! If anything, you made us worry. I'm sorry! You wouldn't have yelled at me if I wasn't being so foolish. You were just trying to protect me, and I shouldn't have left you after that man yelled at you. Forgive me?" Eva said.

"Only if you will me."

"Of course!"

The two stared at each other for a moment then burst out into laughter. Finn sighed, sitting down on a large rock. "We really are something aren't we? It's odd, you know. After all this, we still find ways to keep everyone together."

"Someone has to. We make a great team," she said sitting on the ground beside him.

"Yes, that we do."

"Hey, Finn?"

"Hm?"

"Last night, you kept mentioning the name Mary. Who is she?"

Finn became tense and looked away. "It's no one."

"Does it have to deal with that man from last night? Was she his daughter?"

"It doesn't concern you!"

"She's someone important to you, isn't she?"

"Why do you care? Why do you keep trying to bring up things that don't involve you? Why do you want to know so bad?" he yelled, his face becoming red.

Eva paused, bashfully. "It's obvious, isn't it?"

Finn's temper ceased.

"I like you, Finn…I like you a lot. Ever since this mission started, and we got to know each other, learning from our mistakes and helping each other through battles, I felt like I could trust you. You make me laugh, you've always been there for me, and you've shown me this beautiful world I never thought I would ever see. You made me feel secure and accepted me for who I am, and when I'm around you, I feel safe. After that night at the festival, I thought-"

Finn gently held her hand. "I like you too, Eva," he smiled.

Eva's eyes widened softly, and she smiled back.

"Come. I want to show you something." He tightened his hand around hers and led her further within the forest. He helped her over the large tree that blocked their path and soon they came to a large patch of bushes.

"Where-"

"Shh," he said, pushing away some of the branches. "Look."

Eva gazed upon the grassy plain to see a magnificent creature. Standing almost nine feet tall was a stag. It had large wings delicately folded to its sides, and a long-feathered tail dragging upon the ground. Its hind legs were that of a bird, and its feathered fur filled with layers of lavender and yellow hues. Its matching, red-speckled chest made the creature even more empowering. Beside it stood another one, its appearance completely black except for its tawny lined wings.

"Wow," Eva whispered. "What are they?"

"Perytons. They're considered majestic animals here. They are mainly peaceful creatures, but if threatened, they can cause some serious damage," he said as a new peryton came to drink from the small river that passed through the area. Its wings were rather large, and pink embraced its body, fading into a greyish-white color at the collar. Its semipalmated feet made it easy for the creature to walk upon the moist ground. Eva and Finn watched in awe as the perytons walked about the spacious plain, nibbling on bits of grass and fruit from the bushes and trees. Their movements were elegant and mesmerizing, like that of a ballerina dancing upon the clouds.

A small round yellow bird with black stripes hopped around the perytons, giving little chirps every couple of seconds. When it noticed the large animals surrounding it, it grabbed a leaf and covered its face, as if hiding itself from them.

Eva stifled a laugh. "What is that thing?"

"That would be a bumblesnatch."

"That's a bumblesnatch!" she said awestruck.

"Yep. It's an idiotic bird that can barely do anything. It's too fat to even get itself off the ground and finds the most ridiculous of hiding places when it's in danger. If a leaf isn't nearby, it will dig its stinger into a flower and open its mouth to pretend to be the flower. No one knows how it's survived for so long. I guess that will always be a mystery."

"Rina," she growled.

Finn let out a small laugh. "Did anything strange happen last night? I mean besides my behavior." he said with a weakened posture.

"Well, after Rina and I came to get you, this girl appeared. Verona. Rina said she was the same seer girl the two of you have been talking about. It's strange. She just came out of nowhere and disappeared almost just as fast. Do you know why?"

"Danger is coming," Finn said.

"What?

"Verona must have used all her power to track us to give us warning. We spoke after you left. She said that Valdof is becoming agitated and warned us that we should keep a keen eye for when we head to Vîgarie. Her predictions aren't always correct, so I wouldn't worry too much. There are many possibilities for the future."

A soft rustle echoed around them.

"Someone's coming!" Eva whispered. Finn pushed her behind him, blade ready. From the bushes came a peryton. It walked right up to them to get a whiff of their scent. Its olive-green body had royal blue and white spots along its wings that continued to its short tail. The peryton had a blue and yellow crest between its antlers that trailed down its neck.

"Don't move a muscle," Finn gritted between his teeth. The creature glared at them, unamused by their presence. A sudden wail came from afar. The peryton stood straight, its crest raised high, and walked off to the others.

Eva pushed away the branches of the bush to watch them once more. "That was close!"

The perytons came together, nodding their heads and huffing, as if conversing with one another. They spread apart and lifted their wings, thrusting them down to push off the ground. The massive wind forced them back. In a moment's notice, the four creatures were gone.

"Wow," Eva said, still in shock. "That was amazing! Did you see how they took off! They were all like *WOOSH* and all those colors! They were all so beautiful! I've never seen anything like it in my whole life! What did you think Finn?" she continued excitedly. Her heart dropped at the sight of his sullen posture. "Finn?"

In an instant, he embraced her, gripping the fabric upon her back. His body shook ever so slightly as he pulled her in closer. "Promise me. Promise me that whatever happens, whatever trouble we get in, whatever Valdof or his guards do if he finds us, that you'll never give up! That you will stay strong and fight for what is right! And when this is all over, promise me that you will be okay!"

Eva stood there, frozen by the unexpected request. *He's shaking so much. Verona's prediction must be a high possibility. He's been holding this in for too long.* She wrapped her arms gently around him.

"I promise."

~:~

Heading back, Eva and Finn came upon Verona near the tavern door. She seemed calm and composed. "So, you finally arrived," she said softly.

"Verona," Finn exclaimed. "Is something wrong? Did you have another vision?"

Verona put her hand up to silence him. "Now is not the time. We must move on towards Vîgarie. The others will be coming through the door…now." and on her command Rina, Ijaïh, and Dator walked out.

"I figured you would be out here. Are you coming with us to Vîgarie?" Rina asked.

She only nodded. "With the safe zone only being a short distance, I believe I've saved enough strength to withstand the journey. If I shall disappear at any time, however, know that I may not come back."

"Understood."

"Well, then welcome to the team, Verona," Eva said happily. Verona faced her, and nodded, appearing unphased by her greeting.

"'Tis most tempting t' know that this quest may once and for all be complete," Ijaïh muttered to himself as the group started their trail out of the village.

Verona stopped to face him immediately at his words. "You be wary of what you request. Fulfillment is not the end. For every action there is a price. Something you hold dear may be lost by your decisions."

Ijaïh looked at her, confused and angered. He clenched his fist and scoffed. "Tut. I doth not need thine advice," he said pushing past her.

Eva moved towards Verona. "That seemed a bit harsh there, don't you think?"

"I am a seer. I do not *think*. I know. I only speak the truth and what is to come. The truth will be what it is by its formation that the leader partakes. Ijaïh has crossed his path with fate. His actions will not be forgotten. Just as for you. Your path has been predetermined the moment you were born. It is our choices that give us alternate routes which lead us to our consequences," she said. Ijaïh grumbled to himself, trying to decide upon which road to lead them down.

"Then you have seen what will happen in the future, after all this is over?"

"Yes."

"Then you can-"

"Do not insult me. Foretelling the future to others is indecent and a sin. It is both a curse and a wondrous power that must be kept safe. In the wrong hands these visions can become disastrous."

"So, the prophecy-"

"Is but a glimpse into what has been and what will come. I cannot say what the outcome will be. However, with great strength, I have narrowed the possibilities down to five probable outcomes. Based on our conversation they have become even more suitable, yet they are still a few of many."

"Can you at least tell me if I make it home in any of them?"

"'Home' is a contradictory word in this sense. Still, I see two chances where you reach this 'home' you speak of. The choice is entirely up to you and how the others choose their path."

"I understand. I'm sorry to ask so much of you."

"Do not ask for pardon. You simply are who you are. Curious in nature…almost childlike, but innocent in intent. These traits, while pure, must not be coddled. Strength and confidence will be your ally in times of need. Do not let the worlds around you cause dismay. Show your existence and others will take notice, just as they have with your friends. Our influences impact the lives of others in many ways. Acceptance of our ways is what makes us stronger."

"If we all make choices that change the timeline, then you as well must have some purpose being here with us. Finn mentioned you had sensed danger forthcoming."

"We all have our purposes. I know my own fate and what is to become of me. I am here for that reason, and yet I am not truly here."

"What do you mean?"

"I am merely a presence here. A physical image that can appear as my overall being. In a heartbeat I can go back to my true self that lies within the cell walls of the palace dungeons. I am solely here for the role I am meant to play. Every path must go accordingly for all to go well. We must all make our own choices and follow them to where they lead us."

"We will find a way to get you out. Maybe we can break in and-"

"Don't worry about me. These are foolish actions that will only cause more harm to you and everyone else. I am following the path I am meant to be on. Do not change your fate for the sake of saving me. Do you understand?"

Eva grimaced, nodding slowly.

"Good. We should be arriving shortly. Finn appears to be in odds. Go to him. Only you can help him."

"Hey, don't look so glum, everything will be alright, you'll see," she smiled, intertwining her fingers with Finn's.

"Yeah…"

Beneath them lay a meadow filled with bright pink and yellow flowers in tall grass. The wind blew fiercely as they were near the border. The waves of the ocean crashed upon the edges of the surface, creating a salty breeze.

"There it be," Ijaïh said.

"Vîgarie," Rina said happily.

"We finally made it," Dator yelled.

"All will be as it should be," Verona nodded.

"Come on, then! Let's go! The last one down is a bumbling bumblesnatch!" Eva laughed, pulling Finn along as she ran down the hill.

Rina and Dator followed, picking up speed. Ijaïh and Verona casually walked down the hill, unwilling to partake in the game. Halfway down the hill, Finn tripped, and Eva tumbled down the rest of the way with him. Laughing as they picked themselves up, they noticed they had lost their chance to beat the other two.

"I win! I got here first!" Dator gleamed. "What doth I win?"

"Well, collect all the prettiest flowers you can find, and I'll make you a flower crown. Sound fun?" Eva asked joyfully. Dator agreed and darted off.

"I guess that makes you a *bumbling bumblesnatch,* Eva," Rina snickered.

“No way! Ijaïh and Verona are still making their way down!”

“I don’t think they planned on racing if you couldn’t tell.”

“Whatever. So, what happens now?”

“We should scavenge the meadow and make sure we’re safe. Then we’ll form the barrier," Finn said. “Rina, you and Krimm check out the border and see about collecting some water.”

“On it!” she said. Krimm scurried out of her satchel, and she hopped upon him. The two waddled off to the edge, out of sight.

Ijaïh and Verona headed off to the west side. Eva and Finn walked off in the opposite direction, passing a couple trees on the way.

“I can’t believe we finally made it! It’s so exhilarating to know how far we’ve come!”

“Y-Yeah," Finn stuttered.

“Are you alright? You look pale.”

“Yeah…I’m fine.”

“Okay…Wow, Finn! Look at this tree! It’s huge! It must have been here for decades! And it even has some sort of writing on it!”

“E-Eva, m-maybe we should go back.”

“Go back?” she laughed in confusion. “We just got here. We spent days trying to get here. Why would you want to go back now?”

Finn quickly grabbed her hand and started heading back where they once came. “Don’t ask questions. We’re going back!”

Eva pulled her hand away. “What has gotten into you?” she scolded. “We traveled all this way! What’s going on?”

A swirl of black energy formed behind her. A tall dark figure stood behind her. He wore black and burgundy attire with

matching armor. His face lay hidden by the draping hood from his tattered cloak.

"Bertram," Finn gulped.

"Well done, Finn. Valdof will be pleased," Bertram said, his voice shrill and grated.

Eva turned around to see the figure and then faced Finn with wide eyes. Her heart pounded with fear. "YOU SET ME UP?"

"No! Eva! It's not like that!"

Bertram gagged Eva from behind and wrapped his arms around her to hold her still. "Now, now. It will all be over soon. Stop struggling," he grinned.

"Let go of her!" Finn shouted, pulling out his dagger.

Bertram laughed at him. "Don't test me! I could just slit her throat right here and now," he said holding a knife to Eva's neck. Eva whimpered, trying to reach for her dagger.

Finn's eyes widened in rage.

"You made a deal. Don't forget what your consequences will be if you fail."

"EVA!" Verona screamed.

"WHAT? HOW DID YOU GET OUT OF THE DUNGEON?"

Eva took this opportunity to grab her dagger and thrust it into Bertram's leg. He growled in pain, releasing her. She ran, and he pulled her back. "Oh no you don't!" Eva let out a cry. Dark energy began to surround them. As the darkness drew closer, Verona pushed her out of the way. Eva hit the ground as the energy vanished and Verona was gone with the guard. Eva shook in fear and anger. She tore off the gag and looked at Finn.

"How could you?" she said.

"Eva…I-I-" he stuttered.

Her body boiled and her eyes welled up with tears. A loud clasp ran across his face followed by a stinging sensation. "I trusted you," she said, her face red and puffy, before running off. Ijaïh, Rina, Krimm, and Dator stood a little distance away in shock. Rina ran after Eva, calling out her name.

Eva continued running when suddenly another dark mass formed in front of her. The guard was back and ripped the satchel away from her. Eva went for her dagger, but Bertram grasped her, tightening his hold amidst her cries. "NO! LET ME GO!" and in a split second they were gone.

"NO!" Rina screamed slamming her sword into the ground where the guard once stood. She ran back to where Finn and the others were and grabbed Finn by his collar.

"WHAT HAVE YOU DONE?" she said, throwing him to the ground. "SHE TRUSTED YOU!" Rina punched Finn continuously. He took it without opposition, feeling numb inside out. "She was our friend, you bastard! How could you do this to her? After all we've been through! After all we put her through! She told you her feelings and opened up to you! Do you have any idea how hard that was for her? How could you do this?"

Finn put up his hands to stop Rina's fist. "I didn't have a choice!"

"The hell you didn't!" she screamed. She quickly pulled out her chimera blade and held it to his neck. "You've been lying to us the whole time! That's why you've blocked me from reading your mind! You planned it from the start, and you dragged me into this! What happened to protecting everyone we could? How many girls have died because of you? I thought we had a plan to protect her at all costs!"

"I did what I had to!"

"BY TURNING HER IN? YOU TRAITOR!" Rina leaned in close to him, forcing the blade close to the skin's breaking point. "Give me one good reason why I shouldn't kill you right now!" she spat.

"I DIDN'T HAVE A CHOICE! VALDOF TOOK MY FAMILY!" Finn screamed, tears beginning to form. Rina's eyes widened as she backed away from him. "He took my parents and my little sister Mary! He approached me when I found Eva that night of the car crash! He said if I didn't bring her here by today that he would kill them! YOU KNOW HE WOULD! He forced me into silence until we handed E-E…her over…I'm so sorry! I didn't want any of this to happen!" he cried. He buried his face in his hands. "I'm so sorry…"

Rina stood up and covered her head with her hood. "We will get them back, your family and Eva. We must. But if she gets hurt, I will never forgive you," she said coldly. "Krimm, let's go. There's no time to waste. Valdof's castle is on the other side of the kingdom. If you truly care for her as I thought you did, you'll fight for her like a man." Krimm spread out his wings and they took off.

Finn wiped away his tears and picked up Eva's satchel. With his hands shaking, he wrapped it around him and looked at the sky. *Eva...I will find you.* He ran after them. Dator started after Finn then came to a halt. Ijaïh did not follow.

"Come on, Ijaïh! We have t' go! We have t' save Eva!" he said desperately.

"No."

"What?"

"Our mission is done. We came here t' deliver her t' Valdof's guard, and now that 'tis complete, we hath no purpose continuing," Ijaïh said coldly. "Come. We leave for Elnaïr."

"NAY!"

"Pardon?"

Dator stared down at his feet, shaking. "I said nay! I will not be leaving with you t' go back to Elnaïr! Eva is our friend! I'm not leaving without her."

"How dare thou speak t' me that way! Thou impish creature! Thee nor I will be fighting. 'Tis a foolish action that will cause naught but dismay," he said in disgust. "We leave now," Ijaïh turned around and started to walk away.

"Coward," Dator muttered under his breath.

"What didst thee say?"

"Thou art nothing but a coward! A recreant! Thee always say what *be foolish*, or *motley-minded*, or *ill t' do*, but the only foolish one is you!"

"Fighting this battle is suicide! What would father bethink if it proves I hath brought thy lifeless body home?"

"I care not what father think! I wouldst rather die knowing I help save mine friend than run hence in their time of need!"

"I will not fight for some wretched human! Hast thou forgotten what those vile creatures hast done t' our tribe and kingdom?" Ijaïh spat.

"She is not like the other humans! Eva has helped us this entire mission and she stood up for us when we got in trouble! Thou art blinded by thine own hatred t' see what very much is going on! Thee speak of courage and bravery like 'tis thy nature, but courage means nothing when thee doth not stand up for what's right! I will not deal with this anymore! Thee disgust me…and t' think I called thee brother. I…I HATE YOU IJAÏH!" Dator screamed. He quickly darted off towards Finn and Rina.

Ijaïh stood there clutching his heavy-beating heart. A scorching pain spread through his hand. The pendant his father gave him burned his skin. Multiple scars of the imprinted symbols covered his palm from when it scorched him before.

Something you hold dear may be lost by your decisions.

He looked back to where Dator ran off and then turned around with a scoff. "The impish creature," he said calmly as he walked off back the way he came.

Chapter 20
Valdof's Castle

Eva opened her eyes to see she was no longer in the beautiful fields of Vîgarie, but rather in the center of a massive bedroom. A fireplace as tall as her filled with flames that warmed the frigid interior. Stained glass windows brought in little light through their depictions of death and shadowed figures. Sitting between their gloomy reign lay a large bed, with its draperies swaying amongst a nonexistent wind. Dark floral carvings lined its frame, matching the burgundy linens seeping from the sides.

"What is this place?" she asked as she picked herself up. A familiar sound reverberated through the room. "That piece…that music," she said softly. She walked through the shadowed doorway, finding a stone hallway dimly lit with spiked torches. Following the sound through the winding passages made her feel dizzy. Her heart raced as she came upon a large wooden door where the music seemed to be coming from. There was a moment of hesitation as she placed her hand upon the handle, for Eva became filled with the unnerving feeling of being trapped; escaping was no possibility. Pulling the door forward breathed a creaking noise.

The room lingered in darkness except for the pale blue and grey light that shined from the windows that rose several feet tall. The stone walls formed a round room encasing her like a mouse in a cage.

Eva let out a gasp at the horrifying sight that lay in front of her. A pipe organ rose from the side of the room, its long pipes grew up the walls releasing air through the skulls of those slain. Some were unnatural with their pointed teeth, curling horns, or elongated faces, while others resembled that of a human. The clattering of teeth echoed throughout the room from one of the skull's broken jaws flapping against the pulsing air that sounded from the pipes. The music, while enchanting like that of a piano-esc xylophone, had a demonic feel of never-ending doom. A man sat beneath the structure, running his lengthy fingers across the keys.

“Don’t be afraid. Come into the room. I won’t bite," he said in a calm manner.

As if on cue, the door closed behind Eva who squealed. Knowing there was no luck in fleeing, she stepped forward. “Y-You’re King Valdof," she stuttered.

The man smirked with a soft chuckle. “Smart girl. You’ve proven that much, but you’re still quite *naive* as it is.”

Valdof stood from his chair, leaving the music to play on its own. His soulless golden eyes sent shivers down her spine. A single silver lock hung from the fringed ends of his pulled back dark wavy hair that fell past his shoulders. His warm ivory skin paled under the light, drawing attention to his exhaustion. Crow’s feet lined his eyes above his heightened cheekbones that angled his face to a rigid point. He wore a classy periwinkle buckle-down tunic with extravagant black and silver striped sleeves that cuffed at the neck. He walked up to Eva, humored by her fear, and ran a hand down her cheek and through her hair.

“Come, dance with me," he said.

With a snap of his fingers, a sudden wind gushed around her changing her attire from a leathery exterior to an elegant gown. Its iris blue bodice fitted against her skin flowing into a ball gown figure. The sleeves flared halfway down, with long draping material flowing partway down the skirt. Elegant and full of grace, but with her dagger now gone, she was left defenseless.

Valdof pulled her close as they spun together. His pungent cologne encased the two in a sickening spell of musky rosemary with a sweetened twinge of putrescine. Eva shook beneath his hold, unsure of what lay ahead.

"You seem so frightened. You need not be though. I will not hurt you," he said. He glanced at the organ for a moment. "*Moonlight Sonata*, one of your favorite pieces, isn't it? Written by Ludwig Van Beethoven after the loss of his hearing."

"H-How do you know that?" she asked, trying to pull away. Valdof leaned in closer.

"I know everything about you Eva. Things you know not of yourself. Your fears, hopes, dreams, and so much more. I've waited *so* long to meet you."

"What do you want with me? You want to kill me?"

Valdof released her, giving a wispy cackle. "Oh, Eva, Eva, Eva. You're such a naive child! I wouldn't dream of killing you. You're much too *precious* for that," he said as he began circling her. "You see, Finn, Rina, Ijaïh, and Dator, they all *lied* to you. They probably told you stories about me *murdering* girls around your age. Oh yes, they do tell some *tall tales*. You see, the only reason why those girls died was because they didn't give me what I wanted, but you can! You have the potential! You have the ability I've been looking for!"

"What do you mean?" she said.

"Well Eva, you're not like the other girls. You're different, unique. I think we could rule together, you and me. Forget the other worlds. Forget your family and friends. Rule with me, and you'll never have to suffer again. We can tear this place apart as well as the Human World and live in happiness together. Anything your heart desires, I will grant to you."

"This…this isn't right," she said. She dug her fingers into her arms as her stomach churned.

"Oh, but it is Eva. It is very so much. People have hurt you throughout your life! They don't care about what they've done to you! But you, you're *pure* of heart. You've done nothing that could cause you or them harm. You've stuck to your righteous ways, and in that process have become…pure."

Valdof came close to her, staring into her eyes intently. "You possess a strength I haven't seen in anyone…in a very long time. That strength, that goodness…it all lies here in your heart, and you can use that however you wish. So why don't you use it to make your dreams come true? Make every last person who made you suffer *Punish Them*. Make Them Feel The Way They Treated You! MAKE THEM SEE WHAT IT'S LIKE TO BE THE UNDERDOG! They *deserve* it, and you deserve peace! Don't you agree with me Eva? You would never have to suffer again. Everything that you ever *known*, everything that has ever caused you *harm*, or *pain*, or *suffering*, it can all disappear. Forget about those times when people hurt you. Forget about it. Live a happy new life, and *never* let others treat you that way again! Just shake my hand, and it can all go away."

The feeling of the betrayals and hardships she once faced crept back into her memory.

"You looked flustered. You really are such an *innocent* soul," he said, caressing her shoulders from behind. "You haven't a negative thought in your mind, have you? Well in that case, is it worth all the pain?"

"But…T-They didn't know all the time, they…" she stuttered.

"Why do you support them? Ignorance is hardly an excuse. They've hurt you from the beginning and you're letting them walk upon you now!"

"Get off of me!" she gasped, but his grip only tightened. He smelled her hair; its sweet scent of vanilla and rain intrigued him.

"You'll see the way I see things soon enough. Forget about *Finn*. Forget about *Rina*. Forget about all those people who hurt you," he said. He planted soft kisses upon her neck and ran his tongue along her pulsing artery. Eva shivered.

I feel strange. Finn...who? Rina?

"Oh…n-no, no," Eva groaned, placing her hands upon her throbbing head.

"Forget about them and live the way you want. Then none of us will suffer again." Valdof whispered in her ear. "We can release them all. We can be *free*."

"None of us will suffer?" she said in a daze as he released her. "We can be- Ugh! No…What did you-!"

Something's wrong!

The room span before her. Her thoughts and memories bounced around in her skull screaming to find a way out. In a moment of sudden pain, all her breath was taken from her. Darkness blurred her vision and with a release, her body gave way. Valdof caught her as she fell. He glared down at her, carrying her fragile form in his arms.

"If you won't listen to me, I'll force you to listen. I'll make you mine own. And if you refuse, you'll end up just like those other girls…*screaming…begging…pleading* for mercy. I can give you that mercy. Listen to me! Forget your so-called friends. And listen to my voice."

"I-I won't do it," she said trembling.

"Eva…you're so foolish. Don't you see? You've already succumbed. You've already forgotten. You're mine now."

Chapter 21
Memory Trials

Her day started just like any other. Eva walked over to the vanity across the room. A soft towel laid next to a gothic pitcher and basin. She poured water into the basin and gently dabbed a cloth to her cheeks. A middle-aged woman entered the room; her eyes widened as she gazed upon Eva.

"Who might you be?" Eva asked.

The woman shook a moment and placed her hand upon her wrist to calm her. She put on a fake smile, that to anyone would look real, and straightened the sheets of the bed.

"I am but a humble servant to you, milady," she said. She walked over to Eva and sat her down in the chair in front of the vanity. Grabbing a brush, she began removing the knots from Eva's frizzy hair. "King Valdof sent me to prepare you for today."

"He is very generous, isn't he," she smiled.

The woman's hand stiffened at her words. She let out a sigh and continued to fix her hair.

"Yes, milady."

"He told me that he would be sending me a new handmaiden today. Mentioned there being '*issues*' with the other one. Whoever she was, I'm sure she's a good person at heart."

"Yes, milady."

"What is it that I may call you?"

"Maudy, milady."

"Well, Maudy, it is great to make your acquaintance."

"The pleasure is mine, milady."

"Must you call me 'milady' all the time? Please call me Eva."

"I would rather not, milady." Maudy said. "It is most improper! What would King Valdof think?" She braided Eva's hair, weaving ribbons through its design and pulling it up partway.

"Then don't say my name around him," she laughed. "Valdof may be ruthless at times, but he cannot control my personal conversations. I'd much rather you call me by my proper name. Besides, I'd like to get to know you better since we will be spending time together."

"You would l-like to know me? M-Mila-"

Eva looked at her sternly.

"I-I mean…Eva. I'm just a servant."

"Oh, pish-posh! You seem like a wonderful person. I'm sure we could be great friends."

"B-But your status-"

"We are all the same, so do not treat me like I'm special just because Valdof has sent you as my servant. If you wish to serve me, I would like you to be yourself. Embrace who you are. I want us to be friends, to be able to share our feelings with one another. Do you understand?"

"Yes," she smiled softly.

"Good," she said, twiddling her fingers through her hair. She grabbed a small bottle off the table. Removing the teardrop lid lifted an aroma of iris roots. She patted a few drops behind her ears, rubbing the rest between her wrists.

"Lady Eva…may I ask you a question?"

"Yes."

"Why do you stand up for him? King Valdof, I mean."

Eva glanced at the mirror. "That's because he saved my life."

"H-He did? But how could such a despicable-?"

"Oh, I wish you wouldn't call him that! He's not as bad as people make him out to be! Valdof took me in when others treated me poorly. I don't remember much, but he said that there were people who had kidnapped me and held me prisoner for months." She placed a hand to her cheek. "The memories hurt so much to think about, but I can still remember their faces. There was a sorcerer with bright green eyes and a freckled face, two elves, brothers I believe, and a rebel Intellect girl with a dragon. Valdof said I was in bad shape when he found me. He took me in, healed my wounds, and treated me with the utmost respect. I may be some girl from the streets, but I owe him my life."

Maudy gritted her teeth, begrudgingly.

"Is something the matter?" Eva asked.

"No." said Maudy. She grabbed a small jar full of white powder. "Perhaps we shall start with your makeup?"

"Oh, that's a bit extreme don't you think? I've never been one to put much on."

"Wouldn't you want to look *nice* for the King?" she said, snidely.

"I would like just to be myself."

"Then maybe a little lipstick. Simple and formal."

"Okay."

Maudy gently took out a smaller jar filled with a fruitful fluid the color of cranberries. She took a small brush and painted Eva's lips until they were stained and full. "There, all done. You know I used to look like you when I was your age. Oh, those were the days," she chuckled.

"Thank you." The words rang in her ear like she had heard them before. Maudy helped Eva into her gown and buttoned the back.

"Is there anything else you wish for today?"

"There is one more thing I would like to talk to you about. Please take a seat," Eva said motioning to a nearby stool. "Why is it that you are here?"

"I am here because King Valdof sent for me to be your handmaiden."

"I know you are lying, Maudy. Please, you can trust me."

"I-I can't tell you! If I do, he will surely kill-" she said before covering her mouth, trying to hide her horror-stricken face.

"Kill? Kill who?"

Maudy shook her head, tears rimming her eyes.

Eva gently removed Maudy's hands from her mouth, looking at her with pleading eyes. "Please, if you tell me, I could help you."

Her lips quivered. "My sons…my two boys. If he finds out I said anything, I-I don't know what I would do! You mustn't say a word!"

"I promise. Maudy, I'll find your sons. If he's using them as leverage, Valdof surely has them here. I can't believe he would do something like this…it's so unlike him. If I find out this is true, I'll make sure they're safe."

"Thank you! Thank you so much!" Maudy wept, hugging her. She quickly pulled away, straightening the wrinkles she had made on Eva's dress. "You mustn't be seen untidy. The King is expecting you for breakfast."

"Then I shall be going. I will find them when I find a moment to leave his side. Perhaps after breakfast."

"Good luck, Eva. And please be careful."

~:~

The soft tapping echoed in the hallway. Little droplets rang through the air sliding between the cracks. *I hate walking through these halls. I always feel like someone's right behind me.* A gust of wind brushed against her back. She quickly turned around to find King Valdof standing behind her.

"Where are you going?" he asked.

Eva smiled brightly. "I was just going to find you. My handmaiden mentioned that you had a wondrous breakfast prepared."

"Spoiled the surprise, didn't she?" he smirked.

"I kind of figured it out on my own," she teased.

"Clever little girl, aren't you?"

"Well, I'd like to think so."

"Then let me lead you in the right direction," he said, offering his arm to her. Eva graciously took it, and they headed off towards the dining hall.

Entering the room, Eva came upon a massive feast that rested on a long table. Roasted bird, bowls of fruit and bread, soft boiled eggs and jams lined the tabletop. In the center sat the head of a drawrble with two candles on each side.

The sight of the head disturbed her, but the rest of the food made her mouth water. Valdof pulled out a chair for her then sat down on the opposite side of the table's end. He snapped his fingers and in came a servant to pour her a cup of wine.

"Oh, no, I don't drink," she said. The servant started filling her plate with various servings of food.

"Oh, but you must." Valdof said laying his head upon his hands. "It is made of the sweetest of jubi berries and grapes. It is the finest wine in all Aloncia. It is a delicacy."

Eva glanced at the chalice and gently picked it up with her shaking hand. The deep reddened fluid smelled floral and tangy. She lifted the drink to her lips and let the fluid slide down her throat; its rich flavor bringing a chilling sensation.

Valdof smiled sinisterly.

Eva began to eat from her plate. The saporous meats and berries filled her with ecstasy. She noticed Valdof's plate remained empty.

"Aren't you hungry?" she asked.

"I'm not one to eat much in the morning. However, you seem to have *quite* the appetite."

"The food is so flavorful, and the meat is tender and juicy," she said with a small blush. "And these berries are absolutely delicious."

"It appears I have glorious chefs."

Valdof's henchman entered the room and made his way up to his master. Valdof sneered at his intrusion, but listened to his request. Standing up from the table, he glanced at Eva. "I am needed elsewhere for the time being. I shall be back within a few moments. Stay here until I return."

Eva nodded in agreement. The servant crept back in, picking up the empty dishes. She gently placed a hand upon the man's forearm. "You made a wonderful meal. You have a great talent," she said with a smile.

The man's face went red. "'T-Tis mine duty, milady."

She giggled at the man's timidness. "What kind of meat is this? It is truly scrumptious."

"That would be blue crane, milady. Seasoned with saffron, cardamom, and smothered with an apple-honey glaze."

Eva's face grew pale. Her stomach churned vigorously at the mention of the bird. She pushed away from the table.

"Milady? Art thee alright?"

"Water…" she said softly.

"Ah! Yes! I shalt get thee some water!" he said.

Eva leaned herself against the wall to regain her balance. Sweat dripped down her face. She clutched her chest as her breath quickened.

'But her most loved creature of all was the blue crane.'

'KEEP RUNNING!'

'I ran and ran until I came across mine village.'

Eva grasped her head in pain, sinking to the floor.

A bloodied floral crown hit the ground. A shadow of a boy being pinned down hovered above with hundreds of others looming over.

'I knew mine actions were in vain...'

Nausea engulfed her; she heaved, lurching over.

'And that I would never see mine mother again.'

Glaring eyes from two tall figures gleamed down upon the shadowed figure that wept.

A sharp sound rang through the crisp air followed by a soft patter.

'I cut mine hair...I deserve mine punishment for mine betrayal.'

Bile seeped from her lips.

"MILADY!" the servant screamed. "Milady, what happened? How now! Thy mustn't be seen like this! The King will have mine neck!"

Eva glanced up at the man, her vision clearing as she came to her senses. Valdof stood behind them and pushed the servant to the side. He grabbed Eva's arms to stabilize her. Using his thumb, he wiped the fluid from her chin. He gazed down at her in a serious manner, as if to look for any signs of ailment. He pulled her close.

"You're safe now," he said. He gently pressed his lips upon her forehead.

Eva shivered momentarily. She blinked, looking around to take in her surroundings. Her eyes met Valdof's, and she smiled softly. All was well.

Chapter 22
Storming the Castle

Over the edge of a jagged crater lay Valdof's castle. "There it is," Finn breathed. In the center rose a steep mountain of blackened earth. Its rigid exterior twisted and turned, curling its way into a cold hardened gate that encased the towering castle. A stone pathway led to its forefront, drilling through the mountain that led up to its stone wall entrance. Guards stood at every post, making sure no one passed. A misty fog dwelled from the bottom, darkening the sky, and bringing death upon all floral beauties. An infectious layer of rotting roots climbed the mountainous border, protruding spikes so thin, one would not know they had been stuck until delirious illusions of horror formed before them.

"I will give you more later. 'Tis all I have," Dator said, handing a sack of berries and a few gold coins to the fairies. The fairies scowled then flew back through their closing portal. "'Tis a long way up,"

"How do we get up there?" Rina said. Krimm curled out of her bag and growled at the castle. "Easy Krimm," she cooed. "I can't exactly make a portal to the dungeons like I did when we went to see Verona while Valdof was in the Human Realm. We'll be caught instantly!"

"It won't be easy that's for sure," Finn said. "And from what has happened, Valdof probably has his guards on the lookout for us. Not to mention that if I step foot in the castle, they'll likely kill me on the spot…"

"Then we must set up a diversion."

"We'll have to be quiet. Once we're inside, Valdof will be able to sense my magic easily. We'll have to take out the guards, and find some way in."

"Alright. I can handle the guards. Then-"

"Then you could enter secretly!" Dator said.

"What?" Finn and Rina said in unison.

Dator smiled and pulled them in close whispering his plan.

"That…is actually a great idea," Finn said.

"Let's do it," Rina said.

~:~

Standing at the bottom of the crater by the main entrance was a rather large guard. Hiding within Finn's barrier, the three headed towards him. The closer they got the more nervous they became, heightening their determination to get past. They came only feet away from the guard and sneaked close to the side of the door. Dator scrambled through his satchel and pulled out a tiny silver orb. The guard became alert to the sound of the orb clinking upon the ground. He moved towards the small object and poked it with the tip of his sword. The orb burst and silver glitter exploded all over him. The guard stumbled backwards, ripping his helmet off to free him from the sparkly blindness. Rina grabbed the man, holding him in a headlock until he went still and pulled him inside the corridor.

"You just had to use glitter!" Rina said, patting down her dress.

Finn let down the barrier and started undoing the man's armor. "Damn, it's Nota. Of course, he had to be twice my size," he scowled. "Ugh, at least he's about the same height. Sorry, Nota. I'll pay you back somehow."

"Hush up!" Rina growled. "I got you a guard, now hurry up!"

"Don't rush me! Armor takes time to take apart and put on. Just keep a lookout for any other guards coming our way."

Moments passed and Finn finally got his armor together. It hung on him like a baggy jumpsuit, with only the ties connecting each piece holding it together. Rina tied up the guard, who now

lay in only in his undergarments, and tucked him in the far corner behind a pillar.

"He should be out for a while. At least long enough to grab Eva and get the hell out of here," Rina said. She snickered at Finn's unruly appearance.

"Oh, shut up Rina," he said.

Rina grabbed some rope and tied it around Dator's wrist tightly. "Use your teeth to pull on this part here and the whole knot should fall apart."

Dator nodded. "Do you think it will work?"

"It has too," Finn said, tying the same knot on Rina's wrists. He led them further down the path towards the castle entrance. Finn's armor clanked with every step. *This isn't going to work! This isn't going to work!*

"Calm down," Rina quietly scolded.

"Halt! Who goes there?" a guard said.

The guard stood at the next post, pointing his sword towards them. As they approached, Rina and Dator pretended to struggle.

"Nota? What are you doing?" he said.

"I found these two roaming around the castle grounds," Finn said with a deep voice, trying to mimic Nota. "I'm taking them to the dungeons."

The guard stiffened and moved aside. "Understood," he said.

Guard by guard, the three passed, leading them closer to the main gate. The guards appeared even more anxious as they watched them pass. Dator gave Rina a worried look as they headed towards the main gate.

Finn saluted the head guard.

"Get back to your post, Nota."

"Sir Everard, I would like entrance into the castle to deliver these two to the dungeons," he said, jerking on the ropes.

"What crimes have they committed?"

"W-What crimes?" Finn stuttered. "They were found trespassing the castle grounds!"

"Take them back."

"Sir, these are dangerous people!"

"Nota, may I remind you who oversees the royal guard? I said, take them back."

"But Sir-" Finn said, beginning to shake.

"Honestly, Nota! I knew you were dense, but even you should know what has been happening behind these walls. Take them back before you regret what you've done."

"But Sir, these are the ones King Valdof has been asking for! They committed treason against the Kingdom of Aloncia!"

Sir Everard took a step back. He stood there, eyes wide at Rina and Dator. "Where is the other one?"

"T-The o-other one, Sir?"

"Barrett! Where is Barrett, their leader?"

"B-Barrett?" Finn choked, losing his act. "H-He's uh…he's um…"

"You mean that wimpy little guard of yours?" Rina said. Dator quietly tugged at her skirt.

"Silence you!" Finn said, shoving her downward.

"Stop! I want to hear what she has to say," Sir Everard said.

Rina glared at him. "That little rat never stood a chance against me. I slit his throat the moment he stepped foot in my village," she said, and spat at Sir Everard's feet. "Just like I will do with you."

Sir Everard gritted his teeth and held his sword to her chin. "That was your mistake," he said calmly, raising his blade. Finn blocked the sword as it came down.

"Get out of here!" he said.

Rina and Dator pulled free of their ropes and started toward the exit, when all the guards from the other posts encircled them. Rina opened her satchel, and Krimm flew out. "Get them," she said coldly, and he launched himself at them. Rina drew her weapon and gazed at the guards.

"You think you can resist me?" she mocked.

Two of the guards leapt forward and Rina began swinging her blade back and forth. Front flips, backflips, and headlocks, and soon the guards were dropping like flies.

Dator snuck past the guards and started picking the lock sealing the gate.

"Nota! What has gotten into you?"

"I must get past that gate, Sir!"

CLANK

CLANK

"Do you wish for them to have a death sentence?"

"I am doing what I have to! I must get through!"

SWASH

SHING

Rina struggled beneath three guards. She bit down upon the one's hand. Latching on to the other two, she swiftly knocked their heads together with her knees. Four more guards headed her way.

"Have you completely lost your mind?"

"Sir, I don't want to fight you, but I need to get through!"

"You're not Nota, are you?"

"Who I am doesn't matter! I must get through! Lives are at stake!"

Sir Everard swung his sword, pressuring Finn back.

"I know that! That's why I'm asking you to leave!"

"I hath unlocked the gate! Hurry!" Dator yelled.

Finn glanced at Rina. Letting go of a guard's motionless body, she attacked the last standing guard, knocking him down in a split second. Sir Everard took this chance to knock the sword from Finn's hands and remove his helmet.

"Barrett..." Sir Everard said. He stepped back and dropped his sword.

Finn held his wrist, and then stared at his leader.

"Come on, Finn," Rina said, waiting for him by the gate.

He grabbed his sword and shut the gate behind him. He melted the lock and the three ran off towards the castle.

"Please come back! You don't know what you're up against! You don't stand a chance!" Sir Everard cried.

~:~

Entering the castle, Finn, Rina, and Dator looked around cautiously. They kept their weapons close, awaiting an ambush that may be lurking in the halls.

"Where do you think she is?" Rina whispered.

"She could be anywhere. We should check the throne room and dungeon. It's our best bet. I hate to think what he may be doing to her," Finn said.

"I could seek her out."

"No! You'll get us caught!"

"Do you think she is okay?" Dator asked.

Finn and Rina stayed silent.

Dator hung his head.

"Rina-"

"Shh! Someone's coming!" she said, pulling them into an entryway. Two guards walked down the hall.

"I'm sure I heard something over here," a guard said.

"You're probably just hearing things. No one could get into the castle with all the guards outside," said the other.

"Well, I'd rather be sure just in case. You never know-"

Rina slammed her sword handle into the back of his head, knocking him out. The other guard grabbed her from behind. She flipped backwards, twisting his arms back. Using her legs, she knocked his helmet off and cut off his circulation. The guard soon collapsed, and Rina tied them up. Finn and Dator helped drag them into a nearby storeroom.

“We can’t keep doing this. Someone’s going to notice," she said.

“Well, we can’t get caught either," Finn said.

“Shant we hide in a room ‘til we come across Eva?” Dator asked.

“By the time we find her, it will be too late!”

“Finn’s right. We’ve got to be strategic with this. Every move will make a difference. I say we get out of this room and find Eva before more guards come.”

“Right," Finn and Dator said together.

Suddenly the door burst open. “Hey! What are you doing in here?” a guard yelled.

Finn shoved the guard to the ground. “Run!” he said.

Rina and Dator hopped over the guard, followed by Finn, and ran down the hallway. They came across a circular room with hallways and rooms leading in different directions. The sound of footsteps echoed in the room.

“Scatter!” Rina said.

Chapter 23
Abandoned

"Bring in another one," Valdof said in an inhospitable manner, descending into his seat.

Two guards dragged a bloodied man from the room, leaving only stains across the floor.

"Isn't this marvelous, Eva?" he said with a baleful grin.

Eva kept her head down, and gently rubbed her thumb across the back of her hand. "Must we always portray violence?"

Valdof smiled smugly, his eyes gleaming down at her as she sat beside his throne. "This is merely the act of leadership. A King must always abide by his rules and follow them through. The only way to keep power is through fear. And to create fear, there must be punishment for one's mistakes."

"But all that b-blood…who deserves-"

"He will survive. Perhaps he will learn better than to lash out at one of my guards."

The two guards pulled in a struggling man and threw him on the floor.

"Ah! Based on your facial expression you must have seen your brother. No matter. I'm sure you know that you, too, will meet the same fate," he said. Valdof slowly rose from his chair and came toward the boy.

"I swear upon my tribe, you will pay for this! If you ever lay a finger upon my mother-"

Eva's heart skipped a beat as she heard the man's words.

This…this can't be true…

"Hush now." Valdof said grabbing the man's jaw, his fingernails tenderly digging into his skin. "Look at you. You are nothing but a pathetic waste of flesh. Any good son would have taken the deal which was given to him: you and your brother's life for your mother's. Now you'll never see your mother again, and your lineage will die due to your selfishness."

Their life for their mothers! They weren't supposed to be here! How can this be? Maudy was...right? No. No! That can't be right! Valdof isn't that way, he couldn't have...ugh my head!

He summoned a silver mace and smashed it across the man's face. Eva let out a cry for him to stop, but Valdof refused to listen. He paused for a moment, letting the pain settle. Waving his hand over the bloodied mace, its metal exterior became hot. Its molten material formed a long chain that dangled; at the end was a teardrop-shaped mass encased in a twisted spiral of spikes.

"Please…help…me…" the man slurred through the pain of his broken mandible.

Eva shook in fear.

If I try to stop Valdof, he'll surely find out Maudy revealed her secret to me and kill them. None of this makes sense! How could...why would...

"Silence! You are not worthy of speaking to her!" Valdof scolded, smacking the flail into his gut. Blood splattered across the ground. Valdof struck the man repeatedly, each time making Eva flinch. She shakily covered her ears. Soon only silence dwelled in the misery.

Icy hands embraced her own.

"Do not cry because of a sight such as this. There is nothing for you to fear. They are but insects looking for a chance to spoil our lives. We must look out for ourselves to survive. The world is cruel and will do anything to take away our happiness. I am only here to protect you. We cannot feel for the others."

Eva nodded slowly.

"That's a good girl," he said, wiping away her tears. "I have something special for you." Valdof took her hand and walked her to the center of the room. He snapped his fingers and a black mass formed in front of them. As the mass flushed away, a woman in bloodstained rags knelt beneath them. Bits of thickly scarred flesh-covered stitches lay over where her eyes should have been. This was the real Verona.

"Eva…" she whispered. "Don't you remember me?"

Eva looked at the woman.

"Heh, of course you wouldn't," she smirked. "Not with-"

CRACK!

Valdof stood over Verona, a thorned whip in hand.

"You think this will change anything?"

Valdof clenched his fist and let his anger rage.

CRACK!

CRACK!

CRACK!

"Stop it…please stop!" Eva cowardly cried.

With a wave of his hand, Verona grasped her head and began screaming.

"VALDOF, STOP IT!" Eva yelled, pushing herself in front of him to reach the girl.

"EVA, DON'T!" he said, reaching out for her. Eva embraced Verona. Her body froze and her eyes became dazed. Then everything went black.

~:~

Dark shadows encased a dimly lit village. Eva found herself floating down to the ground. A small, cloaked girl ran into a house. The shadows swirled around her, changing the scenery.

"Where am I?" Eva asked. "Who are these people?"

Inside the house, four people stood. The parents of the girl were greeting her arrival home, while her older brother sulked in the corner. Their eyes were completely white, but they could see the lights and shadows of the world around them. They all seemed upset, but neither Eva nor the little girl could figure out why.

“Mother? Father? Why are you crying?” the little girl asked.

Her parents hugged her. “You must be strong, Verona," her mother said.

“I don’t understand.”

“We have seen the future, Verona," her father said. “You will be safe, but…”

“You must always know we love you!” her mother said.

Verona started tearing up. “I love you too.”

“Verona? Is she-”

BANG! BANG! BANG!

Verona’s father shoved her into her brother’s arms.

“Venice, take her upstairs and keep her safe!”

“But what about you?” he said.

“We must never change fate. In doing so will cause great distress,” his mother said, placing her hand on his cheek. “It is our time to go. Protect Verona and never stop fighting.”

Venice nodded his head.

BANG! BANG! BANG!

“Go,” his father said.

Venice ran up the stairs with a crying Verona in his arms. The door burst open, and five bandits swarmed in. They swiftly killed the parents and began ransacking the place.

“W-Why?” Eva cried.

Shadows engulfed the scene and faded into the bedroom where Venice took Verona. He put her down and locked the door with a wooden plank.

“Where’s mother and father?” she cried.

Venice dried her tears. “They’re okay. Everything will be okay, but now we must be quiet.”

“Veni, I’m scared.”

"I am too, but you know sometimes it's okay to be scared. Think of happy things like how we caught that big fish in the lake at the Lunar Festival."

"Heh...that fish was pretty big."

"You know what? After all this is over, we'll go fishing again. We'll go and catch the biggest fish in all Aloncia. Won't that be fun?" he whispered, tears rimming his eyes.

Verona nodded with a sniffle.

"Hey, you hear that?" one of the bandits said. "Check upstairs!"

"Shit!" Venice said. He scooped up his sister and placed her in the closet.

"Veni? What's going on?"

"Shh! Stay in there and be quiet! Whatever happens, don't come out, okay?"

"But Veni-"

"I love you, Verona. You be brave just like mother and father. Everything will be okay."

The door burst open.

"Hiding up here, are you? Where's the other one?" he asked.

"You stay away from them!" Eva yelled, coming in front of the bandit.

"Other one?" Venice said.

"The other child! I know you're not alone!" he said, stepping right through Eva.

"Why can't they see me?" she said to herself.

"There's no one up here, but me!"

"Liars pay a price," he said. The bandit attacked Venice. Venice struggled beneath the bandit and felt a sharp piercing in his side. He let out a cry as he fell to the ground, grasping his wound. "I'm going to find the other child, and when I do, I'm going to make you watch her die. This is on your hands," the bandit said, then spat on the boy. The bandit searched the room and when he came close to the closet, Verona let out a small gasp. The doors creaked open.

“There you are," the bandit grinned. He yanked her hair and threw her on the ground.

“LEAVE HER ALONE!” Venice yelled.

The bandit ran his hand up Verona’s skirt as she cried and screamed.

“GET YOUR HANDS OFF HER!” Eva said, phasing through the man. She took a step backwards in shock. “I-I can’t do anything…”

Venice tried to pull himself up. Another bandit came and slammed his pommel against the boy’s head.

“VENICE!” Verona wailed, watching her brother fall to the ground.

“Shut up!” the man screamed, punching her.

“Sir! We’ve raided the house, there’s nothing but junk here.”

“Go ahead and leave then. I’ll be out in a moment. I need to teach this one some manners," he growled.

Verona sobbed, placing a hand to her throbbing cheek. The bandit started undoing his belt when she noticed her father’s razor under the bed. Verona reached for it. Her fingers grazed the blade as the bandit raised the belt. She finally grasped it and slashed his face.

“WHY YOU LITTLE-” he screamed. Out of rage, the bandit pulled Verona up and slammed her into the ground. Her vision went in and out. She tried to escape his grasp, but the bandit pinned her down. He pulled out his knife and started slashing out her eyes. The scuffle soon ceased as Verona’s body lay still. The man lifted himself from her and left the room, leaving her to bleed to death.

Eva walked over to the young Verona and wept.

The room turned dark and soon there was nothing.

~:~

Eva blinked a couple times and pulled a panting Verona close. She stroked her hair, her hands clammy and shaking.

Valdof glared down at her. "Are you happy?"

"How could you remind her of something so awful?"

"She needed punishment."

"No one deserves this!"

He pulled Eva away from her. "So, you would stand up to someone who betrayed you?"

Eva's eyes dilated. "What?"

"Why do you think she's here?" he spat. "She is the one who sent your captors to find you! She's the one who told them your location."

Eva looked back at Verona in shock. *I don't understand...all those horrible memories...how could she...in her state...*

"I've been trying to tell you. Everyone has a reason for their punishment. I was only trying to protect you," he said.

"Eva I-" Verona said.

"Is it true?"

Verona hung her head down in guilt. "It is."

Eva's heart raced, pain flowing through her chest.

Valdof placed his hands on her shoulders and lowered his lips down to her ear. "See? She even admits it. What do you think we should do?" he whispered.

"Let her go," she said, seething with anger and empathy.

"This woman betrayed you! She made you suffer through the bitter doings of others! They tortured you and treated you like dirt!" Valdof said, slipping the handle of a whip into her hand. "She *deserves* it."

"Eva, listen to me! He's lying!" Verona pleaded. "None of us kidnapped you! We were trying to protect you!"

"She's just trying to get out of what's coming to her! She knows she did wrong! Don't let her get into your head!"

"Trust me! He's not your friend! I want to help you!"

Valdof sent a gust of black powder into Eva's eyes. She quavered with anger.

"Lies. All lies. She's nothing but a coward. She's making excuses. You know what you have to do."

"Eva, remember it is our choices that give us alternate routes which lead us to our consequences! You don't want to do this! You know this will haunt you! He has you under his control, don't you see?"

Eva's grip tightened.

"Are you going to let her walk over you like that? She's messing with your head! Who has been there for you all this time? Who rescued you from those evil peasants? Who has treated you with the utmost respect and give you everything you wanted?"

"EVA, PLEASE!"

"You can trust me. I am here for you. I am telling you the truth. Believe in me, Eva."

"Eva!"

"EVA!"

CRACK!

Eva gripped the whip and lashed her repeatedly, rage and fear taking over. By the sound of the fourth whipping, Valdof snapped his fingers, and Verona fell to the ground, dead. Tears of blood seeped from her scarred face, draining into the puddle beneath her. A glowing white orb flowed from her body. It gracefully rose to the ceiling, seeking a way out. A black essence wrapped around the orb, bursting it into flames. Silent screams rang through the room, as it quivered in agony. Its energy peeled away in flakes of burnt flesh, sizzling into nothing before reaching the ground.

Eva stopped, her scattered breathing echoing within the room. She let the whip fall to the floor, tears streaming from her eyes.

"I'm sorry! I'm so sorry!" she cried, dropping before Verona's lifeless body. Mortified by her actions, Eva reached out towards her. "I-I didn't mean to! I didn't-"

"There, there, Eva." Valdof said, pulling her up into his arms. "You've done nothing wrong. All of this is over now. You did well."

Eva shook, clenching to his vest, letting her emotions go. "I-I k-killed her."

"Yes. You need not think any more of it. You will be alright," he said stroking her hair. Eva's eyes glistened black for a second, and her body relaxed. "Sometimes we must learn lessons through a harder path."

Chapter 24
Behind the Door

In the back of the castle stood a large wooden door covered in black vines. Valdof led Eva inside, revealing a withering mess of what once had been a wondrous garden. Blackened bushes laid bare, intertwining together, forming large thistles that surrounded a tattered fountain. Brown water dripped from its tip, creating ripples in the stagnant puddle beneath. Dead vines encased the stone walls, entrapping the arbor. Thistles surrounded plots of petal-less flowers, leaving nothing but empty soil between the cobbled pathways.

"Eva, I have some matters to attend to. While I'm gone, I want you to stay here in the garden," he said.

"Must you go?" Eva asked. "It's quite dreary here…"

"There are some *things* I must tidy up. I won't be long. You should be safe here, but I'd rather you not worry yourself about unnecessary troubles. In the meantime, stay here. Do not leave until I return. Understand?"

"Yes."

"Good. Oh, and be wary of the thistles. They're rather sharp this season."

Valdof walked out leaving Eva alone in the dark gardens. She nervously glanced around. She walked over to the bare flowers, touching one of the blackened buds. Its feeble stem disintegrated under the pressure, leaving nothing but dust.

Eva caught the bud and sat on the ground. "You poor thing. If only you had a chance to show your true beauty. I bet you would have been the prettiest flower in the garden," she said, running her finger along its edge.

She sighed, laying the bud down on the ground. She started down the path, when suddenly a rumbling crackle came from behind. A hole materialized where she had placed the bud. A small stem climbed from the crevice, twisting around itself to form a diamond shaped pod. Eva leaned toward the plant curiously. As her finger touched the tip of the pod, it sprawled open, revealing a vibrant orange flower.

"Did…I do this?" she said. Its petals were thick, layered upon each other like scales. "Valdof said he'd grant me whatever I wish. I wonder…"

Eva placed her hand upon the flowerbed soil. As she gently drifted her fingers upon the baron bush that surrounded it, a wispy light dug into the soil, bringing forth new life.

Eva giggled and twirled in excitement. She danced around the garden, ridding it of its deathly embrace. Hundreds of flowers sprung from the soils and bushes, expressing their elegant designs. From the vines, dangled fluffy blue blooms with long pistils and stamens holding clear droplets like that of morning dew. Bright green bushes bore soft barbed petals that grew luscious ivory berries. Across the other beds rose flowers whose blossoms took various shapes that of birds, butterflies, and fairies. The arbor glowed like it had been recently whitewashed; its vines decorating it.

The entire garden had been recovered, except for the fountain and the surrounding bushes. Eva carefully stepped around the thorns, making her way to the edge. She hesitated, feeling a presence nigh. She laid her hand upon the fountain's base. A blue light spiraled around the base, creating a soft breeze as symbols glowed brightly. Their radiance seeped into the murky water and up the center, reforming the broken pieces. The water became clear. High at the top of the fountain, rested a large blue orchid made of stone; golden and silver orbs floated from the bloom. They spiraled around the water, slowly sinking to the bottom of the reservoir. From these orbs sprouted purple water lilies. The surrounding bushes burst into bloom, forming a beautiful, knotted pattern around the fountain.

Eva's heart pitter-pattered at the sight of its lustrous scented orbs. "It's beautiful," she said softly. She cupped her hands under the rushing water and threw it into the air, gleefully enjoying her glorious creation. "Valdof will be so pleased!" she said. She lifted her skirt and pranced between the bushes towards the exit.

Running through the halls, Eva felt a sickening guilt for leaving the gardens. *Oh jeez...I shouldn't have left. Valdof told me to wait for him. He was very strict about it too... Maybe I should go back.* She realized she had no idea where she was, or which way she came from. The walls narrowed in a dizzying state full of suffocating entrapment.

"Well…looks like I'll have to seek him out myself," she sighed. From the side, she heard a soft creaking of a door. Taking a glimpse, the door shut quickly. Goosebumps formed upon her arms, and she hurried to the end of the hall, away from the door. Turning right led her down a spiral stairway. The cold air sent shivers down her spine as she headed further into the castle depths. At the bottom extended a hallway with two doors. A scream echoed throughout the hall. She stepped closer to the door at the end of the hall, regret boring in the pits of her stomach. Her hand shook as she clasped the handle. A strong smell of iron and musty rot gushed through her.

A thin humanoid creature crouched over a corpse, whose blood puddled beneath, seeping into the cracks between the stones. Its leathery sage skin held tight to its body, revealing its bone and muscle structure. Eva let out a gasp, standing frozen in fear as she watched the creature tear apart the juicy flesh. The creature lifted its head swiftly, flicking its lengthy, pointed ears at the sound before turning to face her. Its black sunken-in eyes beamed at her as it panted, blood and black fluid oozing from its decaying teeth. In its hand were the entrails from a body that would be almost unrecognizable if not for the scarred tissue that covered the eyes. The creature let out a blood curdling shriek, scuttling towards her. She opened her mouth to scream when black energy formed around the area, and a cold hand pulled Eva back, covering her eyes, as the door slammed shut. The creature growled and squealed behind the door, trying to claw its way out. Eva trembled, unable to move.

"I thought I told you to stay in the gardens." a familiar voice said in fury.

"I-I-" Eva stuttered.

"I do not like the mindless meandering of those who do not obey."

"V-Valdof, I-I'm s-sorry!"

"What were you doing down here?" he growled, turning her to face him.

"I-I w-wanted to s-show you the g-garden."

"You mean the garden I told you explicitly to stay in?"

"T-The flowers! T-They've-"

"I don't care about some stupid flowers!" he screamed. Eva flinched, trembling within his hold. "Perhaps you will do better in the library, where you can ravage your time with books instead of tourism."

Valdof clenched his hand tightly around her forearm, dragging her away from the door. With each step, Eva's heart doubled in pulse. He huffed and snarled, twitching with rage.

"W-What was that t-thing?"

"That's none of your concern."

"B-But it was e-eating that g-girl f-from before…"

Valdof slammed her into the stone wall. Eva winced, sharp pain climbing up her arms as his nails dug into her skin. His skin sagged upon his discolored face. "You'll be better off forgetting what you just saw before you wind up chained in that dungeon where I know where to find you!" he said pointing to the second door in the hall. "And trust me, you wouldn't like that."

Valdof pulled her up the stairwell and to the main floor. He threw open the door and shoved her in. "Now stay in there, or you will rue the day you crossed me!" he said.

Eva rubbed her arm. Dust lined the shelves and wooden floor. Across the room stood a small table with a single book lying open. A feather quill hovered above it, scribbling down various symbols on the pages.

Curious of its magnificent nature, Eva examined the strange book.

Typical. It would be illegible.

As if the book had heard her, it flipped to a page somewhere in the middle and formed words she could read. Eva gazed upon the words. Her heart raced with curiosity and apprehension. On the page it read:

Rumor has it that the Enaïrian tribe has been hiding summoned girls within their village. Investigation was a must, not that I knew not of their actions prior. Being a patient man that I am, I gave them the option to release the girls, or suffer the consequences. They are terrible liars. I set forth a few of my guards to seek out their queen, and what did they find? The little wretch had snuck off to another part of the kingdom with her boy! An insolent pair they are, but to create an outcast of the leader's son will do its part. What better way to bring more shame to the tribe than for the queen to die at the hands of her own son? It is only fair for their actions. What joy it brought when I sent my guards to scavenge their homes, burning the village to the ground. It is a simple request; one any ought to obey.

Eva stepped away from the book, almost tripping on the chair behind her. Her stomach swirled in disgust from the story told.

Her attention shifted as a small object glimmered behind a bookshelf. Picking it up, she realized it was one of many pieces lined up properly. *A suit of armor? What would it be doing here? And better yet, who was wearing it?*

Eva became alert at the sound of books tumbling to the floor. She grabbed the breastplate and walked over to the source of the sound. Behind the corner crouched a man. He looked at her way as she took a step forward, coming face first with the breastplate.

"Ow!" Finn said, rubbing his cheek.

She moved far away from him as she could.

"Eva? Eva! Oh, thank goodness!" he said leaping to his feet. "I've been looking everywhere for you!"

"Y-You stay away f-from me, or I-I'll scream!"

Finn stopped, worry filling his eyes. "Eva…I know I did wrong! I shouldn't have let them take you. It's my fault you're in this mess," he said. With her guard down, he took a step towards her. "I was so worried I'd never find you! I thought Valdof-"

"Don't you speak ill of him!" she yelled.

"W-What?"

"Valdof has treated me with nothing but respect! Unlike you, and the rest of your disgusting crew who kidnapped me, he seeks to protect me!"

"P-Protect you! Eva what are you talking about?" he said, inching closer. "He's the reason you've been through all this. He's the one we were trying to protect you from."

"D-Don't you come near me! He's told me of your mistakes! How you kidnapped me with two elves and some savage Intellect! Y-You tortured me, leaving me to rot in the streets! I-I'm not going back!" she said, moving to the bookshelf's edge.

"Torture you? We never hurt you! Where is all this coming from? Don't you remember the good times we had traveling through the woods? The fun we had at the festival?"

Eva's lower lip quivered. Her mind began to race with moral contradictions.

"We were just trying to keep you safe," he said, placing a hand on the breastplate.

Eva's heart pounded with fear. She shoved the breastplate forward and darted for the door. Finn grabbed her wrist, pulling her into his arms.

"No! Let me go!" she screamed.

"Eva, don't you remember me?" Finn said gently, his voice full of concern.

She gasped, remembering how Verona spoke the same words. She gazed into Finn's eyes, questioning whether to trust him.

Why do I feel safe all of the sudden?

"Eva, it's me Finn," he said softly. "Rina, Dator, and I have been looking all over for you. The moment that guard took you…Oh, I'm so sorry, Eva! I was so stupid! I shouldn't have turned you in! I tried to find a way out of it, but I worried about what would happen to my family if I didn't obey Valdof's rules. I should have never let them take you! Maybe Rina and I could-"

"Stop!" she said. Eva clenched her head, her thoughts colliding with one another. "I don't want to hear any more of your lies!" Eva ran to the door. *Valdof will surely be mad when he finds me gone, but I must search for him. He warned me of that man! I need to find him now!*

She ran down the stairwell, hoping if she came to the room she had before that he would appear once again. She placed her hand on the handle and paused. She looked at the door near the stairs. *What if he was telling the truth? Maudy's sons would be down there too…* Reluctantly, Eva walked to the dungeon door. Opening it revealed a second stairway. She sighed. *It's too late to turn back now. Either way, a promise is a promise. I have to know.*

Descending further into its depths made Eva anxious. Blood dripped from the walls, enticing the spiders with a free-for-all buffet. The cries of people could be heard as she came closer.

"Whoever you are, leave us alone!" a man said.

"No! No! I will not go through it again!" a little girl screamed.

"Quie' you! You'll only make i' wo'se!" another man scolded.

"Shh…it will be okay. Shh…It's only a bad dream," a woman cooed.

"It's okay Sarin, I can handle it," a fourth voice sounded.

"Don' be s'upid! You can' even s'and!"

Eva came to the bottom of the stairs. The two brothers remained in neighboring cells. They looked almost identical except for their hair. Across from them sat a family of three. A blonde freckled woman sat, holding her crying daughter in the far back while the father stood protecting them. He had scraggly curling hair the color of bark with black locks. Their eyes widened at the sight of Eva, who appeared mortified.

"Who are you? Get out of here before you get caught!" the father yelled.

"You'e that gi'l from the th'one 'oom! Wha' pu'pose do you have he'e?" one of the brothers growled.

"Sarin, calm down."

"Calm down? CALM DOWN! SHE JUS' SA' THE'E N' WA'CHED US BE SLAUGH'E'ED, FAL'ON!"

"There was nothing she could have done. Listen to yourself. You can barely talk. Getting upset will only increase the pain."

"NO! SHE COULD HAVE S'OOD UP FO' US, BU' ALL SHE DID WAS LOOK AWAY! SHE MIGH' AS WELL HAVE BEEN LASHING US HE'SELF!"

"Would you have rather her hurt herself in the process? She did what-"

"He's right…" Eva said.

The brothers looked at her.

"I should have stepped in. I'm sorry."

"Do not apologize. It's not your fault. If you helped either of us, he would have punished you too," Falton said.

"I'm not sure he would. He's been generous to me, but I can't say I agree with his tactics."

"If you'e so lovey-dovey with Kingy up the'e, why did you come down he'e then?"

"Sarin!"

"I came to find you actually…"

"Find us? What for?"

"Are you by chance Maudy's sons?"

"You know our mother? Is she okay?" Falton said, full of concern.

"WHA' HAVE YOU DONE 'O HE'? I SWEA' IF-"

"She's fine. I met her this morning in my chamber room. She's been worrying about you two very much. I promised her I'd find you. I hoped it would have been under better conditions."

"Thank goodness," they sighed in relief.

"Now if only I could find a way to get you all out."

"No can-do miss." said the father from the other cell. "These cells can only be opened by the King or the guards, so unless you know of anyone up there who'd be willing to help, you're out of luck."

"There must be another way," she said.

"There are no ways out. Papa's tried everything," the little girl sniffed. "Magic doesn't work behind these bars. We'll be trapped down here forever."

Eva knelt to her height. She looked just like her mother, but shared the matching bright green eyes as her father. "Don't cry. I'm sure we can figure out something. What's your name?"

"Mary."

"Well Mary, my name's Eva. I know times are hard right now, but you must keep hope."

"I wish Finnie were here."

Eva's heart skipped a beat. "Does Finnie have blond hair with brown strands, a freckled face, and green eyes?"

"Yes! You know my brother?" Mary said excitedly.

He was telling the truth! Her stomach began to spin.

"Finnian's alive?" the mother said, rushing to the cell bars.

"Where is he? Is he alright?" the father said his words full of concern.

Thoughts began bouncing back and forth in her head. She latched onto the cell bars. "I feel sick."

"What? Where's Finnian? What's happened to him? Tell me!"

"H-He's alright," she gritted between her teeth. She sank to the floor grasping her head. *The pain! It's unbearable!* "Make it stop..." she said under her breath. Sweat dripped from her forehead as she gasped for air.

"Make what stop?"

"Papa, help her!"

"Sarin! The water tray!"

He grabbed the water tray and squeezed it through the bars, placing it down as far as he could. Eva's thoughts clouded up; the noise around her sounding ten times louder than it was. It took everything not to scream.

"What do we do?" Falton screamed.

"What's wrong with her, Papa?" Mary said.

"Don' you qui' on us!" Sarin said.

“Honey, do something!” the mother cried out, placing a hand on Eva’s head.

“EVA!” Finn screamed, running over to her. Rina and Dator followed behind. He pulled her up into his arms. She shook, burying her head in his chest.

“What is the matter with her?” Dator said.

“Finnian!” his mother called out.

“Mother! Father! Mary! Oh, thank goodness you are safe!”

“What happened to her?” Rina asked.

“She just collapsed," she said.

“It must be Valdof. He’s been messing with her memories! She didn’t even recognize me and ran off before I could find you two.”

“Dammit!” Rina said.

“Everything’s spinning," Eva gasped.

Finn stroked her hair. “Shh, it’s alright, Eva. It’s me. I’m here.”

The pain began to dissipate as her body relaxed. She blinked a couple times and looked up. “Finn?” she said, laying a hand on his cheek. “Is it really you? Are you really here?”

“Yeah, it’s me," Finn laughed. “How are you doing?”

Eva hugged him tightly. “I’m so happy to see you! How did you ever find me? Valdof showed me such awful things and... Wait!” she said pulling away. “I’m still mad at you!”

“There’s no time for that!” Rina said, lifting her up. “We have to get you out of here!”

“It won’t work. Once Valdof realizes I’m gone, there’s no way he’ll let me out of his grasp again,” she said.

“Then what do we do?” Dator asked.

“Well, Finn, you’re a guard. Can you open these cell doors?”

"No can do, but I did sneak these off Sir Everard!" he said, twirling a set of keys. He promptly unlocked the doors. Mary tackled him, tears of joy soaking his shirt. "Oh, my sweet Mary! I've missed you so! I'm so sorry you had to go through all this!"

"Rina, I want you to heal them. They've been through a lot today, and I made a promise to their mother that I'd make sure they were safe," Eva said.

"What are you going to do?"

"I have to go back to the library before Valdof finds out I left."

"What? No way! I'm not letting you risk your life to make some diversion!"

"I'm not asking you to. There's no other way."

"We could come with you!" Dator suggested.

"Dator's right! We're not leaving you alone!" Finn interjected.

"If Valdof finds you, he'll kill you! He's not going to cause harm to me. He said so himself. I-I can distract him until you're done and find a safe place for everyone to hideout."

"Eva." Falton said calmly. He held out a muddy purple ribbon and a small scroll to her.

"Th-This was Verona's…" Eva stuttered.

"She wanted you to have these."

Eva grabbed the items with a shaky hand. Two tiny symbols were scratched upon the scroll's edge. The scroll was damp, frail, and smelled of mildew.

"She told me to tell you that 'when the moment is right,' to 'wrap the ribbon upon your weapon for this will bring great chance.' And Eva…there's one more thing," he said. She looked at him, teary eyed. "'This wasn't your fault.'"

"Eva, what's he talking about?" Finn asked.

Eva bit her lower lip.

“What does he mean? Where’s Verona?”

She stood there in silence, afraid to face him.

Finn’s shoulders sunk. “No. It can’t be.”

“Time’s running out. I must be getting back," she said solemnly.

“I don’t like this one bit," Finn said.

“I don’t either, but what choice do we have?” Rina said.

“None," Eva hugged the three of them. “Meet us in the gardens in ten minutes," she said. She turned around and hurried up the stairs.

Making sure the coast was clear, Eva darted out of the dungeons and headed back to the library. Closing the door behind her, she let out a sigh of relief. *I’ve got to make this look convincing.* She quickly shoved the armor pieces into the cabinets beside the corner bookshelf. She slipped Verona’s ribbon into her sleeve and placed the scroll in her stocking. The soft sound of footsteps echoed from the hallway. Eva frantically looked around to search for a book to read. There, upon the desk sat the self-writing book, now closed. She quickly sat herself down in the chair and opened it to the last page with writing on it. On it flashed *‘A marvelous feast’* before returning to its original symbolized form. Eva’s heart began to race. Suddenly, the door opened.

Chapter 25
Beware the Thorns

"Find an interesting read, have we?" Valdof said with a smirk. His posture seemed rigid and disjointed, as if he was walking on shards of glass.

"Y-Yes," Eva said. She placed the book down.

Valdof ran his hand down her cheek. "You seem unnerved. Did something happen?"

"No…nothing," she said, her face paling.

"Now do not lie to me my dear, sweet Eva. Falsehoods are distasteful. We wouldn't want anyone getting hurt, would we?"

"O-Of course not! You just startled me, that's all."

"I see…" he said with a sneer. "I presume you have done what I requested, and remained here since I last left?"

"Yes. I wouldn't disobey you…not again. I guess I just got carried away because the garden bloomed," she laughed nervously.

"The garden bloomed?" he said in disbelief.

"Oh yes! You should have seen it, Valdof! The flowers started sprouting all over and the thorns turned into berries! Even the fountain is working!" Eva said. She grabbed his hand and started toward the door. "Come, you must see it! It's absolutely marvelous!"

Valdof swiftly removed his hand from hers. "Perhaps it would be best to leave the gardens alone, and rest for a while. You have had quiet the day so far. I wouldn't want you getting too *unwound*."

Eva's heart felt as though it hit a brick wall. *Oh no...has he figured me out? There must be some way for me to get him to the gardens!* She put on a smile. "Rest? Oh, I couldn't possibly rest at a time like this! You've finally come back! I've wanted ever so much to show you the gardens since you left me there! You must see it, Valdof. The flowers are so beautiful!"

"Yes. I'm sure they are," he said with a sigh. "Very well, your words intrigue me. It may be *wise* to look upon these *flowers* you speak of."

Valdof opened the door and led her back towards the gardens.

"You know, while I was finishing up my work, I thought I heard someone sneaking around the castle halls. Any idea on what that could have been?"

"W-Well, I'm sure I don't know. I've been in the library since you left…"

Valdof placed a finger to his chin. "Hmm…it could have been the spiders. They have been quite a nuisance as of late. Or perhaps it was the presence of your kidnappers wandering about the dungeons," he spat. "You wouldn't happened to have helped them, would you?"

"Why would I help someone who betrayed me?" she said with a quickened breath.

Tell me this isn't true! I was just there! He couldn't have possibly found them, could he?

"Never you mind," he said opening the garden doors. He examined the peculiar flowers.

"W-What happened to them," Eva said, nervously.

Please let them be okay.

"They have been *disposed* of. I wouldn't want you dealing with *unnecessary* troubles such as these. This is precisely why you must obey my every order. Do you understand?"

Eva's heart sank. *No! This can't be true! Finn, Rina, Dator! They c-can't be d-dead...*

"Y-Yes…"

Valdof looked at her with suspicion.

"Although, I-I've been thinking. Perhaps you are right. People d-deserve punishment for their actions," she said, each word creating a bad taste in her mouth.

"It pleases me to see you come around."

The door creaked open. Finn, Rina, and Dator walked in.

"Just as it will please me to see the look on your faces when I destroy every last one of you!" he said, yanking Eva to his side to face the trio.

"Let her go, Valdof!" Finn said, a green flame floating above his palm. Rina grabbed her chimera blade, as Dator twiddled a metal ball.

"My, my, such a *temper*. You really *must* watch that tongue of yours, Barrett. We wouldn't want you getting *out of sorts* would we now?"

Finn gritted his teeth, taking a step forward.

"Ah, ah, ah. Remember? We had a deal. Your family, for this *lovely* treat," he said, caressing Eva's chin. He twirled her hair between his fingers.

"DON'T YOU TOUCH HER!" Finn barked, sending a green flame past Valdof's face.

Valdof stood straight, unamused by his actions. "You try my patience boy," he flung his arm upward, creating a swarm of black energy around Finn. He collapsed, withering in electrical convulsions.

"FINN!" Eva screamed. She jumped on Valdof's back and slammed her fists upon him. "Valdof, stop it! Leave him alone!"

With his attention broken, Finn was released from his wrath.

"How dare you disobey my commands!" he said, shaking her off, and slapping her. Eva fell to the ground, becoming miniscule in his presence. "I should have gotten rid of you while I had the chance!"

"Oi! Half breed!" Rina said.

Valdof turned to face her, his face enraged. Dator threw the metal ball, causing an explosion of fog between them. Rina swung her blade with haste, but her moves were no match for him. In a swift second, Valdof grabbed Eva's wrist, and escaped into a cloud of black smoke.

Black-thorned roots shot from the ground, blocking the gates to the castle.

"Stay away from the walls and whatever you do, don't touch the roots!" Finn said. He sent a burst of green energy towards the door. A sizzling sound rose from the burnt fixture, leaving the roots untouched.

"It can't be…" he said. He sent another flame, but the roots did not budge. Rina grabbed her sword and rammed it down the center of the thorny blockage.

"Rina, don't! The needles!" Finn said.

"Look it's beginning to fall apart!" she said. The roots mangled themselves together and wrapped around her leg, sweeping her off her feet.

"Rina!" Dator yelled. The roots shot towards him, and just as they were about to strike, Finn pushed him out of the way, slicing the root through its core. The roots shook, twisting to reform their loss. They darted towards Finn, who dodged them one by one. Swinging his blade, he cut through the roots, careful as to not encounter them. Then suddenly, the roots dropped to the ground. Dator stood near the fallen root, Rina's sword in hand. The plant receded back into the ground, unblocking the entrance. Finn rushed over to Rina, who sat cowering beside Dator.

"Rina! Dammit! I told you not to mess with it! Did it grab you, Dator?"

"N-No. Is she going t' be okay?" Dator asked.

"Do you hear that?" Rina said, grabbing Finn's wrists tightly.

"What? Ah!" Finn said. Finn ripped away from her grasp. He rolled up his sleeve up, revealing a tiny piece of the root lodged into his skin. He pulled the thorn out and threw it to the ground. His head started to spin.

"Shit…" he said.

"Finn? What do we do?"

"We need to find Eva," he said helping Rina up. She quickly drew her chimera blade and swung it toward Finn.

"Don't touch me, you vile dingus!" she growled.

He sighed, knocking the blade from her hand, and giving it to Dator. "Keep ahold of this. Both of us will be dangerous once the toxins set in. Dator, I need you to make sure we don't separate. Hopefully the hallucinations will wear off soon, but we must stick together."

"Aye," Dator nodded.

Dator and Finn walked a struggling Rina into the hallways of the castle. Drops of sweat ran down Finn's face as they continued down the path. Dark shadows formed in his peripheral vision, whispering ambiguous requests. Soon they came before a three-way corridor.

Rina became still. "There it is again!" she said. She glanced at the three paths and darted off towards the left. Finn grabbed her arm.

"Let go! Eva! Hold on!"

"*Help me, Finn!*" Eva's voice rang out.

"Eva?" Finn said, releasing Rina to look at the right corridor.

"Finn! She's getting away!" Dator said, trying to catch Rina.

"*Finn! Help!*"

"EVA!" Finn ran towards the voice.

"Finn, wait! That's not Eva! 'Tis not-"

"*Dator*." a womanly voice called out.

"Real…" he said. Dator looked around to find the source of the sound. *I must be losing my mind!* He searched his arms and legs. "No needles…then how?"

"*Dator. Over here, my child,*" the voice called out again. A thin, youthful woman stood in the center corridor. Her long creamy hair braided loosely under her floral crown.

"M-Mother?"

The woman walked down the hall, her thickly layered skirt flowing with every step.

"Mother!" Dator said, running after the figment. Krimm, having escaped Rina's satchel, scurried after him.

~:~

Eva gasped for air as the overpowering mist vanished. The room overflowed in murk. Valdof was nowhere to be seen. She rested her hand upon the curved wall, trying to see a way out. With her eyes adjusting, she came to find herself standing face to face with a skull. She let out a scream. A soft crunching sound came from beneath her and she soon realized it was not just the walls that were filled with skulls; the whole room was lined with bones, trapping the small wispy souls that dimly lit the room.

A cynical chuckle came from the other side. "My, I would have thought you'd enjoy a change in scenery," Valdof said. "Do you like it? I made it myself."

Eva stumbled upon the skulls as he came toward her. "Y-You're a monster!"

"Now, now, there's no need to be rude. I've treated you well," he said. He leaned in close to her, fiddling with her hair. "You're alive, aren't you?"

"Don't you touch me!" she said, smacking his hand away. "Y-You stay away from me!"

Valdof laughed, dissipating into the darkness. Eva quickly stood up, looking to see where he was going. As she turned around, he appeared in front of her, and threw her backward.

Hitting the wall, she tumbled to the ground, bones falling upon her from impact. Valdof shoved her into the wall, clenching his nails into her arms.

"What a pathetic excuse. Why don't you fight?" he said, slamming her back again. "Let me guess. You like having others walk upon you. Well two can play at that game." Valdof grabbed her hair, pulling her head back, and gently licked her collarbone up to her shoulder. Eva's breath quickened as his grip tightened.

Across the room something small and sharp stuck out from between two skulls. Upon its handle was a symbol of luck. *My chevalier! If I can just get it, then maybe...* Her eyes widened with the grazing of his teeth against her flesh. Eva rammed her knee into his stomach and pushed him away. She darted towards the blade and in an instant, was pulled down to the ground.

"Heh...playing hard, are we? You're so naive." Valdof said. He snatched her arm and jumped up to the ceiling, dangling her like a puppet. Eva squirmed, trying to free herself from his grip. "My dear, you are *quite* amusing," he said with a laugh. He released her for a second, then burrowed his nails into her wrist. "Ha, ha, seems my grip is slipping. I did warn you that I'd grant you whatever you wish." A twisted grin ran across his face, and he let her go.

Eva felt the bones beneath her snap on impact. She let out a moan as she lifted her aching body. Valdof dropped to the ground beside her, watching her scramble in amusement.

"Stop it! Please just stop it!" she said backing up to the wall.

If I can just distract him a little longer!

"Pitiful. Begging for mercy already? Stand up and fight!"

"What do you want from me?"

"You still haven't figured it out yet? Why hide it, Eva? What purpose does it serve?"

She slowly pulled Verona's ribbon from her sleeve and began wrapping the handle of the blade behind her back. "What purpose? What are you talking about? I'm not hiding anything!"

Valdof's blood began to boil. "Oh, yes you are! You have been hiding this a long time!" he said, taking hold of her shoulders. "I don't know how you obtained it, but you did! You can release them! You can release them all, someway, somehow! I will figure it out even if I have to tear you apart, limb from limb!"

Eva clenched the chevalier and swiped it across his side.

Valdof stumbled back, clenching the slice. "YOU INSUFFERABLE FOOL!" he screamed as he launched at her. The blade swung back and forth as if it had a mind of its own.

Cut after cut, Valdof became even more enraged. In a moment between swings, he slashed her arm. Eva let out a cry, dropping the dagger to hold her burning wound.

"You doltish child. To think such a weapon could do this much damage. Too bad you don't know how to use it," he said, picking up the chevalier. "What a waste." and with a snap, the blade broke beneath his hands. Eva gasped, watching the pieces fall. He towered over Eva, admiring the blood that dripped down his hand. "You really are an innocent soul," he said licking his fingers. His wounds began to heal, mending the once broken skin. "Almost *disgustingly* sweet. You truly are delightful, Eva. I've been waiting for this moment for a long time. I can't wait to hear you scream. It will be so *appetizing*."

Valdof grabbed her arms then suddenly stood up straight, releasing her. "It seems that they have arrived. Now the real fun begins," he said coldly before disappearing.

Eva sat there in silence, unable to move. Snapping out of it, she rushed over to the cracked bones and tried pulling them apart. With no avail, she grabbed the ribbon and blade shard and started cutting.

~:~

Running through the hall, Rina found herself in a dark room with a few torches. Eva dangled by the end of a rope, her body still and lifeless.

"No..." she said in shock. She reached for her blades to find both gone, and Krimm nowhere to be found. Confused and distraught, she let herself fall to the floor. "Why? WHY DID YOU DO THIS? WE COULD HAVE WORKED THINGS OUT! IT WASN'T YOUR FAULT! I COULD HAVE HELPED YOU!" she screamed, slamming her fists into the ground as tears streamed down her face. "It didn't have to be this way...why didn't I notice sooner...Eva...please don't leave...I could've been a better friend...I should have done something!"

Eva's head moved to face her. "*You were a terrible friend. You betrayed me,*" she said in a cold manner.

"N-No! It isn't true! I-"

"*You lied to me. Told me you'd be by my side through thick and thin. Look where that led to. You never even tried. You are just as much to blame as they are. It is as though it was you who tied this rope around my neck. You are no friend of mine.*"

"I just wanted to protect you! You have to believe me!"

"*Why should I believe someone who can't even trust herself?*"

A black oozing substance drenched the floor, encasing Rina from behind. She struggled beneath its hold as it dragged her from the room.

~:~

Finn burst through the door to see Eva dangling from a broken plank of a balcony.

"*Finn! Help!*" she screamed.

Finn ran up to the balcony and reached out his hand. "Grab onto my hand!"

Eva reached out and began to slide. "*Finn, I'm slipping!*"

He reached out his hand even further until her fingertips reached his. Suddenly, the board fell. Finn grabbed her hand, barely able to hold himself. "I got you! Hold on!"

"*Don't let go!*" she cried.

He moved his hand further up her arm to get a better grip, when suddenly, she gave way. She let out a scream of terror. Her body hit the ground with a crack. A puddle of blood formed under her mangled body.

"NO!" Finn screamed. He jumped down, creating a field to break his fall. He lifted her head into his arms. "Eva! Please wake up! I'm so sorry!"

"*You dropped me. You broke your promise. You're nothing but a liar,*" she said, turning her broken neck to face him.

"I didn't mean to! I'm so sorry!"

"*You never cared.*"

"That's not true! I do care about you! We can find a way to help you!"

"*You waste my time. Who would ever want to be with someone like you? You can't even save your family, yet alone your friends. You're absolutely worthless," she* hissed.

"What?" he said, dread consuming him. Suddenly the bloodied bodies of Mary and his parents surrounded them, staring at him with soulless eyes. Finn's heart began to race, and his body shook in terror as he stepped away from the bodies, letting out a scream.

A black substance hardened around his arms. It started to drag him away from the lifeless bodies that began to disappear. "LET ME GO! I HAVE TO SAVE THEM! MARY! EVA! DON'T DO THIS! WAIT! EVA!"

Chapter 26

A Battle of a Timely Manner

"Well, now! It seems we have a few stragglers running amok." Valdof said with a sneer as the guards dragged in Rina and Finn. Shackles bonded their legs and wrists. Their hallucinations subsided. Underneath the throne, stooped a sullen Dator chained to the floor, weeping for his mother.

What should we do? Finn thought.

If you can get me out of these shackles, I'll start an attack. Krimm is nearby. When I give the signal, he'll ambush the guards. Then you can free Dator and we attack. Valdof won't stand a chance. Rina replied.

We can't just attack them! What purpose will that serve? Fighting them will be committing treason against Aloncia! It goes against everything we worked for!

We've already committed treason, Finn! You said so yourself! We don't have a choice! If we don't fight, we'll die right here and Valdof will win!

There must be another way!

Shh! Listen!

"We found them in the east and west wings, my liege," Sir Everard said.

"It appears they escaped the thatorine," Valdof said. "Kill them."

"No."

"What?" he spat. He rose from his throne, inching closer to the guards. "You dare defy me? I am your King! Have you forgotten what happened to the last one of you who disobeyed my command? I said kill them!"

Sir Everard stepped in front of Finn and Rina. "Barrett is one of our own. He took a chance only the bravest and most loyal to Aloncia would make, and we will not stand to fight against our comrades anymore!" The guards started to unlock Finn's chains.

"Very well then, I shall take matters into my own hands," he said. Valdof grabbed Sir Everard by the neck, digging his fingers through the flesh until the sound of a snap rang through the air. Sir Everard's body fell to the floor. Valdof thrust away the blood from his hand.

One of the guards grabbed his sword and charged toward Valdof. With the raise of his hand, roots shot from the ground. They slithered around, entangling the guard in the thorny thatorine. They constricted like a snake as he struggled until only silence remained.

"Although, I must admit, it will be amusing seeing the blood run down your palms as you murder the ones you desperately wish to protect," he said, and in a single wave of his hand, ripped the souls from the guards. Their bodies dropped like hornets in a storm.

"You bastard! You will pay for what you have done!" Finn spat.

"Oh no, Barrett. It is you who will pay." Valdof cackled, disappearing into smoke.

Finn, with chains almost loosened, squeezed his hands free. He sent sparks toward Rina, removing the screws holding her chains together. They stood back-to-back. The guards rose to their feet, as if attached to strings.

"They're not your friends, Finn. Their souls are gone. Don't let them distract you from reality," Rina said. Finn shook behind her.

The guards pulled their weapons. Finn crossed his hands over his head, creating an impenetrable shield. He pushed their attacks back, lacking the confidence to fight against them.

"I don't want to fight you," he said.

"I know they were like your family, but now is not the time!" Rina said. She came upon two guards, snapping their necks. They rose again, seemingly unaltered by their disfigurement. She sliced through their chest plates. The guards dropped. "It's the heart! Without it they can't move! Shit! Finn, on your left!"

Finn blocked another attack. He sent green ropes around the guards surrounding him. They sizzled, falling to the ground. The largest guard charged, swinging a battle axe. Finn blocked him, trembling under the pressure. The guards broke free of the ropes. Cracks slithered up his shield. Finn quickly hurled a bolt of energy, knocking back the guards.

Suddenly, Krimm flew in biting the guards. The guards stiffened from his venom and fell to the floor. His tail whipped the others back.

The guards headed toward Dator. Finn sent a gust of wind that pierced through their bodies like bullets. He chanted and the chains surrounding Dator turned bright green before disintegrating into dust. Finn pulled him up and shoved a dagger into his hands.

The guards encircled Rina and Krimm. She rammed her chimera blade through one of the guard's chests. The blade chipped and stuck in the armor. Rina placed her foot on the guard. She pulled on the blade, trying to free it from his chest. The other guards grabbed her. With a few punches and kicks, she pushed them back momentarily. Krimm bit down on his tail and curled up into a ball.

"EVERYBODY DOWN!" Rina screamed, letting go of her blade and dropped to the floor. Finn and Dator mimicked her and in an instant, Krimm let out a horrendous growl. Scales flew throughout the room. They ricocheted off the walls and shot through the guards' bodies.

Dator lifted his head. "What was that?" he said. "Mother!"

"She's not here, Dator. It was just one of Valdof's tricks," Finn said.

"Nay! I know 'twas she! She was here!"

Rina signaled for Krimm to come. "Dator-"

"Nay! We have t' find her!" he said.

"Listen to-"

"Rina…look," Finn said, pointing to the ceiling where a dark mass spun above.

Descending before them, it slowly reformed into Valdof. "You really do surprise me. I figured the guards would have maimed at least one of you. No matter. It will be far more entertaining killing you myself," he said with a grin. He snapped his fingers and a dark cloud shot towards them.

Finn put up a forcefield, protecting them from the electrical explosion. Green flames pinwheeled towards Valdof who smothered the flame in a gust of wind. Krimm scooped up Rina and flew towards the ceiling, swerving past the thatorine. Finn formed a long whip, and with a quick lash, pulled Valdof's hand back. Flames traveled down the whip, Valdof hissed in pain. Dator threw a couple orbs that burst into smoke. Rina jumped off Krimm's back, aiming for his head. Valdof sent black energy through the smoke. He grabbed Rina's blade, unscathed, and threw her back with force. Krimm quickly flew behind her. They crashed into the wall, bits of stone crumbling upon them.

Valdof sent a flaming demonic figure towards Finn and Dator. Finn counteracted the attack. Valdof stumbled backward, smoke pouring from his abdomen.

"ENOUGH!" he screamed, sending a black energy through the room. The power swept everyone off their feet. The energy wrapped around them like a rope. The three struggled beneath the tightening hold. "You really think you can defeat me? How pathetic!"

A wooden rack appeared with a wave of his hand. Chains surged from the rack and grasped Rina, latching her to the board. Valdof's energy entrapped Krimm in a cage with spears penetrating through the holes, poking through his scaly flesh.

"It's okay Krimm! Stop struggling! We'll get out of this! Just try to stay calm!"

"Let them go," Finn said pushing himself up. Valdof smirked, kicking him. He summoned his mace and swung it down against his back.

A crackling sound came from above. The ceiling opened and a human skull toppled to the ground. The wooden frames splintered. With the snapping of the center beam, the ceiling broke free and thousands of bones fell through. A chain snapped and the pewter chandelier fell. They scurried out of the way. Weakened, and unable to move in his bindings, Dator was buried within the bony avalanche. The chandelier slammed into the center of the mound. Dangling from the ceiling was Eva.

"Oh my god," Rina said.

Finn gaped; his body petrified. Valdof grabbed the chain from the chandelier and threw it at Rina. It's ends clamped around her wrists. Eva cried as her hand slipped from the ceiling's edge. The chains twisted around the sturdy beams, forming tiny skulls that bit down upon her wrist, bringing her to a halt. She wailed as blood dripped down her arm.

"Eva!" Finn screamed.

"Finn? Oh boy, am I glad to see you!" she said.

"Hold on, I'll get you down!" he said and broke free of the ropes.

Valdof snapped his fingers and Eva fell a few feet, the clasps tearing away at her flesh. Rina grunted as her arms jerked upward.

"My, my, Barrett. It seems you've found yourself in a predicament, haven't you? I consider myself a reasonable man, so

I'll make you a deal," he said. He put his hands together and formed a silver hourglass. "If you can save all of your friends before the last grain of sand falls, you may leave. However, the longer you take to save one, decreases the chances of the other's survival. Little Dator will surely suffocate if the pressure of the bones hasn't killed him already. As for our miraculous ladies, every hundredth grain that falls will signal another drop. If the last grain falls, Rina's arms will be torn from her body, causing *poor Eva* to fall to her *untimely* demise. And the hybrid, well, he'd make a wonderful cape don't you think? Better choose wisely." Valdof said. He turned the hourglass upside down and disappeared.

It's obviously a trap, but I have to try. There's no way he'll let Eva die. Not yet anyway. If I can get Dator out, then I can save Rina and Eva together. He sent a blast of energy at the bones covering Dator. Rina gasped and Eva fell a couple more feet.

"Oh, and by the way, I forgot to mention that any use of magic immediately removes a hundred grains of sand." Valdof's voice echoed. Finn snarled and ran over to Dator's hand. He quickly pushed away the remains until he could see his head. Dator was unconscious, but still breathing. Finn pulled him from the boney casket. Valdof grabbed Dator by the hair.

"LEAVE HIM ALONE!" Finn said, a ball of green fire in his hand.

"Do you really wish to waste more of their precious time by fighting me?" he mocked. "Don't worry, I'll take good care of the little imp."

A whistling rang through the air as an arrow lodged itself into Valdof's arm. Dator dropped to the ground, shattering the bones beneath him.

"No one calls mine brother an imp!" a familiar voice said.

"Ijaïh!" Finn said.

"Ah, the *noble* elf returns." Valdof said. He tore the arrow from his arm. "I must say I am surprised a coward, such as yourself, had the courage to appear before your friends. How vain. Is all this to prove a point? To prove your *worthiness*?"

He pointed his sword at Valdof. "Finn, save the others. I shalt deal with him."

"Oh, a new attendant? Let's even the odds, shall we?" Valdof said as tiny demon spirits appeared. They circled Eva and Rina, tugging their limbs. "Tick-Tok. Your time is running out," he said, sending an electrical mass at Ijaïh. He stiffened under its embrace and with little energy, thrusted the blade at him.

Finn rushed over to Rina. The spirits hissed and made their way towards Finn. He pulled out the Lux Spirituum and opened it. He threw it far, and the light spirits terrorized the demons. Finn hurriedly fiddled with one of the chains on Rina's wrist when suddenly Eva dropped again. Eva screamed and the demon spirits rushed toward her, twisting her chain.

"Finn, stop it!" Rina said, angrily. "Listen, you must help Eva! Use your magic to break the chain at its pivotal point. The chain will collapse, and you can catch her before she falls!"

"But if I use magic-"

"Trust me! It will work!"

Finn nodded and took a step back. He shot an arrow at the point where the chain met the ceiling, sending a flame down its links. Eva dropped and a loud snapping sound came from behind. Rina screamed as her left arm ripped from its socket. The demon spirits rushed toward her. As the chain fell, she threw her arm to her side. The chain sliced through the spirits, dissolving them in a fiery agony. She snapped the chain from her limp arm and legs and ran over to free Krimm.

The ceiling collapsed, and the chain broke away. Finn hopped upon the falling rubble and caught Eva. He quickly tore the skull chains from her wrists and created a green energy beneath him, breaking their fall. Eva wrapped her arms tightly around his neck.

"Oh, Finn, I thought I'd never see you again!" she said.

"I'm not that easy to get rid of. The fight's not over yet."

Rina unhinged Krimm's cage.

Across the room, Dator regained consciousness.

"Ijaïh," he said. He pulled out the rest of his glitter and smoke orbs and threw them. The orbs bounced off Valdof. A sparkling smoke cocoon encased him. The moment Ijaïh's blade touched the smoke, a tar like substance climbed up its metal frame. Ijaïh dropped his weapon and in a burst of energy, the black goo latched him to the ground.

"Time's up." Valdof said as the last grain of sand fell. He lifted his sword and pulled Ijaïh's head up. "You were never worthy of the title of vaward," he said. He raised the blade, only for Krimm to tackle him, latching onto his arm and clawing at him. Krimm's teeth touched his blood, and he jumped away. Stumbling backwards, he fell to the ground in a sleep-like state.

Rina ran up behind him, jumping upon his back. She pulled her sword against his neck. His skin, so thick, could not be pierced. Valdof clamped his hands around her arm and flipped her over his shoulder. He pressed his foot against her shoulder, tugging her arm. Rina wailed.

"Not much of a fighter now when you only have one arm, are you?" he scoffed.

"I only need one," she said and with her other arm, she sliced through the black mass, releasing Ijaïh. Rina slammed her blade through the fabric of Valdof's shoe. "Now Finn!" she screamed, grabbing Ijaïh and Krimm and running away.

Finn emptied the contents of the small brown sac on the floor. Four small beads rolled out and formed a square around him, leaving behind a trail of dusty white symbols. He formed a green flame and shot it towards the ground. His body glowed and in an instant, the flames burst up from the ground, forming a horned wolf with wings; its transparent figure flickered with aggression.

The wolf growled. Valdof struggled to remove the sword. Forcing all his energy into the fiery beast, Finn let the creature loose. It viciously barked and ran towards Valdof, snapping its jaw down upon him. The wolf's wings encased him, erupting into a wind of energy.

As the flames dispersed, Valdof knelt, grasping his face.

"No way… What the hell are you?" Finn said.

Valdof chuckled. Half of his face had melted off, revealing a soulless sunken eye upon decaying green skin.

"I am the evil that lurks beneath, the fear that slithers through your soul, and you will not escape me!" he said and disappeared into black dust. The torches around the room went out one by one, leaving only darkness.

Ijaïh, Dator, Rina, and Finn surrounded Eva.

"Finn, what do we do?" Eva whispered.

"Stay calm. Don't make any sudden moves."

Demonic whispers echoed through the room as a black mass danced around them.

"You're nothing but a pathetic *waste* of flesh." Valdof's snapped. Finn formed a flame in his hand. "Yet so *tasteful*." his voice sounded again from the opposite side. "*So tender. So luscious.*"

"He's over there!" Rina said quietly.

Finn hit a black mass. It dissipated into smoke, revealing a cage built of thatorines. Maddie lay there unconscious, covered in bruises and lacerations. The mass lurked towards Eva.

"Maddie!" Eva cried.

"Eva, don't!" Rina said, pushing her back. The mass latched upon Rina's feet and dragged her further into the darkness. Then there was silence. Ijaïh grabbed his bow. Heavy steps sounded from behind them. Finn pulled Eva behind him, who clung to his shoulder.

Rina shrieked, her voice surrounding them. Finn threw a couple of flames into the air, dimly lighting the room. Over by the wall, Rina clenched her head in agony as a dark mass loomed. Beside her lay Krimm tied up in thatorines. Dator ran, thrashing his dagger at the mass. The mass threw him back.

Ijaïh shot an arrow at the mass, and it squealed in pain. It reformed into a rotting creature and lunged for him, releasing a spine-numbing growl. Finn sent flames, the creature slipping past them. It threw Ijaïh across the room. Dator jumped on the creature's back, jabbing it with his dagger. The creature snarled and squealed, tearing Dator off him. It clawed at his clothes. Finn shot it with a blast of energy. The creature latched itself to the one of the remaining columns, baring its teeth.

"Thou hath finally shown thy true self, Valdof," Ijaïh said. "How disgraceful. Thy presence is eye-offending."

"Foolish elf!" The creature growled.

"Didst I make thee mad? Mine mistake. Thou art nothing but a vile, ill-bred, miscreant!"

The creature screamed and launched at Ijaïh. Grasping Ijaïh's blade, the creature shattered it then swiftly thrust its claws through Ijaïh's stomach. He wrapped his hand around his spine, crushing it beneath him as he sent electric smoke through his body.

Finn blew green wisps at the creature. It tore his hand from Ijaïh's body and scurried towards him, hungry for blood. The creature panicked as a transparent cage surrounded him. Ripples formed as the creature tore and slammed its hands against the cage. He was trapped.

Ijaïh stumbled backwards and collapsed upon the cold ground, black smoke pouring out his wound. He wheezed in anguish.

"IJAÏH!" Dator screamed, running to his brother's side. Tears fell down his face.

"Doth not c-cry, thou im… I-I shalt be alright," Ijaïh said.

"Ijaïh! Nay! Nay! 'Tis not alright! 'Tis mine fault! We must get thee help! Rina has some medicine! We can mend-"

"Nay. 'Tis t-too late."

"Nay! Nay! Speak not o' such things! Why didst thee come? None o' this wouldst have happened if thee traveled back t' Elnaïr! What shalt father think? I wilt-"

"Datorajï," Ijaïh said. Dator became silent. "'Tis not thine fault. Thy words be true. I w-was motely-minded and cowardice. I see that now."

"Nay! I was only angry! If I had not spoken t' thee as so, thou wouldst be safe!"

"Always taking the censure," Ijaïh laughed, blood dripping from his mouth. He placed a hand on Dator's head, giving him a soft smile. "Thy hair hath grown. Thou hast p-proven thyself brave as a true Elnaïrian. F-Father would be proud."

"But how can I-"

"Gaze upon mine hand, and thou shall see the sins I have committed. I have scorned my fate and thus shall be p-punished for it. Thou suffered dearly for our m-mother's death. She would not hath wished for this."

"Speak not, Ijaïh! Thy must get up! I won't lose thee too!"

"Doth not cry, Datorajï. T-Thee must stay stout. I am honored t' calleth thee brother."

Ijaïh's body became limp.

"Ijaïh? Ijaïh! Nay! Nay! Don't leave me! IJAÏH!" Dator screamed, burying his face in his brother's chest.

Eva staggered towards Ijaïh and Dator. Finn finally cut through the thatorines binding Krimm. He shook with tears, hearing Dator's cries. Black mist spewed from the creature, destroying the barrier. Its teeth gleamed in victory.

"Eva, watch out!" Finn yelled.

The creature tackled her. She screamed beneath its grasp, struggling to break free. Finn sent flames toward the creature. The creature bore shadows over the flames and sent it back flying at Finn, wrapping him in chains. A dark mass surrounded Eva.

"EVA!" Finn said. With all his energy, he burst through the chains.

"QUIET!" The creature hissed. New skin crawled over his body with each step, returning him to his familiar form. "You never know when to give up do you?" Valdof said. He melted Finn's dagger into a silver maul, and slammed it into his leg, shattering the bones beneath.

Finn screamed, withering under the pain.

"Perhaps now you will take heed of my advice and follow through when making a deal."

"Go to hell!" Finn spat.

"Tsk. What a *thoughtful* request. However, I see it more fit to bring it here. Too bad you won't live to see it come."

Chapter 27
The Strength from Within

Eva's heart raced. Murk encased her like a caged dog.

"Look over there! Little Miss Eva's doing homework during recess again! How pathetic!" the voice of a young girl called out.

A spiral of memories from her past played before her. Two girls huddled over a four-year-old version of herself. A version who imagined the joys of youthful enthusiasm, yearning to play with the other kids.

"She obviously doesn't have any friends," the second girl said.

"Who would want to be friends with her? She's so weird! All she ever does is work by herself. She's always sucking up to the teachers too! I mean, how stupid can you get?"

"Let's ask her to play with us. It will be fun to mess with her."

The girls asked if she wanted to play tag with them.

"You want to play with me?" she said excitedly.

"Yeah, you look SO bored doing homework over here. Live a little, girl."

"O-Okay! Yeah, let's play!"

Images zoomed to a couple days later. The recess bell rang, and little Eva ran to the girls.

"Hey, want to finish our game?"

"Pa-lease. As why would we want to play with someone like you?"

"Yeah Eva, you're such a wimp!"

"W-What?" Eva said, her smile fading.

"How gullible can you get? You really think we'd be your friends? It was all just a game to mess with you. No one would ever want to be friends with you."

"You don't belong here."

"She's right, so why don't you just go home."

"Yeah, that's it! Run home to mommy!"

The two girls laughed as they watched her run off.

Eva dropped to her knees. Her eyes locked with the screen, dread simmering through her.

She worked at home for hours on a project. She covered it in pictures and writings about herself and her family. The next day it was posted upon the bulletin board next to the others. By the end of class, a picture of herself had been torn from its paper form and replaced with a drawing of the devil.

Sitting in the front of the classroom, Eva worked diligently on her homework as kids behind her whispered terrible things about her. Paper balls hit the back of her head. The acts were left unnoticed by the teacher.

As she walked home from school, the neighborhood kids offered to play with her, but she soon learned that their meaning of fun was to push her around, forcing her to do things she knew were wrong.

An eight-year-old Eva spent countless minutes in the bathroom, crying. She struggled to pull dozens of staples from her unruly hair every other day. The tangled mess made it almost impossible to find all of them.

Years passed. Her friend sat with one of the other kids on the bus. A sleazy boy slipped in beside Eva. He pursued her, teasing her about wanting to take her home to his place and spend the night drinking and smoking pot, while cuddling on the couch. Eva scooted as far away, begging him to stop, until finally the bus came to the school. She hopped over the seat, escaping his immodest embrace.

Hiding behind the pillars of the school, she talked to her friend when one of the bullies came over and snatched a lunchbox from his hands. They chased down the girl until they finally pulled it from her grasp, and she chased them. She pushed Eva into a pillar where the cameras could not see. Taking Eva's purse, she wrapped its chained strap around her neck. "If you ever do that again, you'll be sorry!" the girl hissed, tightening the metal noose.

Tears fell down Eva's face. The chains of her past slowly wrapped around her.

It was her eighth-grade choir concert. Eva finally got a solo. She tended to sing quite loudly in an almost forceful manner. She worked so hard to prepare for the night, taking heed of her teacher's advice. Before she entered the stage, a curly haired girl stopped her.

"The microphones stopped working in the last performance. No one could hear the soloist. You'll have to sing louder," the girl said.

"No, no, it's okay. My voice is loud enough...I-I'll be fine."

"You don't understand. No one heard her. They won't be able to hear you either."

"It's okay, really!"

"Don't you want the audience to hear you sing?"

Her solo came up. Eva walked to the center stage and thought about what the girl had said. She took a breath and sang her part as loud as her voice would allow. The microphones vibrated, echoing her voice. Not one person in the audience clapped.

The next day, the video of the concert was played in class. The students turned to face her after her solo was complete.

"Why did you sing like that? You sounded awful!" a kid said, followed by an uproar of laughter. Eva's heart pounded in her chest.

"She told me to sing that way! She said the microphones were off!"

"I didn't say anything," the girl said.

In a split second, Eva ran out of the room.

Eva's breath quickened. The air felt like it was being sucked out of the room. "Make it stop! Please! I can't take any more of this!"

The house phone rang over and over. Prank calls poured in every hour. Her so called 'group of friends' said they didn't know who it was, but deep down she knew they did.

As she walked up the stairs to get to her next class, she rushed past a girl. Eva felt a hand on her back, and she was shoved down upon the stairs she climbed. Her books and paper scattered across the ground. The girl kicked her, leaving Eva to cry as she scrambled to pick up her belongings.

Eva clutched her arms, rocking back and forth.

At lunch, Eva sat with her group of friends when one started to pick an argument. Him and Eva would often bicker about nonsense. Today was different. He stood up towering over her, his body fueled in rage.

"At least I won't end up alone like you! No one could ever love someone like you!"

"YOU TAKE THAT BACK!" Eva screamed, bitter tears rimming her eyes.

"What's going on?" one of the others asked.

Eva explained the situation and they all laughed.

"Why are you laughing?"

"Because it's true! Who would want to be with someone as worthless as you?"

Their words rang through her head. She hyperventilated, covering her ears.

"It was only a joke!"

"Gullible!"

"If you speak of this to anyone, I'll really make you suffer!"

"You don't deserve to live!"

"You just think you're all that, don't you! You little goody-two-shoes!"

"You're absolutely worthless!"

"The world would be better off without you!"

Eva closed her eyes, leaning on the ground. A soft hand touched her shoulder and instantly the voices stopped.

"Are you okay?" a familiar voice said.

"Maddie!" Eva said, throwing herself into her arms. Long, tender fingers ran down her hair as she wept, sending shivers down her spine.

"Don't worry, you're safe now."

Eva pulled away. Valdof was where Maddie once stood. She distanced herself from him.

"What did you do to Maddie?" she asked.

"You need not worry about her," he said. "She is in good hands."

"Tell me where she is! Now!"

"My, what anger! Wouldn't you rather see what has happened to your so-called *friends*?"

A small image revealed Rina, Finn, and the others walking free from the castle.

"The plan worked perfectly!" Finn said.

"I can't believe she actually believed everything we told her! Protecting a human? Yeah, right! I'd rather die than save one more of that disgusting species!" Rina laughed.

"I can't wait t' tell father o' our mission! He'd be so pleased t' hear of our actions towards bettering the kingdom! No human could stand a chance against us!" Dator said.

"Vile creatures they are. Come, Dator, we shalt make our ways back home," said Ijaïh.

The picture faded as the four entered the woods.

"No. I-I don't believe it!"

"Don't you *see*, Eva?" Valdof said, coming closer. "They never liked you. They've been lying to you from the very beginning."

"N-No! No, they wouldn't!"

"Hmph. So *naive*! Eva, think about it. Why else would they have travelled this far? Ijaïh wanted nothing to do with you because he was *so noble* and *prideful*! It was *too* much for such a low life, as you are, to require an elf's aid. His little brother, on the other hand, *so angry and full of rage*, wanted revenge against Ijaïh for taking *all* of the attention, the *deserving* pride he wanted for himself!"

"No! You're wrong!" she said.

Valdof laughed. "Ever think to wonder why Verona, so *quiet*, so *isolated* from the group, never wanted to talk about anything to you, or pretty much anyone. She only aided with the actions, knowing there was no way that she could stop what was coming. She didn't want to harm you! She didn't want attachment! She knew what would happen, and she just stood by watching. Every seer knows that to talk about the future is a *dangerous* task. She could have stopped this, you know. She could have ended your suffering. But now, you see, she did nothing! She wanted nothing to do with you!"

Eva's guard weakened, her heart painfully pounding against her chest.

"And Rina. Oh, *sweet* Rina. You think she wanted to be your friend? You think she asked to take the position? She knew who you were and knew that if she helped bring you to this realm, she would be rewarded with high *honor* and wonderful *luxuries*! You act so shocked to realize that she was part of the whole thing! How else could she have known?"

Eva clung to his every word, entwining his thoughts into her memory.

"And Finn, the *mysterious* man who showed up at the festival. Isn't it odd how Rina knew who you were talking about with his 'bright green eyes' as your only description! She wanted it for herself, the glory of turning you in to the king, so that she could help in the revolution that will be."

"S-She wouldn't d-do that!" Eva said. "S-She is my f-friend."

"Friendship means nothing to those who don't feel for others," he said. "And to think, your dear, sweet Finn, the boy who started it all through sorcery and magical-spun lies! He meant to turn you in from the start. Do you actually think he loved you? You thought he cared? He made a deal with me on that night of the crash."

An image of Finn carrying Eva, unconscious after the crash, appeared in the mist.

"I'll bring her to your castle," Finn said.

"He made you believe you were special. It's as you said: you are a *stupid little nobody*! Nobody ever wanted to be your friend. You were too *pure*! Too *innocent*! You barely lived a life at all! You were too *good* to have any fun! They all hated you! Except for one."

Eva gasped.

"Wouldn't you like to see your little friend?" Valdof said, moving aside to reveal Maddie tied up behind him.

"NO! MADDIE!"

"So *easy*. So *fragile* are the lives of humans. You had your chance. Why don't we see how *sorry* you can be?" he said.

With a wave of his hand, a black substance consumed Maddie.

Eva rushed forward. Chains latched to her wrists, pulling her back. She collapsed before her friend. "OH GOD! PLEASE! NO! MADDIE!"

The gooey blackness left nothing, but a raging mass subdued.

Outside the mist, Eva's screams echoed through the room.

"EVA! DON'T LISTEN TO HIM! IT'S NOT REAL! FIGHT AGAINST IT!" Finn screamed. He snapped through the chains and sent a gust of energy to the cloud. Catching in its current, the energy dissolved into the darkness. The chains multiplied and pinned him down.

Valdof circled her like a vulture seeking its prey. "You're weak! You grieve over the loss of a mere human, subject to lies and betrayal, yet you refuse to fight? What a disgrace! You're completely worthless! Tell me, do you even care? Does life matter that little to you that you'd let your friends suffer?"

Eva covered her head, his words pounding through her mind. A green light glimmered in the dark. '*Don't give up, Eva. You're such an amazing person. You just have yet to realize it. No matter what happens, I'll always be right here, beside you.*' rang Maddie's voice.

"You could have had everything your heart desired, but you threw it all away! Only a *fool* would be that careless!"

Her tears subsided. *Maddie? This isn't real...this can't be happening!*

"We could have created a new empire, you and I! We could bring greatness to this world, but you would rather give up everything out of your wretched *good will*!"

She held the small orange quartz charm, feeling an unnerving sense of clarity.

'*Hooest threaded the needle attempts an action worth pursuing, but only when the spool is through, will one learn to sew.*'

That's it!

"Perhaps the world would be better off without someone like you!" he spat.

"You're right," Eva said, grasping her necklace.

Valdof stopped in his steps.

"Maybe it would have been better that I didn't exist, but there's one thing about me that you still don't know."

"And what is that?" Valdof said.

"I've learned how to sew." She stood up. "You speak of greatness in the means of bringing terror across the land! You torture those weaker than you to prove your strength! It is true that I have suffered through the hardships of my youth, but if there's one thing I learned from my friends, it's that the only way to move forward is with hope! Maddie believed in me, even when I thought no one cared! She brought back faith and love into my life when she could have just followed the crowd!"

"You really think she-"

"And Finn, Rina, Dator, and Ijaïh stood by my side, even though they knew very little about me! They risked their lives to escape your reign! And you're right, I don't deserve them, but I would give my life for theirs! None of them ever stopped fighting for what was right, and neither will I!"

Her necklace glistened, releasing a feathery white wind. Its tender warmth intertwined with the blue aura that radiated from her.

"No…it can't be!" Valdof said, stumbling backward. *That aura...how could she- how is it possible?*

Eva's body rose above him. Blue energy poured from her fingertips. Her eyes filled with the energy, shining bright within the darkness.

"Your time is through," she said.

A burst of light erupted, breaking through the black mist. Valdof screamed as the energy encased him. His body disintegrated before his eyes. Valdof was dead.

Finn and Rina gasped, blinded by the light that released them from their chains. The thatorine crumbled, freeing Maddie from her cage, and retreated into the ground. Rina rushed over to tend to Maddie's wounds. The energy surrounded the throne room, then spread across the land. Land grew green, buildings repaired, and the skies brightened. Aloncia had reformed.

The light faded, and Eva collapsed.

"Eva!" Finn said, halfway crawling to her. He lifted her up into his arms. Eva's face was pale, and her body turning cold beneath the static force surrounding her. He gently shook her, but her eyes did not flutter. "Please wake up!"

Rina rested Maddie against Krimm. She shook, knowing she could not hear Eva's thoughts or feel her emotions. *No...tell me it isn't true! This wasn't supposed to happen!*

Finn placed an ear against her chest. There was no heartbeat. His heart raced. He laid her down gently and formed an electrical green orb in his palm. *I can't let her die! If I send this energy through her bosom, it could save her! It has worked before, so maybe-*

"Don't!" Rina said, pulling his hand back. "There's too much magic coursing through her veins. If you send in more, her heart will rupture and then it will be too late."

Finn shook under her hold. He shoved Rina's hand away and compressed her chest. *Eva, don't do this! Come on, open your eyes! You promised me you would be okay! You said you wouldn't give up! Please...don't leave me.*

Chapter 28
Back to the Human Realm

Warmth surrounded Eva as she opened her eyes. She was back at Finn's house, safely found in the comforts of his bed. A slight pain spread through her chest as she sat up.

"'Tis valorous t' see thee wake," Ijaïh said. "Thou very much gave us fright, resting these past few days."

Eva gasped. He stood straight and unscathed, as if he had not been near death at all. "Ijaïh! H-How did you-"

"Ah, the flesh wound. Hath left a terrible scar, it did. Although a mere spirit I hath become, I be most grateful for thee. Was it not for thee, the others and mine brother would not stand here. Mine father and village thank thee. If thou ever need safe refuge or seek assistance, the tribe o' the Elnaïrians will be by thine side."

"Ijaïh…" she said. "Th-"

The door burst open. Rina panted heavily, her arm in a sling.

"Don't you ever do that again!" she said, embracing her.

"I'm glad to see you too," Eva smiled. Tears rimmed her eyes as she hugged her friend, her tightened hold erasing the horrifying memories of their past endurance. Eva glanced up at Ijaïh, who placed a hand on the bedpost.

"Thank me not. Words need not describe thy noble deed. Thou hast freed me, but doth not speak o' mine presence t' the others, for it wouldst make them sorriest. Prithee, protect mine brother Datorajï, and ne'er let him forget how proud I am o' him" Ijaïh said, leading himself out of the room.

"Rina? Wherefore didst you go? Mary says the tea is almost-" Dator said. "EVA!" He threw himself at her. "Thank the stars you art alive! I was so worried!"

Eva stroked his head, giving a little chuckle. "Thank goodness you're both okay. I couldn't ask for better friends," she said. Dator's hair fell well past his shoulders. "It seems you've earned your way back into the Elnaïrian tribe. Long hair suits you."

Dator blushed, rubbing the back of his head. "Father will make the final decision when Ijaïh and…I mean, when I return t' mine village. It hast been so long, I hath forgotten what 'tis like t' be part o' a tribe…and how difficult long hair is t' maintain. 'Tis messy and quite sweltering!"

Eva laughed. "Well maybe Maudy can give you a few…Maudy! Her sons! Finn's-"

"They're alright," Rina said. "Falton and Sarin are a little rough on the edges, but doing well. Although, his jaw has given him a lisp. They're safe at home with their mother. Finn's parents and sister are still settling in."

"And Maddie?"

"She won't remember a thing. She seemed to have been unconscious for a long time. Maybe even days given how deep the thatorine needles were. I healed her wounds and sent her home. Seems Valdof sent a doppelganger in her place. Took a hefty fee to make it leave."

"So, everything that happened…"

"She'll think of it as a bad dream."

"Thank goodness. It must be hard coming back to a warm house after being in a cell for so long. I'd hate for her to relive the memories every day."

"Yeah…"

"H-How's your arm?"

"Nothing time and ginger root can't fix."

"And Krimm?" Eva asked. Krimm was curled up in the corner of the room. He growled playfully in his dreaming state.

"Still sleeping off the toxins. Thankfully, he didn't take in too much of Valdof's blood. It should wear off in a few days. The real question is if you're okay?"

"Yeah, Eva. You almost died!" Dator said.

"I'm fine. I mean…things could have gone smoother during the fight, but I think…I think things will be okay," she said, feeling numb. Dator's face swelled from all the tears, and Rina stayed silent more than usual.

"Eva…what's the matter?" Dator asked.

She smiled, placing a hand on her forehead as tears streamed down her face. "I'm so grateful. I never thought I'd meet so many wonderful people who'd be so kind as you, who would risk their lives and put everything at stake. I'm j-just so happy you're all alive."

They hugged once more.

"Look at us," Rina said with a chuckle. "All blubbering like a bunch of bumblesnatches."

Laughter surrounded them.

A tall blonde woman walked into the room. "Oh, it seems you're awake! Mary and I made some tea. Come, we'll dine in the kitchen."

Rina and Dator helped Eva walk from the room. They sat down at the kitchen table. Finn's mother poured everyone a cup of tea. She resided next to her husband and daughter.

"Thank you, Helena," he said.

"Jarob and I would like to thank you for freeing us from Valdof's castle," Helena said. "You put your life in grave danger in doing so, all of you. I want you to know that you're welcome here whenever you wish. In gratitude, we would like to give you this," she said, handing them each a small hand-stitched cloth. Underneath its delicate embroidered seams was a silver brooch with the symbol of valor stamped on top. "With this brooch, everyone in Aloncia will know of your great deed."

“Thank you," they said. Rina and Dator fastened it to their cloaks.

Eva admired its intricate design. “I shall cherish it always.” Finn was nowhere in sight. “If I may ask, where is Finn?”

“Finnie hasn’t stepped foot in the house since we returned,” said Mary.

“He has been quite desolate lately," Dator said.

Eva’s heart filled with worry for him. The sheer window curtains danced upon the wind. A warm smell of grass circulated through the room.

Rina sighed. “He’s taken this whole situation rather hard. After the battle, Finn carried you all the way here. He wouldn’t let you out of his sight even for a second. It took everything Dator and I had to convince him to rest and let me mend his leg. I was able to heal your wounds, but as you can see, Valdof’s marking still remain. Normal cuts are a cinch, but ones from dark magic aren’t as easy.”

Four nasty scars ran under her shoulder, still red and swollen.

“We stayed by your side, hoping you’d wake, but Finn couldn’t handle it. I think he blames himself for what happened.”

“But that’s not true! He-”

“I know…” she said, solemnly. “Fighting Valdof was bad enough, then suddenly you rose into the air and this pure energy burst out of you, repairing everything…I’ve never seen anything like it. Your heart stopped, Eva. Finn saved your life.”

~:~

The gentle breeze blowing against her chemise soothed her. Finn leaned on a tree trunk at the end of the orchard, twiddling the blue orchid. She came closer to him, the soft grass running between her toes.

"Hey," she said.

Finn jumped up, stumbling backwards. "E-Eva! I-I didn't know you w-were awake!"

She sat down beside him. "Your leg looks better."

"Y-Yeah…Rina really knows her stuff."

"Are you okay?"

"Me? It's nothing, really. It barely even hurts anymore…"

"I mean, are you doing alright with what happened?"

"Oh…that…" Finn said, avoiding her eyes. "I-I'm really sorry, Eva…damn. I'm such an idiot! If I hadn't made that deal with Valdof, none of this would have happened!"

"Finn…" she said, placing her hand on his. "It's not your fault-"

"Yes, it is!" he said, pulling his hand away. "I had no business listening to Valdof's conversation that night in the tower! I shouldn't have been there, and if I had been more careful in trying to find you, Valdof may have never known! That night of the car crash, I took his stupid deal, knowing full well what would happen! And where did it lead? The whole damn guard is dead, my family and the others are a mess, and you almost died!"

"And Valdof is gone," she said, taking his hand again. "Look at how many lives you saved! Finn, you did something no one else even thought to. You rebelled against Valdof, seeking a way to stop his horrible plans. You, and the others, risked your lives to end his massacre. Without you, who knows how long this would have lasted? Do you think he wouldn't have continued even if he killed everyone in the kingdom? Look at the changes that will come, the peace the people will have as time passes! So, we ran into trouble and experienced awful things I wouldn't wish upon anyone, but what we did…it will change the future."

Her hand tightened upon his.

"I can't forgive you for lying to me," she said. Finn winced. "But I will never forget what you did. You saved my life, and everyone in the kingdom, and I-"

Finn pushed his lips against hers, his hand trailing up the nape of her neck. Eva's face reddened. His tender lips made her heart race and chills ran down her spine. She gently placed her hand upon his chest. His warmth enveloped her as he pulled her in closer. He ran his fingers through her hair. Their hearts beat rapidly, like they had never before, yearning for this moment. Yet moments, as they are, must come to an end.

They pulled away bashfully. Finn placed the blue orchid in her hair, running his hand down her cheek. "You're so beautiful," he said.

Eva's cheeks flushed, and her eyes sparkled. She leaned her forehead against his.

"Stay with me," Finn whispered.

"What?" she said, full of disbelief.

"Stay with me, Eva. Stay here, in Aloncia."

Eva pulled away. "Finn…you know I can't."

"Why not? They've never treated you right over there! You belong here, with us. Don't you see? No one would treat you improperly and-"

"But what about my parents…and Maddie?"

"They can come too!" he said cupping her hands. "I could take care of you! I could find you a place to stay with your family! I could teach you everything you could ever want to know about magic and this world around us!"

"They wouldn't know what to do here! They wouldn't understand!"

"I could make them understand! You wouldn't have to worry about a thing-"

"Finn…" she said. "I-I want to stay. I really do but…I have to go home."

“You’re right," he sighed with a weak smile. He pulled her close, stroking her hair.

“I wish there was another way," she said, resting her head against his chest.

“I know…I do too," he said. “Come on, I’ll take you home.”

~:~

Back in Finn’s room, Eva found her clothes upon a chair beside the bed. She slipped on her shirt and shorts and pulled her hair part-way up. Looking in the mirror, she could barely recognize herself. She was someone new; a girl with an adventure returning to her past.

How could she possibly explain to everyone where she had been? What she had seen? No one would believe her. Fairytales weren’t reality at home. She held her necklace in her palm. Would she ever be able to live a normal life after everything she had been through?

Inside her satchel was Maudy’s comb, the celestite, and a few silver balls Finn had given her. She set the balls on the nightstand. She shoved the broach and Verona’s note in the bag, then pulled the flower from her hair. She traced its purplish-blue petals with her finger and pulled it up to her nose. She placed the flower gently in her bag. Eva gave one last glance at the room, memorizing its layout. With a smile on her face, she closed the door.

Rina, Dator, and Finn walked her to the edge of the forest, out of view of the villagers. The sky shined bright, and the trees glistened beneath the sunlight.

“Well, this is it," Eva said sorrowfully.

“Must you go?” Dator said hugging her legs.

"It's for the best," she said. "Everything will be alright. Ijaïh would be so proud of you. You got to promise me that you'll stay strong. I'm going to miss you. All of you."

"I promise. I will miss you too," he said, rubbing his eyes. Ijaïh placed a hand of his brother's shoulder. He nodded his head at Eva and disappeared.

"I wish I could stay. There's still so much I don't understand. Where did my powers come from? Will they be difficult to control? What-"

"You will be fine. There's nothing for you to worry about," Rina said, grabbing her hands. "Eva, there's something I need to tell you. There's more to my powers than altering emotions, reading minds, and seeing bits of the future."

"What do you mean?"

"I can change what the mind chooses to believe."

"You mean I won't remember any of this?" Eva said.

"I hoped this day wouldn't come, but you must understand that we must take precautions. If anyone were to find out about Aloncia, it would put our whole world at risk."

"What if I just didn't tell anybody?"

"Do you really think you could withstand not speaking a word of this for the rest of your life? Even to Maddie or your parents?"

Eva sighed. "Probably not."

"Rina, are you sure this is necessary?" Finn said, shifting uncomfortably.

"There can't be exceptions…not even for those we care about."

Eva hugged Rina tightly.

"Woah, hey now! Don't be so emotional. It's not like goodbye is forever, right?"

Eva sniffed. "Will I ever see you again?"

"Ha, ha. I'll see you, but you may not see me."

"Your so mean, Rina!" Eva said pursing her lips like a child.

Rina laughed heartily and ruffled her hair. "Well, someone has to watch over you and make sure you don't mess up. Besides, who will clean up the aftermath of your klutzy behavior."

"Rina!" she said. Eva's face filled with embarrassment.

"Alright, alright! Enough of this mushy stuff," Rina said, gently shoving Eva away. "Finish up your goodbyes before I force you through the portal myself."

Eva came up to Finn, fidgeting shyly. "I guess this is goodbye."

"I guess so," he said placing a hand on her cheek. "I'm going to miss you, Eva Dawkins."

"I'm going to miss you too," she said.

"Hey, don't look so glum. You're going to have wonderful times over there. You'll learn so many new things and make new memories. I can already imagine what joy and happiness you will bring to others. The Human Realm is lucky to have a girl like you," he said. He pulled out the lux spirituum. "Here, take this. That way you can feel the love and warmth of those around you, even in the darkest of times."

"Thank you, Finn," she said, placing it in her satchel. "But, what about you?"

"Ah, I'll be fine. Maybe I'll start a new guard or take off on new adventures. I could start my own bakery or produce shop. The world is full of mystery, but there's one thing that will never change."

"What's that?"

"I'll always be thinking of you."

Eva smiled. She placed her hands on his face and kissed him.

"Okay, you two, let's move before my skin walks off on its own," Rina said.

Eva came over to Rina. She opened the portal.

"Will it hurt?"

"It will be like a dream. The memory may fade, but what happened will still be true."

She placed a hand upon her head, sending a wave of energy through her. Eva felt the cold essence wrap itself around her mind.

I won't forget them. Not really.

"Bye," she said.

The portal closed. Eva was gone.

~:~

Eva stood in her neighborhood, only a block from her home. A sense of déjà vu encased her. She stumbled towards her house, feeling cold and distant. A woman sat within the garden, pulling weeds between tears. The soft sound of feet approaching made her mind race.

"Martin?" she called out. "Martin! Get out here!"

She pulled Eva into a hug. "Eva! Oh, Eva! Is it really you?"

Eva accepted her mother's hug.

"Eva!" her father screamed, embracing her. "Oh, my little girl! Thank goodness you're okay! Are you alright? Are you hurt?"

"Where have you been? Your father and I have been so worried! We thought we'd never see you again! It's been three months! When the cops stopped searching for you, we thought… Oh, I'm so happy you're back!"

But I've only been gone for a week! A week? Where did that come from? Her memories of the last few days became transparent. She sobbed, unable to think of what to say to her parents. They held her close and led her into the house.

Chapter 29
A New Beginning

Students crowded the halls, meeting up with old friends. Eva walked into her first class, finding the perfect seat in the front. Across from her sat Rina, with her head on the table. Eva gently shook her awake.

"Let me sleep, Eva…" she groaned then lifted her head up quickly. "EVA?"

She smiled at her. Suddenly, Eva was embraced by her friend.

"Where have you been? It's been so long! I started getting worried when I didn't hear back from you, and then the news reports came in and-"

"It's okay, Rina. I'm alright," Eva said with a laugh. "It's good to be home."

"Are you sure? I'll find whoever did this to you and make them pay! I will!"

"Yeah, sure… You know, I'm a lot stronger than you think," she said, playfully punching her shoulder. Rina winced from the pain that ran down her arm. "Are you alright?"

"Just an accident. I flew off my bike riding over a ditch. It's nothing, really."

"Oh my gosh, Rina! You should have that checked out! What if you broke a bone or tore a muscle or something?"

"Ha, ha, break a bone, yeah right," she said plopping a piece of ginger root in her mouth. "Now let me sleep before the bell-"

A sharp ringing ran through the room.

"Rings…" she sighed.

The teacher came up to the front of the class. "Welcome to American Literature. Here we will be studying the works of famous American authors to interpret their ideas and philosophies to gain knowledge about our past. Before we begin, I have a special announcement. We have a new student starting this year, so I want you to treat him with respect. Please take a seat wherever you wish."

A tall man with sandy hair came in wearing a polo and dress pants. He sat at the open desk next to Eva, giving her a grin. Eva blushed. He was quite handsome and had beautiful bright green eyes. Rina rested her head in her hand, murmuring idiocrasies to herself.

"Don't mind Rina. She gets cranky when she doesn't get enough sleep. I'm Eva, by the way. Eva Dawkins," she said holding out her hand.

Finn took her hand and gently brought it to his lips. "Finn Barrett," he said. Rina groaned, slamming her head on the table.

"You're perfect!" Eva said with a giggle.

Finn's face paled.

"Mrs. Smith said we'd be reading Huckleberry Finn this year! I'm sure if you ask, she'd let you play the part! I can't wait! I've been waiting to read it all summer!"

Finn sighed with relief.

"You would be excited about reading Huckleberry Finn, Eva," Rina said rolling her eyes.

"Quiet down," Mrs. Smith said. "We'll start by opening our textbooks to the first page."

~:~

One Friday, Maddie and Eva headed towards a tree in the park. When Maddie found out of Eva's return, she rushed over to her house, spending the next few nights out of fear of losing her again. Nothing could separate them now.

"I'm so glad you're back. It was so lonely without you over the summer," Maddie said.

"It's good to be back."

"I see you still have the necklace."

"Of course! I never let it out of my sight," Eva said. "In fact, I think it's what made me keep going all that time. I don't remember much of what happened, but I just kept hold of it, hoping we'd see each other again."

"It must have worked then! I knew that necklace suited you!"

Eva paused a moment. A large bush covered in aging white flowers stood beside her. The blooms were mesmerizing in their fragile beauteous state. She ran her fingers through the leaves, taking in its soft waxy texture.

"Eva? What are you doing over there?" Maddie said with her foot propped up on a tree.

"Nothing…I'll be there in just a sec."

The flowers began to brighten. All except for one.

As I gaze at the withering flower that begins to fall, I realize my life, my experience, is that flower. The end of my journey, as depicted by the bloom's release from the high branch. A death of a beautiful memory that would soon be forgotten. However, just like the flower, a new beginning will come when spring brings forth a new bud, and thus a new chapter will begin.

Made in the USA
Middletown, DE
03 November 2024

63765568R00166